LOVE HELD HOSTAGE

Jim Simmen

ISBN-10: 0692999868
ISBN-13:9780692999868
Library of Congress Control Number: 2018900424
Love Held Hostage, Key West, FL

This book is dedicated to soldiers suffering from PTSD (posttraumatic stress disorder).

We make a mistake, and some guy doesn't walk away.
—John Wayne, *Sands of Iwo Jima*

I want to thank the members of the Key West Writers Guild, especially Ann Gallagher and Bernie Kaplan, for sharing their wonderful insight. Amanda Shearer, thanks for being so supportive. Doug Shuler, social worker, and Dr. Douglas Eaton, my psychologist, you helped me see the difference between comedy and tragedy. To the members of my PTSD group, thanks for sharing your thoughts and feelings and listening to mine. To all the Miami Veterans Affairs doctors and nurses in the PTSD program, thanks for devoting yourselves to making my life better. Major Benton, you did a fabulous editing job. Thank you. Wilhelmina Harvey, thanks for letting me use your name. A big hello to my children: Eric, Russell, and Melissa. Russell, you were there once again when the best storytelling took place. Hey, Ryan.

CONTENTS

1

WHERE THE HELL IS MARLEY?

My bladder was about to burst, and it was all Dr. Howe's fault. When she told me I had to take my medication before attending court, I took it all right, and just to spite her, I downed the four pills with half a gallon of water.

Dr. Howe sat at the table to my right in the courtroom. We both faced the judge. Dr. Howe looked up from her clipboard and smiled weakly at me. I crossed my legs and squeezed, smiling as I envisioned her head between my legs.

It wasn't that I didn't like Dr. Howe. She had always been nice to me in the Veteran Administration Hospital in Miami, right from the start, with kind words that made me feel special. But I'd had enough of the mental hospital, and I wanted to go with John Marley, my platoon leader from Vietnam. If she were to understand my intentions, I feared she would think of me as a traitor, and if I didn't escape her clutches, upon returning to the hospital, her attitude might change from love to hate forever. From this point on, she would always know I hated it there.

Her thin face transformed into the head of an octopus, and tentacles reached out and touched every part of my body. I shuddered. She wore a white smock over an ivory-colored blouse. Her bra was much too large for the size of her chest. She disguised her femininity with an Elvis Presley slicked-back hairdo and a styling-gel curl over her right eye. She caught me looking at her, and she said, "It's five minutes after two, Mr. Donovan. Your friend is five minutes late."

I felt like letting loose and peeing all over the courtroom, her, and her aides and team of nurses. I hadn't known the judge long enough to include him.

The flowing black robe on the arms of the Honorable Judge Lester Sharp rustled as he read my briefs. Judge Sharp was a black man with short peppered hair and reading glasses. Acting nonplussed and gentle, he sat with his elbows on the bench, head resting on his clenched fists.

My appeal proceeding was now the most important day of my life up to this point, and all I wanted to do was go to the bathroom. Dark and windowless walls buttressed with ornate wooden pillars surrounded me. The six spectator benches behind me were empty (that made me feel special). The wooden jury stand was equally squeaky clean. The air smelled like lemon-scented bleach. I sighed.

Where the hell was my old Vietnam platoon leader, John Marley? He promised he was going to sponsor me out of the mental ward of the Miami veterans' hospital, and I believed him. I risked a lot by believing, because if he failed, I knew Dr. Howe would hold it against me for the rest of my life. She took everything personal, reinforcing her inferiority. She would probably double dose my BuSpar medication, and I'd spend the rest of my life sitting in the ward on Sixteenth Street in downtown Miami, watching the paint on the walls grow misty green.

Dr. Hensheman, known as the Medicine Man, sat on the other side of Dr. Howe and counted his fingers. He mouthed the number one and watched the index finger straighten on his left hand. He counted each finger that sprang up. At the pinkie finger, his head jerked to the right hand as the index finger straightened. His white gown resembled a fisherman's vest with pockets galore, now all empty of pill bottles but stretched to bare thread.

Dr. Hensheman stopped counting and said in his baritone voice, "Calisthenics starts in fifty-eight minutes, Dr. Howe, and if I don't dispense medication in thirty minutes, all the patients will be bouncing off the walls instead of touching their toes." Poor Dr. Hensheman was worried about missing his afternoon workout: stuffing Prozac, Zoloft, Paxil, or BuSpar into the mouths of the stressed-out patients. Into the mouths of the openly depressed patients, he shot capsules of Darvon, decapula, diphenhydramine, or nefazodone. Whenever the little quiet voice of an emotion peeked open in any patient, Dr. Hensheman, the intuitive person he was, countered with a combination of multicolored basketballs. For the emotionally handicapped, there was the Thorazine drip.

The khaki-uniformed bailiff stood to my left, his right hand resting on a holstered nightstick.

The judge said, "I'm afraid, Mr. Donovan, that we are going to postpone this hearing for at least another six months. Obviously your sponsor is not coming."

Dr. Howe's head bowed. Was that relish? Was she smirking?

"He's more than a friend, Dr. Howe," I replied. "He was my platoon leader in 'Nam."

"So you say," Dr. Howe replied, "and I had some questions to ask him about that as well. You've been my patient since time immemorial, and I love you dearly. I don't want you to fall in harm's way."

You don't have to worry about harm's way on a drying green wall, I thought.

I whispered, "George Custer killed his own men and blamed it on Sitting Bull." I quietly repeated what I had just whispered, and I realized it didn't make sense. It certainly wasn't what I felt. Uh-oh! Not now, I prayed. Please, don't lose it now. Don't have a panic attack now."

"What did you say?" Dr. Howe asked, her notepad and pen poised.

I hated her. I felt like standing up and hosing the lot of them, but if I didn't roll with the punches, I'd be the entree. My brain throbbed like a kettledrum, and the Hulk inside of me tore a sleeve. Time became boulder-size rocks that crunched and cracked against each other, pressing, splitting, and rolling. Vibrations in my head, although slight, blasted my subconscious and deafened my sense of duty. My breathing grew deeper, and my eyes wandered to the scratches on the table, the cup and pitcher of water at hand, my shaking fingers, and the deep parallel grooves in my nails. The leather seat felt tacky, and the incandescent lights caused my forehead to drip sweat. Water rumbled. I swallowed, and my ears popped; my esophagus vibrated, and I swallowed again. I didn't know what I was going to do if they tried to return me to the hospital. I was scared, and I realized I was just one point from losing myself.

The two doctors turned toward each other, fussing and whispering as they gathered their stacks of paperwork.

An explosion behind me made me turn to see the back doors of justice suddenly fling open, and John Marley walked in as brazen and confident as the wooden horse into Troy. John winked at me, clicked his tongue, and walked straight to Dr. Howe as if she were a luminary. He complimented her full-bodied Don Boulierie fragrance and shook her hand. She acted shocked and taken aback. The Medicine Man shrank back. John moved to the judge and tried to shake his hand as the judge started pounding his wooden hammer. John shook hands with the bailiff, who acted shy and timid. John turned around and smiled at me, waving a long white envelope histrionically. He said, "Today is the big day for you, brother, and here are the papers that will set you free." He slapped the envelope against his other hand and laughed as the doctor's attitude turned to one of standoffish deference.

I had never seen John look more handsome. He was six feet tall, a Grecian warrior figure of insurmountable dazzle. He wore a dapper pinstripe business suit with a mauve starched shirt and a colorfully playful tie. The tie was a little bit not tied right, but it looked new. His ponytail was sparkling, slick, and as handsome as his spit-shined shoes. But the shoes had deep creases in them, like they were nearly worn out. The only flaw in his attire was a small and weathered leather pouch, the size for sunglasses, looped through his belt buckle and zipped closed. The pouch fit the decorum of a backpacker astir in the forest, not a lawyer, or whatever John was looking to be.

The pressure in my head melted away with a sigh. A sense of regard warmed my feet and exploded up through my body with a smile to shame a caiman. If anyone could pull it off, John could.

"You betcha," I replied. "You betcha." He saved my ass in 'Nam on more than one occasion, and he was going to save it again. I believed in John.

John placed his right hand on mine and asked, "How you doing, brother?"

"I have to go to the bathroom," I whispered.

"Then I better get down to business." He whipped around like a matador revealing a sword.

The judge started with a wave of his elbows. "If you would, Mr. Marley, please be seated." He pointed to the conference table alongside Dr. Howe and continued. "As you all know, this is not a trial. There are no witnesses. This is a hearing in which Mr. John Marley has petitioned the court to reverse the involuntary commitment of Mr. Bryan Donovan to the Veteran's Administration Hospital, where Mr. Donovan has been residing the last eight years. Mr. Marley has appealed to become the legal guardian of Mr. Bryan Donovan, since Mr. Donovan has no other family to speak up for him. Mr. Marley, would you like to proceed and tell us your plans?"

All eyes were on John.

"Your Honor, it is with pride and respect that I stand before you this eighth day of May 1995, twenty years after the end of the Vietnam conflict…"

I couldn't hold it any longer. I looked again to see if anyone was watching. They were all focused on John. I picked up my glass of water and quickly downed it. I refilled the glass, three times in all, and downed the lot.

I looked at the bailiff, and he was staring at me as if I had lost my mind. Possibly, I had made the situation worse.

John continued. "I am so relieved that I finally found Bryan, who, twenty years ago, was my M60 machine gunner in the jungles of Vietnam. My machine gunner!" He pointed at me with a benevolent pride. I grimaced and smiled back. He continued. "Nobody else in the platoon was big enough to carry that machine gun and bandoleers of ammunition. Nobody but Bryan. For Bryan it was a piece of cake, and when he opened fire, there wasn't a VC brave enough to look up and watch." John pointed at me and said, "Bryan was my own personal dragon, fire-spitting killer, and those VCs feared him like a cobra would a mongoose. He saved my life on more than one occasion, and when Bryan was wounded, all bloodied, he reached out to me for help, and I dragged his ass back to safety. Today, Bryan's hand is out there for me, again, and I'm here for you, brother."

The bailiff shook his head in wonder.

I moved the pitcher to the ground between my legs, unbuttoned my pants, and let the cloud rain. My eyes floated back into my head, and I nearly fainted with relief. I kept going until I figured the pitcher was nearly full and looked down. I wasn't empty but close enough. I cut off the valve before I flooded the floor.

The bailiff played with his name tag. The rest of the audience seemed transfixed by John.

I placed the pitcher back on the stand in front of me and proudly eyed it. My God, it was the wrong color. I quickly grabbed the pitcher and placed it on the floor again and hoped to God that nobody would notice.

As John spoke, he waved the white envelope high and landed it on the judge's bench as neatly as an Apollo landing on the desert sand. John said, "This should about wrap it up."

The judge opened the envelope, quietly read the first page, flipped to the second and third and fourth pages, and said, "This is your tax return for 1994."

"That is correct, Your Honor." Genuine pride.

"Yes," the judge said, holding the document at arm's length and tilting his head back for the bifocals to work. "You did all right for yourself."

"Just all right? I would say more like excellent. I made over one hundred thousand dollars in the commodities market last year, Judge. That's better than all right, and I accomplished that working only four hours a day, five days a week. The other four hours I fffff-fancied a life of leisure and pleasure."

The judge looked to Dr. Howe and asked, "Linda, what do you think?"

John interrupted. "And there is more. Here are three character references." John placed another envelope within Dr. Howe's grasp.

Dr. Howe took the envelope and asked, "Are there telephone numbers included?"

"Yeeees, sir," John sang sarcastically.

Without looking inside the envelope, she handed it to Dr. Hensheman as she withdrew her cell phone from her belt. She said to Dr. Hensheman, "Please call these numbers, and verify these contacts. You can step out of the courtroom to do so."

Dr. Hensheman took both items and waddled out of the door, fumbling with the papers and phone like they were a puzzle, still counting on his fingers.

She turned around, set down the clipboard on her chair, and approached John, inspecting him suspiciously.

John took a hold of his suit lapel and tugged. Instead of looking like Clarence Darrow for the defense, John resembled a milk farmer stretching his suspenders. His suit looked a little baggy.

She slipped her fingers around the IRS forms and scanned the pages, one after another, twice as fast as the judge did, like a cop inspecting a bookie's alibi. Acting unimpressed, she flipped the package to John, saying, "This is not a certified document, nor was it signed by an accountant."

John's forefinger tapped the Formica-capped rail, and, with disgust in his tone, he flipped his fancy tie under his jacket and replied, "Hopefully you are a better doctor than a businessperson. I don't share this confidential information with just anyone, and certainly not to be challenged. I am not about to question your interests in retaining Bryan nor your credentials as a doctor."

The line was drawn, and the swords unsheathed. The air smelled of perfume and spent gunpowder.

Her head snapped to attention as the pole that ran the length of her body stiffened. She asked, "Mr. Marley, you say you were in Vietnam in 1968. Is that correct?"

"Yes. Three tours, and when the NVA (North Vietnamese Army) tanks came rolling south from Hanoi on Highway One, I boarded the last Huey helicopter from the Presidential Palace in Saigon with my top security clearance from the CIA."

"I just want to understand your relationship to Mr. Donovan."

Be careful now, John, I thought as I clenched the wooden rail and felt it surprisingly ungiving. She'll crack you open like a walnut and feed the ants your meat.

In John's silence, she continued. "When I was at Harvard doing postgraduate work, I studied Vietnam veterans at the nearby Hillsboro Clinic. One thing you all have in common: you never grieved for your losses."

John squirmed. "What are you talking about? What good would that have done?"

She laughed derisively. "Even now you cannot grieve. You are totally denying grief, as well as, I am sure, many of your other emotions."

"What is grief?" His shoulders shook.

Oh no, I thought, don't become defensive now. This is her game.

She twisted her neck condescendingly, inhaled through one nostril, and replied, "Deep mental anguish...from a loss."

"What makes you think I lost a friend? You'll notice Bryan was just wounded." John's neck swelled, and he started to scratch his forearm and then his neck. "And I didn't grieve Vietnam..."

"No one?" she asked.

"OK," John replied. He stared at his shoes and took three deep breaths. "I did lose a very good soldier, Hank Laser, but he was my first. Shot through the head. Dropped like a sack. Didn't have a chance to say hello or good-bye. Dead."

John, I thought. You told me just last week that Hank Laser was alive and living in Key West. What are you saying?

Dr. Howe asked, "And there was no one else?"

He stared at her a moment before replying, "I quit counting after that."

"You suppressed your feelings. Even now, you are not ready to deal mentally, emotionally, or spiritually with the loss."

She'll never let me out. If she cracks John, he might be my new roommate.

"I am sure your life is full of anger turned against yourself, which is depression, since you never recovered from the loss. You didn't grieve?"

"Why should I? Like I said, he died."

"See, that is what I am talking about—stuffed feelings."

"You didn't hear what I said. He got shot in the head on an ambush, just like all the other guys who hesitated or looked the wrong way or chickened out or their luck just turned for that one second, or God wanted them for that one moment. They died. What do you want me to grieve?" He fidgeted nervously. "I don't know why you are talking about me. I'm not crazy."

"But you are going to be responsible for your, and my, dear friend Mr. Donovan, and I believe you have the same symptoms."

They both looked at me, and I could have crawled under a peanut shell. I had just heard John tell my doctor that the only man in our squad who hadn't been killed *had* been killed. John was lying to my doctor. Oh my God. Please don't ask him another question. He'll blow it.

John fidgeted nervously. "OK. OK. I understand. I got it. When Hank was killed, I don't think I ever got over it until right now. I grieve. I'm grieving." His eyes played from Dr. Howe to the judge. "I'm cured for sure. My killing days are over, and I am sorry for every one of them."

Her back straight, eyes focused on eternity, Dr. Howe approached the bench and squeezed out of her lips, "Judge, I know this is not a contested plea. However, I have my doubts about this Mr. Marley and his ability to safeguard Mr. Donovan. I believe this Mr. Marley is riddled with guilt and probably an alcoholic. Look at his shaking hands."

The judge looked at John and then back at the doctor. "When did Mr. Donovan come under your care?"

"He was committed to my care in 1985 because of a posttraumatic stress episode. He attended the twelve-week inpatient program on the fifth floor of the hospital, at the end of which I felt he was gravely disabled, emotionally distraught, suicidal, and incapable of taking care of himself. No family or friends came forward, so I pleaded the court to commit Mr. Donovan involuntarily to my care, indefinitely. I don't think this Mr. Marley is much more responsible than Mr. Donovan."

"But Mr. Marley is certainly financially capable..." The judge's eyebrows arched, but Dr. Howe did not look impressed.

The judge continued. "How did Mr. Donovan come to you?"

"He was arrested for battery and vandalism. Mr. Donovan was walking down Torres Pine Lane in West Palm Beach, Florida, on January 12, 1985, which happened to be the tenth anniversary of his Vietnam trauma. Witnesses said he was mumbling to himself and searching for his lost squad from Vietnam, looking for them behind the trees and under benches. A black Labrador retriever puppy barked at Mr. Donovan. The dog had its front paws on a picket fence. In some fashion, Mr. Donovan expressed an interest in the dog. The dog became excited, crawled under the fence, and blindly ran toward Mr. Donovan.

"The dog was unaware of traffic danger and ran right in front of a speeding car. The front tires of the car ran over the puppy's head. At that point, Mr. Donovan became hysterical and slammed his head into a low-hanging limb of a nearby oak tree. Witnesses say that Mr. Donovan focused on the Porsche stopped in traffic. Mr. Donovan attacked the car, throwing a full garbage can through the windshield and then dragging the driver through the broken glass and stomping on him with both feet. Luckily the driver was not killed, but he was traumatized and hospitalized for a total of seven weeks."

The judge looked at me and asked, "What was going on in your mind, Mr. Donovan?"

I licked my lips before I said anything. "I tried to knock myself out on that tree limb. I really did. I didn't want to hurt anybody."

John stepped forward quickly. "Your Honor, that was eight years ago, and to me that shows Bryan's compassion. Years ago! Let's give Bryan a little breathing room to grow and shake out his socks a little. He's served his time."

The judge sighed and looked at Dr. Howe. A fly landed on her forehead, but she refused to be distracted. The fly circled and, disinterested, flew away.

John approached the judge, put both elbows on the bench, and said, "You know all about how screwed up Bryan is. Now let me tell you how he got that way, because I was there on that search-and-destroy mission with him the day he got shot. I was platoon leader of the Second Platoon, Bravo Company, First of the Sixteenth Battalion, Ninth Infantry Division, and I led him into that village of Ben Tri in the Quang Ngai Province. It was January 12, 1968. Wasn't it, Bryan?"

I nodded my head. (I guess so.)

John continued. "We ran smack into a North Vietnamese Army patrol, and before I even had a chance to call in the artillery or gunships, with the help of Bryan's M60 machine gun, we killed seven of them. What I didn't know was that there were three hundred more North Vietnamese regulars surrounding us. When they opened fire, we ran for cover in this little clay-walled hooch. All hell broke loose. Luckily I had already alerted battalion and the air force, because within five minutes, I was calling gunship fire and one hundred five artillery rounds right on top of my own position. The NVA was everywhere. I removed an empty clip from my M16, threw it aside, and reached into my ammo pouch for another.

"As I went to slam the full clip home with the palm of my hand, a burst of fire exploded in my face, and my hand went flying. Then out of the smoke and fire comes Bryan running at me. He was bloodied up, and his eyes were the size of coconuts and as white as fear could paint them. He didn't have his machine gun, and his arms were flying like a windmill. He dove on top of me, nearly cracking my ribs. I rolled him off, laid him on his back, and saw he was full of bullet holes from head to foot. Later the doctors counted nine in all: one through his right palm and another through the left forearm, his right shoulder"—all this time John was pointing on his own body where the bullets were—"through the left collar, shrapnel in the face, in the ass, in the other cheek, through the flesh of his leg right next to the crowned jewels, another in the foot. Let me see, did I miss any? Oh yes, the big one. Actually the one that did the most damage ricocheted off his helmet. But it exploded like a mushroom and sent shrapnel through his skull and razed the cortex.

"The surgeons in Japan—you see, I was there too because I was shot—explained that if the shrapnel had spun one centimeter closer to Bryan's hippocampus, it would have produced global retrograde amnesia. If that happened, Bryan would be as lively and entertaining as a turnip growing under a full moon. Bryan still has some of that metal in his head. The doctors were afraid to pull it out for fear of tearing up something else and making things worse. When Bryan gets excited and pumped up, the brain starts misfiring, and all hell breaks loose. In clinical terms, panic attacks."

My tongue was stuck to the roof of my mouth. I think John was lying for the second time. Either that, or he was getting me mixed up with someone else. I had gotten shot up on an ambush in a whorehouse.

The judge took a deep breath and exhaled, clearing his head back to reality. "After the war, how did you lose contact with Bryan?"

"After my wounds healed in Japan, I returned to Vietnam. Bryan went home and was discharged. Never could find him. Vanished. Bryan doesn't even know what happened himself."

I butted in and said, "I don't know what happened because I can't remember."

The judge asked John, "And how did you find Mr. Donovan again?"

"To make a long story short, surfing the Internet, under a Vietnam veteran website."

The judge turned to me and asked, "How do you feel, Mr. Donovan?"

I looked to John for the answer. John didn't give me a clue. I turned to the judge and said, "Relieved?"

John said, "With Bryan around, every day is the Fourth of July, and I love celebrations, Judge," John continued. "I don't know if you knew it, but before 'Nam, Bryan graduated from the University of California at Berkeley. He had a degree in botany. His plans after 'Nam were to return to school for his doctorate. He knew the names of all the plants and birds in 'Nam. He was a genius. He knew history like I know the stock market."

Dr. Hensheman returned through the double doors. Smacking his lips, he spoke to Dr. Howe. "The first reference was a Stuart Hood in San Francisco. Mr. Hood is a lawyer. He was unavailable."

"Good friend of mine," John replied. "We negotiated many a real-estate transaction together."

Dr. Howe looked unimpressed.

"The second guy was a taxi driver in Denver, Colorado. Paul Benson said that Mr. Marley owed him some money."

"How could Paul bring up petty cash at a time like this," John fussed.

Dr. Hensheman said, "And Wilhelmina Harvey, mayor emeritus of Key West, Florida. She had nothing but kind words and praise for John. Said he was a war hero and a man to be admired—a hometown hero."

John said, "Mrs. Harvey is my dearest aunt."

The judge shrugged his shoulders.

Dr. Howe asked me, "Are you ready to go out into the world again? Remember all those ghosts of mangled and deformed soldiers that you told me about? The ones that follow you around and talk to you. Nightmares and panic attacks."

"That was my squad," I replied. "I'm not afraid of them. They are my friends."

"Then you want to leave the security of the hospital? Three meals a day…showers…warm bed?"

I wanted to say, "Does a bear shit in the woods?" but instead, I replied, "Uh-huh."

John said, "If you don't let him go now, you won't have enough medication to calm him. You'd probably kill him trying."

The judge frowned and waved his finger for Dr. Howe to draw closer. The judge said, "If you don't agree, there could be a lawsuit."

Motionless, she said, "I just want what is best for my patient."

The judge explained to John, "If Mr. Donovan acts up, it will be your responsibility to find either medical care or hospitalization."

John nodded. "I'm prepared to do both. However, once Bryan is under my care, he will settle down and listen, just like he did in 'Nam. No problems."

Dr. Hensheman said, "Mr. Donovan is the strongest man on the ward."

John answered, "Bryan is also the most positive person I've ever met. In 'Nam, he didn't complain about anything. He was always happy, even there, and I don't think I could be happy another day leaving him here. He's like a brother, but more than that, he's going to be my guardian angel. As a matter of fact, I had a dream about that. I'll spend every last cent I have to get him out."

I smiled sheepishly and agreed. "I am. I really am."

Taking notes, Dr. Howe replied, "Sugar and caffeine are poison. If he doesn't exercise, his brain will swell, and he'll drop into a coma after he destroys his environment. Excess pressure turns his mind to…to gobbledygook. But sugar is the worst—it will kill him."

The courtroom stiffened at her choice of words. She looked up from the clipboard, bit the end of her pen, and said, "Gobbledygook. Mr. Donovan has a phenomenal mind for details, especially some Vietnam events and historical facts and figures, but he can't remember a thing before 'Nam. That metal fragment did more than drill a hole in his brain; it also took a slice out of his memory, coordination, imagination, and articulation. Otherwise, he's quite extraordinary, especially his positive attitude on life. Of course, Mr. Donovan can always have brain surgery."

John chortled. "When I was under the doctor's knife in 'Nam, I heard the two doctors walk out of the operating room, and one said to the other, 'Next time, we'll do it your way.' No thanks."

Dr. Howe coiled like a rattler.

Dr. Hensheman asked, "Would you like some medication to hold him over?" He held forward a pint-size bottle.

"No thanks," John answered. "He has to come down sometime. May as well do it while he's in a good mood."

Both doctors shook their heads in frustration.

The judge signed some papers, and then Dr. Howe and John signed the same papers, and then I did.

I set down the pen and sat there smiling, not knowing what to do.

"Well, come on," John said. "We got some living to do."

I bowed my head, tentatively stood up, and tottered, nodding my head and probably laughing like the idiot I could be. John scooted me out of the door. When I got into the long hallway, I said, "I forgot something."

I turned around, opened the door, stuck my head inside, and said, "Don't drink the Kool-Aid." I slammed the door and ran outside laughing.

In the disabled parking space was a late-model red Mercedes Benz. John walked toward it like he owned it, and I followed hesitantly.

When he stopped and saw me fidgeting, he waved and said, "Get in before they throw a net over you."

I hunched and peeked around until I realized John was just kidding me. I straightened up and asked, "Is this car yours?"

"Obviously you are still medicated. Get inside, and let's get out of here."

I sat in the passenger's seat and looked up at the clean, fresh, luxurious leather headliner and giggled. I'd never felt so wonderful, and this was just the beginning.

2

ROCK BOTTOM

At the Broward Street stoplight, John hung a sharp left into the parking lot of Stanley Tuxedos. Tires screeching, he hopped out of the car and passed through the swinging glass door. I just sat there looking at the dashboard, so shiny and magical, without a scratch. It reminded me of a spaceship. There was nothing in the hospital I could compare it to. I ran both hands along the length of the upholstered seat, smoother than fresh sheets on the hospital bed. The air smelled of Daphne and polished wood. I opened the glove compartment, and it was empty. So were the change tray and the ashtray, sparkling new.

The driver's door opened, and a new John slid behind the wheel. He wore tan canvas pants and a blue T-shirt with a large grouper on the front. John's hair was now shoulder length, and he wore a Marlin's baseball cap. He threw the black pouch that was on his belt into the coffee holder, looked at me with a furrowed brow, and said, "Close your mouth."

I bit my lips, withered in the seat, and finally replied, "You've changed, sir."

He gagged a moment, took a deep breath, and, without looking at me, said, "Let's cut out the formalities, OK? Army protocol was twenty-five years ago. You can call me John. In Vietnam you didn't salute, so don't start now."

I felt confused. "Yes, sir...oh. I'm sorry. I forgot already. Yes, John."

"Oh boy," he smirked. "I can see I'm in for a long one. Just do me a favor though, Bryan. If you ever get mad, don't hit anyone like you did to that poor Porsche driver who ran over that dog. OK? You're so damn big and strong, I'm afraid you'll kill somebody. That's what got you thrown in that loony bin in the first place. Control yourself."

"What should I do then?"

"Get help. Call nine one one. Just don't hit."

"If that's what you want, John."

"That's what I want...and a six pack of beer." He perked up.

"But why did you lie to the doctor about Hank Laser? Two weeks ago you told me he was alive and living in Key West. Now you said he died in 'Nam."

"Well, he is alive, but I don't trust those doctors. I just don't trust them, and I wish Hank was dead. I wish he died in 'Nam, but now I'm stuck with him and his memories, and sometimes I could just kill him myself for what he did."

"They're really not that bad," I said.

"Huh?"

"The doctors."

"It is just the more they medicate, the more they turn normal people into zombies."

"And that story you told the judge about the day I got shot—I don't think that is the right one."

"Now that you mention it...you could be right. Maybe I had too much to drink last night, or not enough. I was under a lot of pressure in that courtroom, and I'm not saying my memory is perfect. I might have gotten some situations mixed up. That's all."

After a long silence, he said, "But they did let you out...or the judge did. I agree. Now forget about all those pills and those hospital rooms and counseling sessions. You are a free man, and we got some living to do."

He sped north two blocks and pulled into a Hertz car-rental lot, ran over the speed bump way too fast, and braked at the door. He said, "This time, you get out."

I did as ordered and just stood there looking at the forest of parked cars, twinkling brighter than the tiles in the hospital's bathroom and radiating with color like the watercolors I painted every morning to relax. I gently closed the door, so softly I had to do it again. John charged inside the building and exited soon thereafter, smiling and stuffing a wad of bills into his pocket. Now the leather pouch was looped into his belt.

"What's in that pouch?" I pointed.

He looked down at the pouch and then back at me and said, "That's my sanity, Bubbah. It reminds me of who I am…"

I scratched my head. "In a pouch?"

"In a pouch. Now forget about the pouch." He opened the door of the Mercedes, reached into the back seat, pulled out a pair of silk socks, and stuffed them in his back pocket. Slamming the door, he went to the trunk, opened the lid, and pulled out a bulging blue backpack and a second bag the same color. He slammed the trunk, picked up a bag in each hand, and asked, "Now if I appeared in court like this, would you be here?"

I smiled. "Maybe not."

"I think not." His forehead furrowed, and he winked, sliding his left arm into the pack, and then handed me the duffel bag. I just stood there and watched him prance down the street. When he signaled for me to follow, I caught up to him.

He asked, "You leave anything at the hospital you want to pick up?"

"Nope."

"No sweet little nurse or anything like that?"

"Just some blurry memories."

"Let's leave those there." He picked up the pace like he was outdistancing those memories.

I asked, "Where are we headed?"

"Where would you like to go?"

I thought a moment and replied, "I'd like to see some trees."

"Then trees it is." He smiled sheepishly and sang, off-key, "North to Alaska, the gold rush is on. North to Alaska…"

We walked up Kearney Street, past the jailhouse, past the Chinese dry cleaners, and I was winded. I hadn't walked that much since 'Nam, and John picked up on it and said, "There's a Hampton Inn up ahead. Let's stop there for the night and get that hospital smell off you."

"You mean I smell?" I asked.

"Yes…figuratively speaking. Well, maybe you do smell a little like a hospital."

John bought a six-pack of beer at a liquor store, and when we checked into the hotel room, he popped open a can for each of us. I held on to the can, sat on my bed, and bounced. It felt a hell of a lot firmer than that crater in the hospital. "My feet used to hang over the end of the wooden bed frame," I said.

John ignored me. He was more interested in the baseball game on television.

I drank half the beer, and I felt so tired, my head began to spin. I collapsed backward with my feet still on the floor. John poked at me in the ribs, but I couldn't move. He lifted my feet onto the bed, set a pillow under my head, and started to unlace my boots. That's the last I remember.

I'd awake periodically, and some sports game would be blaring on the television, or John would be singing in the shower or reading the newspaper or shaving, or the room would be empty. My weight kept me in bed like a tranquilizer, and sleep spread like heavy clouds.

It was dark when I awoke with barely the strength to sit upright. I groggily asked, "What time is it?"

John turned down the volume on the TV with the remote control, scratched his hairy, bare chest, and replied, "Time? Time for me to go to bed. You've been asleep for two days now. How do you feel?"

"I feel like I've been drugged."

He chuckled. "I'm sure you have been. Are you hungry?"

"Starving is more like it."

John made me shower and shave before sauntering down the street to an outback restaurant, where I had the biggest steak on the menu, three small loaves of bread, a baked potato with all the trimmings, and five glasses of water.

When we returned to the room, I slept another day before John roused me out of bed, had me shower again, shave, and dress in a pair of jeans he bought at the Salvation Army, just my size—thirty-eight. I felt euphoric and giddy, even a little bit childish. My consciousness felt fresh and my senses tingly and translucent.

"Are your batteries recharged?" he asked.

"My head feels so clear. I can actually smell things, like the bar of soap."

"Apollo to control, ready for takeoff." John chugged the last of his beer and set it on the nightstand.

"Where are we going?" I asked.

"The last thing you said before you lost consciousness was trees. Trees it is."

Maybe I should have been disappointed at John's meager lifestyle, in contrast to the wealth he bragged about to the judge, but I wasn't. As a matter of fact, I felt more comfortable walking the streets than cruising in that Mercedes. Walking, I could smell. I could smell the salty ocean air, car exhaust, perfume as ladies walked by, restaurant food, body odors, cigarette smoke, burps, and elevator grease. It was all so tangible...alive.

The smells I enjoyed the most were flowers: passionflowers, spathodeas, orchids, jasmine, gardenias, and my favorite of all, frangipani. The hibiscus, red and white and orange, were odorless but prolific and the prettiest. I asked John, "Where are we going?"

"I'm beginning to understand why they committed you," he said, adjusting his pack and pushing the red button on the street corner to make the signal light turn green. "You keep asking me the same question."

I picked up an empty bottle out of the gutter, placed it in the trash can, and asked, "How did you ever find me?"

"Not on the Internet, like I told the doctors. Didn't I tell you the first time I visited you in the hospital?"

I shook my head.

He continued. "It was crazy, and sometimes I think I'm crazy. It's really hard to believe. I should be one of those clairvoyant television personalities. Bryan, I found you in a dream. Actually I saw that skinny little gay guy in our platoon in 'Nam. Remember? His father was a general?"

"Billy Hayman," I replied. "We called him Billy Boy." My nostrils dilated as I took in a deep, happy breath.

"That's him. That's the guy. It's the strangest damn thing in the world. He was standing in the watchtower of a sunken ship. He was actually underwater, and when he spoke, bubbles came out of his mouth. The hair on his head was floating in waves, and colorful fish were swimming in front of him and behind him. He said, 'Bryan lives in the Miami veterans' hospital, and his mind is drifting away.' That was it. I was living in Denver at the time, driving taxis, so I took the first plane out of town. When I got to Miami, I checked the VA hospital and didn't find you. I was about to give up and visit a friend of mine in Bimini when I told myself, 'Hell, why not try the mental ward,' and there you be. Thank you, Billy Hayman." John pointed to the sky.

John loved Mexican food: tacos, enchiladas, rice and beans, and chile rellenos. He loved to wash them down with a Corona beer or a Dos Equis. So we ate a lot of Mexican food all the way across the country to California, where John took me into the coastal hills to enjoy the biggest trees in the world: the wonderful California redwoods, with their soft velvet bark and height that shaded the stars at night and could tell stories of ancient Indians.

After a week in the woods, I got cold under all that shade, and I mentioned to John that I missed open skies. We took a bus ride to Montana, and we camped on the Fork River, and every night I fell asleep counting stars and making my way through the universe, leap frogging from planet to planet.

One morning I mentioned grits, and I'll be damned if we didn't go to Atlanta, Georgia, and eat honey-covered grits and hominies. We ate grits until my mouth turned dry and sticky and my tongue got so relaxed it stuck to the top of my mouth and I could hardly talk.

I told John about one of my hospital friends nicknamed Sourdough. Sourdough was sour on life without the dough to do anything about it. Some people called him Gabby Hayes because he used to smack his lips like he was toothless. John took me to a puppet show in San Francisco and fed me sourdough bread, sourdough French toast, sourdough croutons, sourdough sticks, sourdough soup, and toasted sourdough. After I finished off a sourdough salad, I got very cautious with what I talked about.

The longer I was without my medication, the more nervous I became, edgier and edgier, drifting into my thoughts for longer periods of time. My body started to itch all over, and I couldn't stop scratching.

"You want to stop in the VA hospital in Marin County," he asked, "for a checkup?"

"They might flip a straitjacket on me and not let me out."

He winced. "What were you diagnosed with?" When I didn't answer, he asked, "Why did they throw you in the psych ward?"

"PTSD and chronic depression."

"They Baker Act you?"

"I guess. I just never got out. Had nowhere to go and no way to keep myself alive."

"Things will change now. I'm in charge again. That PTSD ain't all that bad. I've had some of that myself…I think. Just hang in there, brother."

The longer I was away from the hospital, the more I wondered what was going on inside my head. My mind seemed to wander around, and a lot of times when I awoke, I didn't know where I was, like a new birth every day.

Then I lost it at the San Francisco Zoo. I guess it was a panic attack or something. I don't know.

John had asked a Thai waitress named Sarah to spend the day with us at the zoo. Sarah worked with John at the Gino's Italian restaurant in the Tenderloin district. I liked Sarah from the start, because she gave me a present: a pair of salt-and-pepper shakers from Gino's with Gino's name on them. She was really sweet and always laughing, smiling, and sharing good humor.

Trailing behind the two lovebirds, I peeled and ate peanuts, dropping every other one on the ground for the squirrels that trailed me. We reached the spider monkey's cage, and I was just eating away and dropping peanuts when I felt something grab my body really hard, nails pressing through the fabric. I looked up, and there at that mountain of zoo monkeys, instead of monkeys, were NVA soldiers behind the rocks and in the trees. Ever since 'Nam they had been tracking me down, a whole battalion, about eight hundred. They were aiming their rifles and grenade launchers and machine guns at me, awaiting the command to fire.

Those NVA soldiers were Ho Chi Minh's handpicked killers, trained from the age of conception to kill American "dogs," which I was considered. The NVA could be compared to the Gerka soldiers of Korea, the KGB of Russia, or Hitler's SS. They were good, but as long as I looked them in the eyes, they didn't shoot.

When I saw those soldiers behind the rocks, I ran up to John and put a death grip on his arm. His face turned to surprise, and my voice trembled when I said, "We got to get out of here, *now*."

I started dragging John away from Sarah, who was gawking at us. I let go of John's arm and started to run. John followed. After a fair distance, I slowed down to a march and finally slowed down enough for John to keep up. "We got to get out of here," I said.

"OK...OK. I'll get you out of here," he said. "Just don't panic on me."

"I'll try, but they're trying to ambush us."

"If you say so, but all I saw was some monkeys throwing their shit at us."

"Those weren't monkeys," I replied. "That was the NVA."

John understood. We took a taxi to Pier 54 on the San Francisco Bay and then the ferry to Salinas and hitchhiked in the back of a gardener's truck to Muir Woods, north of the city.

Around a campfire that night, in the deep woods where a lone owl hooted, John sat with his legs spread to the fire and his arms dancing with the shadows of the light. I explained to John that at the hospital, the NVA battalion would chase me around the ward, methodically trying to surround me, isolate me, flank me, and block my escapes, slowly and meticulously stalking me for the kill.

"What do they look like?" he asked.

"Whenever I made eye contact with them, they turned into the nurses and doctors at the VA hospital, but once I took my eyes off them…NVA. Oh, they're sharp looking, believe you me. They all look young with starched khaki uniforms, shiny black boots, pith helmets that cover their eyes, and canvas packs. Every one of them has an AK-47 rifle, sparkling chrome. You take your eyes off them, and they'll kill you. Look at them, and they are disguised as nurses or civilians or even children…little bastards…stick me with their communist knives, just like Caesar's assassins did to him."

John looked like a petrified rock. "I think you need some medicine," he said.

The next morning we fled north and ended up in the small Indian village of McGrath on the Kuskokwim River in Alaska, buried under tons of snow and tongue-sticking cold. I acted content up there in our one-room log cabin. The natives were really friendly as long as they weren't drinking homebrew. John said I reminded him of the animals, slow and friendly and harmless unless provoked. But those damn NVA soldiers found us there too, while John was dog-sledding along the southern bank of the Grayling River. The NVA sprung from behind the alders, snapped a marten trap, and nearly cut off my hand. We hightailed it to Seattle to thaw out for a couple of weeks and then headed for Hawaii. After four months between the beaches and jungles, although I never caught sight of the NVA sneaking around our bamboo hut, I felt their presence and smelled the sweet odor of rice cooking over open fires. John told me that the Hawaiians liked rice too, but I didn't want to hear that. I said, "That's what those gooks are doing—hiding, camouflaged. Little bastards." We snuck off the island on a moonless night and drifted to Bermuda, but Hurricane Emily blasted us out of there, through the Bermuda Triangle, and back to Florida.

"You're not thinking of returning me to the hospital, are you, John?"

"No, I'm not. But I've been thinking maybe I should have kept some of that medicine that Dr. Hensheman offered. Since we are here, I want to get some medicine for you. Calm you down a little."

"I'm OK. I'll be fine. Sometimes I think I'm a burden to you."

"You're not a burden. Remember the soldier's code of conduct in warfare. Never leave a brother behind. I'm not leaving you. I feel better with you than I've ever felt in my entire life. No matter what, we'll work it out."

"What say we go to Key West?" I asked.

John shook his head. "One place in the entire world I don't want to visit. I was born there, and Hank Laser is there. Besides, the place is full of ghosts."

I laughed at John. He was always saying I was the crazy one, and now he was talking about ghosts. "What kind of ghosts?"

"That is a figure of speech…that's all it is. Figure of speech."

"Don't you know the mayor there?"

"That is my aunt Wilhelmina."

"Darn." I cuffed my hands. "That's where the squad lives. They'll help."

John stopped in his tracks and swore under his breath. His face turned red with anger. "Bryan, you are driving me crazy with all your nonsense. You keep it up, and we will both be back in that Miami mental ward in the same room. First you got me running from the NVA, and now you say you see the squad. What the hell is going on here? I think I need some of that mental medication myself."

"But, John," I explained, "remember your dream. Billy Boy."

"Yeah…a dream."

"I'm telling you, it's more than a dream."

"Bite my ass," he hissed, his fists clenched shut.

"John, this is our destiny. For both of us. We have to go there."

"Destiny with what?"

"With peace of mind, for both of us."

"All I've got is peace of mind. I need more than that. I need a little sanity. Maybe even a six-pack of beer."

"John, you have been listening to everything I said, and we raced all over the country. Now we are going home…your home…the squad's home. It was meant to be. It is the reason we are here right now. You've taken me everyplace else I wanted to go. Why not to Key West?"

"I didn't take you anywhere. I think you make up half that shit in your head. All your rambling."

"You have to reconnect…with your past, with the person you were…with Hank Laser."

"Screw him. I don't want to see him again. He betrayed us in 'Nam, and as far as I'm concerned, he is no better than a VC."

"We have to dig up all this bad stuff and put it to rest…and Hank is one of them for you. Since you got me out of the hospital, it has been all about me. You are trying to help me stay in control, and you are feeling guilty about all the time I spent in the hospital. But, John, I can help you too. I learned some things in the hospital, and more than how to act crazy. I've seen guys like you there, and I know I can help you."

"Help me? Help me? What the hell are you talking about? You're always flipping out, and you lived years in a loony bin, and you want to help me…the funny farm, and you've seen guys like me in there too. Thanks a hell of a lot, brother."

"Yes. I can help you become the person you were before you went to Vietnam. I can help you bury the past…like Hank Laser."

"Tell you what. We get some meds for you while we are in town, and then we'll talk again. OK? See if you change your tune."

"Sure."

"OK. Sure."

I was surprised at the ease of getting meds from Dr. Hensheman. It took only about thirty minutes. I waited outside the lockable wrought-iron fence that surrounded the hospital while John went inside. Within half an hour, he returned with a bag full of pills. John said it was like Dr. Hensheman had been waiting for him, and the package was ready. John got Paxil for my anxiety, BuSpar for my mood swings, and Nefrin for the hallucinations. I told him I wasn't hallucinating, but he wouldn't listen.

I asked John, "Was that a hallucination that we went to Alaska and Hawaii and Bermuda?"

"Fuckin' A," he said. "We hitchhiked out to San Francisco one time, but all that other shit is just in your head. You are one flipped-out dude."

"I am?" I asked myself. Then I answered, "I am...I am?"

"What do you want to see next?" John asked.

"I want to see the squad, and I want to see Hank Laser."

John took the biggest sigh I'd ever seen a person take, and then he turned and walked away.

We boarded a Greyhound bus four blocks from the Southern District Courtroom, where we had started nearly a year ago. John was pensive.

The bus ride was fascinating. A chain of keys, or islands, or sand spits, as they appeared to be, swung out from the mainland of Florida like the long, tapered tail of a caiman, dividing the Atlantic Ocean from the Gulf of Mexico.

Bait shops and open-aired restaurants advertising "Fresh Fish of the Day," hotels hidden by tropical plants, and souvenir and shell shops sprang up like Ohio cornfields. Island after island, bridge after bridge, the landscape narrowed and the sky grew larger.

We made it all the way to Big Pine Key before I started getting paranoid again. John gave me one of the paranoid pills, and I felt like we had been duped into coming here. It was one big ambush. I forced John off the bus near the Winn Dixie grocery store, and we found our way into the dense dwarf pines of the Key Deer Reserve. The mosquitoes were not too bad at night. Maybe it was the meds I took that helped me sleep.

It took me only a day to get in trouble there. A State Ranger caught me feeding a slice of white bread to a skinny key deer no taller than my waist, its rack the width of tricycle handlebars. I could see the deer's ribs. Ranger Bob wrote a $500 ticket, but when he asked my address and I pointed to the woods, he tore up the ticket and threw it at me. I thought he wanted me to pick it up, and when I did and handed it back to him, he ran us out of there at the blast of his whistle. We thumbed it down the road in the back of a truck with a band of Cubans, down narrowing Highway 1. From the back of that truck, I could feel the world changing. Roadside gas stations and marinas spread farther apart, and the land sunk deeper into the water and exploded with greenery. Palm trees grew into blue skies, scattered mangroves clogged the bright-green waterway, and the skies filled with huge white American egrets and curved-billed ibis. The only signs of civilization were the towering and massive concrete electric towers that were steady roosts for large osprey that perched on the pinpoint top and tore apart fresh mullet. Humidity soaked my clothes.

Finally, we reached the dense metropolis of Key West. Thick vines, towering trees, and fragrant puffs of flowers framed each and every home, built so close together, you couldn't shake them apart. Quaint wooden houses with shutters, overhanging balconies, white picket fences, tin roofs, faded shade canopies, decorative metal fences—it was a study of tropical paradise.

At the southern-most point in Key West, America ended. The next stop was Cuba, ninety miles across the swift and deeply blue Gulf Stream.

I'd read my tourist brochures in the truck and learned that for centuries, this fantasyland had been the home of pirates, fortune hunters, artists and dreamers, millionaires, and eccentrics. Now multitudes of tourists searched for the ghosts of such legends in bars,

T-shirt shops, restaurants, and fishing and dive boats. Everybody was looking for something, including us.

We hid out at the Hamaca Park Missile Site near the Key West Airport, where a platoon of American Vietnam veterans had formed a defensive perimeter in the mangrove swamp thick with no-see-ums, which are tiny, tiny black flies. They packed the bite of a fire ant. Some of the vets called the bugs "ninety/one hundreds"—90 percent bite and 100 percent invisible. John found courage and strength among friends, but the damn place was infested with the NVA. I heard their bushwhacking boots snapping Brazilian pepper trees one night, and I made John take me to Duval Street crowded with Hemingway Festival revelers. Since Hemingway had lived in Key West for twelve years, the residents celebrated his birthday annually, and today was July 23, Hemingway's birthday.

"I think I'm ready," John said. He had been drinking way too much beer to be ready for anything. "To meet those ghosts...to meet Hank again."

"I told you so."

John said, "It's Friday night, and I know exactly where he is."

John led the way down an alley hung with palm fronds, ferns, and elephant leaves. As we approached the noise of inebriated revelers, the air started to smell like humid spilled beer. The bar had no walls, just a grass-thatched roof with wooden columns holding it up. We entered the doorless bar, and out the far side was the moon ray lighting up the Atlantic water. There was a centrally located rectangular-shaped bar in the middle. We headed for the farthest corner.

Bearded, gruff-faced wannabe pirates in flip-flops and sandals occupied most of the seats, and some stood in small groups of three or four, chatting away, laughing boisterously, and waving the beer bottles.

"Stinky's has the cheapest beer in town, and I'm sure Hank hasn't moved up much in style since I was here last." John started drinking nonstop like a Bubba, and his eyes kept scanning the place.

The shapely waitress in short shorts was attracted to John when she discovered he was a conch, the nickname given to people born in Key West. The name came from the first Bahamian settlers cooking conch chowder and conch fritters made from the meat of the local queen conchs, which at that time had been everywhere. Now I understand it is against the law to harvest them, because they are becoming extinct.

Since the waitress had lived in the Keys for only eight months, she was thrilled to befriend a real conch. John said, "Locals used to tell visitors, 'You'll live here forever if you kiss a conch and eat a grunt.'"

"What's a grunt?" she asked.

"The noise I make after sex."

She kept coming back to our table.

The surfboard that hung from the ceiling by two wires belonged to Freddie Powell, who had carried it for five months around the Keys until he realized there wasn't a wave big enough to ride. Before Freddie had thumbed home to California, he had traded the board for a case of beer. That was Gayle Levelock's mask and snorkel dangling over the cash register. Gayle had gotten a nosebleed the first time she dove, and she had traded the dive gear for drinking money.

"What would you like?" Val asked me with a smile.

"A diet coke, please."

Tommy Littleton's daypack hung over a bottle of rum. He had been run over on Highway 1 near the new Sears Center when he had crossed the road for a six-pack of beer. His buddy had donated the daypack as a tombstone. Barbara Schaffer's mini-size bra draped over the ice chest (she had been lucky to get a shot of tequila for that one, because when she had ripped it off and swung it wildly over her head, hardly a head had turned. She had not had much to brag about). Of course John didn't know all the paraphernalia, because he had been gone nearly twenty years, but he knew his share. Some of the smaller memorabilia, like foreign coins and bills, an ivory toothpick, seashells, belt buckles, earrings, tie clips, and rings, were embedded on the bar counter under thumb-deep epoxy. We sat under Arnim's

Alaskan moose rack, a prize that had taken him a lifetime to attain. When he had moved north to Virginia, he had left it here to share with his friends.

I looked up from my diet coke and saw John staring at a man hanging at the bar. The man was a little over six feet tall, with arms buffed and a chest that stretched his sleeveless white T-shirt. His head was shaved bald, and a gold earring sparkled from his left earlobe. His cheeks were covered with a full peppered beard. All he needed was a parrot on his shoulder to make him look like a modern-day pirate.

His partner was equally muscular but darker complexioned, a Cuban, with long, glistening black hair. He had a dark goatee, sparkling eyes, and a gold chain around his neck that would have made Mel Fisher, the famous Key West wreck diver, look twice.

A young girl approached the two of them and began to play coy little touching games with them, running her forefinger around her thin gold necklace, shifting her weight from foot to foot, and twisting shyly.

"Who is that guy?" I asked.

"You don't recognize him? That's Hank Laser."

Hank and his two friends disappeared in the back room and stayed there long enough for John to drink another beer before they came out snorting and playing with their noses.

John got up, approached Hank head-on, and said, "Hank Laser, remember me?"

Hank took a deep snort out of his left nostril, some of the white cocaine powder still dangling there, and looked John over from head to toe. He said, "Lieutenant Marley. What brings you back here?"

"It's home, Hank, remember?" John shot his eyes at the young girl next to Hank and asked, "Is this your daughter?"

The girl smiled, and so did the Cuban, but Hank acted annoyed.

John asked, "How's your wife, Mary?"

Hank answered, "She's down at the birdhouse on South Roosevelt, tending to her lost roost. She's fine." Hank took a head-wrenching gulp of beer, his Adam's apple working quickly to slug it down. The girl whispered something in Hank's ear, and he patted her on the butt, his fingers wide and friendly. Hank said, "Now if you will excuse us," and he and the girl disappeared arm in arm, laughing.

We sat back down, and John ordered himself another beer, and then another and another. I could tell he was taking a walk down memory lane, but I didn't want to bother him. I just sat there listening to the band and watching all the pretty girls shake their flower gardens, and then I helped pick up trash on the floor.

When Hank returned to the bar, he was alone and swollen chested. Hank stopped alongside John, now leaning on the bar. Hank stared at me and said, "Bryan Donovan. I'll be a son of a bitch. I remember you used to love those ham and lima-bean C rations. You'd trade your cigarettes and candy bars for ham and lima beans. You were such a retard."

John lifted his head off the bar and looked shocked and angry.

I said, "Uh-oh," and then I got real close to Hank and whispered, "You'd better not call me names in front of John. He doesn't like it."

"You mean he doesn't like people calling you a big-ass baboon?"

I nodded. "Yeah, things like that. He hates that."

John's back stiffened. His head swung around like it were attached by a spring, and he couldn't seem to hold focus on Hank.

"The birds migrate in the fall and return in April," I said. I knew I was losing it, but I couldn't help it. I was just so darn nervous.

John stood toe to toe with Hank and said, "Ahhh yay goood ddo."

Poor John. On top of everything else, he was an alcoholic, and when he reached the point of no return, he became totally nonsensical, officially inarticulate.

Hank leaned back, cocked his right arm, and threw the fist into John's face. John reeled backward, crashing over a table. Hank ran right after him, picked him up, and hit him again, but this time harder, as John wasn't moving.

I really didn't know what to do, so I called out, "Call nine one one. Call nine one one."

That just got everyone in the bar looking my way, standing up, drawing closer, and laughing.

I kept yelling " nine one one," but everyone was more interested in getting a closer look at John on the ground and started pushing and shoving, and, like a grass fire, a free-for-all fight started. Two blokes grabbed John by each arm, and Hank buried his fist in John's stomach all the way to Hank's wrist. The two men whirled around, dragged John to a window opening, and tossed him outside.

"Welcome home," Hank roared.

John quickly stood up, took two steps, fell off the curb, and landed on his face in the gutter. I rushed outside, got down alongside him, and saw his eyes chase in the gutter little pollywogs that skirted from clouds of pollution to clumps of algae. John could fall no farther, sink no deeper, and feel no less afraid. Warmed in his own piss, he slid calmly into a state of the inevitable. John's hand reached for his side, and he touched the pouch. He patted it awkwardly, and then his fingers stopped moving along with the rest of his body.

3

A DEAD MAN OPENED ONE EYE

I lifted John into my arms, and he groaned softly. His eyes fluttered, he squinted, made eye contact, sighed, and whispered, "Bryan."

I smiled and replied, "That's me…your best friend."

That made him smile. He closed his eyes, and his body grew limp.

Then something very strange and spiritual happened. I looked toward the crowded Duval Street, filled with glittering lights and street vendors and beer-toting revelers. In front of Sloppy Joe's Bar, on the corner of Duval and Green Street, stood Billy Boy. None of the tourists saw him. If they had, they would have screamed and fled in terror, because Billy Boy looked as mutilated as the day he died. His left arm was missing, sinews and muscles dripping blood onto his muddy jungle fatigues and the ground. His fair-skinned face was caked with mud, and his blond hair was spiked. Billy Boy signaled me with his good right hand to follow him.

At last someone to help, I thought. I weaved and wrestled my way through the crowd, trying to catch up, but Billy always remained about the same distance ahead. I quit shoving and bumping into people and slowed down, and so did Billy. I followed him past the Schooner Wharf bar, looked through the open doors, and saw the famous blond singer Sally Foster strumming her guitar and singing "Me and Bobby McGee." I scooted around the Pier House and back along a deserted and moon-swept beach, where a dugout canoe bobbed in the surf. It was about eighteen feet long and carved from a giant cedar tree, like the original Caloosa Indians navigated with. Wider and heavier than most canoes, its polished keel was smeared with black tallow. Billy Boy stood ankle deep next to the canoe and pointed toward the moon's beam on the open water. Then Billy Boy looked into my eyes and mouthed the word "home." He turned around and walked into the water until his head disappeared.

I had to follow.

I placed John in the bow of the canoe, and he slumped against the hard ribbing. I found a knitted cushion on the seat and placed it behind him for a backrest so he wouldn't fall over and crack his head. Moving to the stern, I pushed the craft into the still water. I placed one foot aboard and kicked with the other, balanced myself, picked up a paddle, sat down, and started rowing. I powered the craft with decision and pride, confident of my direction, as if Billy were my point man and the moon were my compass needle. The canoe found its path across the Gulf, through tidal rapids and shallow whirlpools, into the mysterious darkness of light.

If John had been awake, he'd have been ranting about how far we were from shore and the lack of directional lights, supplies, or even a confirmed destination. He would have thought I was nuts. Thank God he was passed out. If John awoke and I told him I was following Billy Boy's directions, he would have jumped overboard and probably drowned himself. The sea turned rough, and the swells became long and steep as I slid down the backside of waves. But after a while, the sea calmed down to a mirror's reflection. My paddle began to touch the bottom, and then I had to shorten my strokes so I didn't hit rocks. Dark billowing clouds filled the sky. Streaking lightning illuminated distant palm trees. The sea sucked me forward. I wasn't in control, and I wasn't afraid. I was curious.

The bottom of the canoe scraped the coral reef. Then the tip of my paddle sunk into deep, sucking mud, the water no more than three inches deep. I stood up and stepped into the water, but I sunk all the way to my knees before I stiffened my grip on the gunwales and prevented myself from being torn loose from the canoe. I struggled back inside, dripping wet and muddy, and cast my fate to fortune. The moon lighted spikes of immature mangroves that grew out of the water in thick clumps, like cigars, and blue crabs waved long pinchers and retreated defensively in puffs of mud. Ahead, the shadow of a key filled the horizon.

This unnamed key was one of one thousand spread amid the shallow backcountry water of the Florida Keys. Soon I was covered in shadows, and the stiff mangrove branches spread apart and formed a channel the width of the canoe. I took one final sweep of the paddle and ducked forward as branches scraped my back. The canoe glided down a slight decline of rippling water that gurgled into an open, tranquil pond. With each paddle stroke, the plankton-rich water swirled in circles of light.

Fireflies shone everywhere.

The canoe slid across the ink-dark water and went aground. For the first time, I spoke. "I think we are home, John."

I docked on the sandy white beach, and, by the light of the moon filtering through the overhead palm leaves, I picked up a seat cushion, and then I picked up John and walked up the beach toward a short lean-to roofed with palm leaves. This was to be John's bed for the night, and I placed him gently on his side, with the cushion as his pillow. The warm summer breeze was his blanket. I lay down beside him, said a short prayer thanking God, the squad, and Billy Boy, and fell asleep.

At first light, I awoke and saw that the lean-to was not a dream, nor was this lagoon. I stood up and wanted to run into the water, splash, and frolic, but I didn't want to wake John. The place smelled of wood smoke, peat, and scented flower buds. I lay down next to John and watched him sleep for what must have been another hour. He didn't move.

"Come on, John," I said. "Let's play." His eyelids fluttered but remained closed.

Frustrated, I sat in the lotus position and watched the jungle slowly awaken. The head and neck of a swimming anhinga bird appeared offshore, creating a large *V* in the still water. A flock of white ibis, distinguished by their decurved red bills, flew in line formation, wings beating rapidly, and then glided in unison. Their necks were extended and feet dangling. A pair of prehistoric wood storks, bald headed and with scaly necks, hissed at each other on the opposite shoreline. Flying toward me was a white skimmer with its lower mandible slicking through the water. It gulped its catch and continued its plowing flight. The black crown on its head reminded me of an English professor's hairdo. The high screech of the long-tail tropical bird, the laughter of gulls, and the splash of a diving cormorant filled the morning silence. A green palm warbler flitted from branch to branch. A flock of scarlet ibis skirted the distant shore, pecking here, pecking there.

I looked back at John. He was still in the deep throes of alpha sleep. He had hours to go. I stood up and explored on my own. Not more than ten feet away was a dugout fire pit filled with dark mud, half-burnt coconut husks, and driftwood sticks. An old dented metal coffee pot was perched on a rock, tilted. I picked it up and looked inside. It was filled with spiderwebs and sand. I set it back down on the same rock.

A rare and mature baobab tree in full bloom caught my attention. Within its huge, thick gray trunk—coarse, knobby, and wrinkled— were wooden planks and more palm leaves resembling a jungle tree house.

I couldn't believe my eyes. I ran across the sand to a grand railed staircase that hung nearly vertical from the tree. Apparently the stairs became steeper as the tree grew. I shook the handrail, and it wobbled precariously. I knew better, but I cautiously climbed the steps, counting them as I tested each one before proceeding—seventeen in all. I stuck my head through a hatch in the overhead floor and saw the gray trunk of the baobab tree protruded in the middle of the room. The tree provided a dilapidating foundation for the floor's strength.

I climbed inside the room filled with flowering tree limbs and vines, and I worked my way around the tree house, breaking limbs, uprighting two chairs, removing a tree limb from a hammock, and clearing a bamboo tabletop. There were no doors or room partitions, but the circular trunk provided spacious delineation. The walls, waist high, were open to the jungle. Solid beams held up the sagging roof. This tree house provided a breathtaking panoramic view, a welcomed breeze, and cooling shade.

A pair of multicolored Cuban macaws, a species that had been considered extinct for fifty years, flew between vines. "Raaaaaak... raaaaaak."

"Home," I said. "Home."

When I turned around, a shiny glint caught my attention on top of a peeling yellow cupboard shelf. I stared at it in wonder, drew closer, and saw it was a cigarette lighter like the ones our platoon in Vietnam had bought at the Dong Tam Army Exchange in Saigon twenty-some years ago. My fingers surrounded the lighter. On the front side was an engraved etching of the cartoon character Snoopy, scarf askew, goggles in place, and a leather cap tightly over his ears, steering wheel in hand. Snoopy was flying on top of his doghouse. Above the engraving was the inscription "5th, 60th, 9th Inf. Div., NAM, 1968." I flipped the lighter over and read the inscription "IF YOU CAN'T EAT IT, DRINK IT, OR FUCK IT, KILL IT."

Catching my breath, my fingers dropped the Zippo like a hot iron, and I backstepped, farther and farther, until I flipped over backward, my legs entangled in vines and my fingers clutching a sagging timber.

A good twenty feet below was a congested pile of logs and coconuts, resembling a pungi trap, which was a VC hole filled with sharp sticks infected with cow dung and human excrement. If a soldier had fallen into the pit, he'd have been immediately evacuated before infection set in.

"John," I screamed. "*John.*" When I tried to pull myself up, the timber cracked and drew closer to collapsing. "John." I couldn't see him, but I could hear his long and steady stride, his feet hardly making an impression. He was grumbling like a paratrooper.

Within seconds I was looking up at his red face, puffy and stern, a hand reaching out and pulling me to safety.

As I sat on the floor, puffing away, he continued. "I leave you one second, and you nearly kill yourself. You have to give me a break here pretty soon, Bryan. I can't watch every move you make."

I ran over to the lighter, picked it up, and pushed it in his face. "Look," I said. "Look."

His hungover expression turned curious, and then he was annoyed. "Now don't start talking about the squad again," John said, grinding his teeth. "I've about had it. You got your medication. Now I need some medication."

But I couldn't help it. "Nobody else in the world would have this." When John didn't reply, I closed in and asked, "Who do you think left this here, huh? Who? Who?"

John scowled. "It wasn't an owl, which I'm surprised that you didn't suggest." He was stone sober by now. He touched his swollen face and winced.

"It was Billy Boy. He led us here. The squad is out there just as sure as the NVA is out there, and they're coming, all of them."

John acted like he had gotten shot in the butt. He jumped into the air, came down pointing a finger in my face, and said, "Hey, Peter Pan, I'll take you back to that hospital in Miami. You understand me? I swear to God I will. I'm getting tired of this, real tired. I mean enough's enough." He took two deep breaths to calm himself.

I got so flustered that I didn't know what I was saying, but I said it anyway. "I wasn't funning you."

"I mean it." He pointed. "One more word, and you are going back to the funny farm. Let them deal with you. You are driving me nuts."

I thought of those faded green walls and the bars on the window and the smell of depression suffocating me like a plastic bag over my head. At the same time, I could feel myself losing control. I said, "But the Africans didn't know what they were doing either. They ran away and thought they were going to a better life."

He calmed down a little, adjusting his baseball cap and sniffling. He said, "Now don't go getting yourself all worked up and your wires crossed. Just calm down."

"But goldfish love the water too," I exclaimed.

"Of course. Yeah, I bet they do." John went over, picked up a banana out of a fruit basket, and peeled it.

I closed my eyes and took five deep breaths. I didn't need a panic attack right now. When I opened my eyes, John was staring at me. He asked, "And why didn't you help me out last night?"

"I brought you here," I replied.

"But I got the shit kicked out of me, and you didn't lift a finger."

"You told me not to get in trouble and hit anyone. You told me to call nine one one. I remember."

"OK. OK. I did. I admit that. But next time you see two thugs whaling on me, lend me a hand. Please. OK? At least pull them off me."

"I'll kill 'em, John. All three of them."

"No. No. See, there you go. Don't kill anyone. Don't crush anybody's skull. Just help me. Please...please."

I nodded my head and sighed. "Even if there are five or six, I'll help you."

"That's right. If I ask for help, *help*." He shook his head and continued. "I tell you...trouble finds me wherever I go."

He accidentally spit in my face, and I closed my eyes and took a couple more deep breaths. When I opened my eyes, I was alone. I looked out the window and saw that John had returned to the lean-to and was falling asleep again. I climbed down the staircase, sat on a log, looked out at that magnificent lagoon, and calmed myself even more.

I don't know why I saw Billy again. The only explanation is that my brain, being half-dead, doesn't catch everything it is supposed to and probably catches some things it isn't supposed to. I grabbed a hold of my right ear and pushed it into my inner ear. It was a peculiar bad habit, but it gave me something to do when I got nervous. I never could get my whole ear into that little hole, but I was compelled to try. I played with my ear, working to fit it all inside.

Of all the squad members, I'd liked Billy Boy the most, because he'd been so marvelously different and interesting to watch. He'd teased me a lot about getting injured first. He'd said it was because I'd been the biggest. I'd thought that was peculiar, because I'd seen lots of short guys blown up too. Size hadn't seemed to make a difference. If you'd been in the wrong spot at the wrong time, you'd gone to the right place, which is heaven, I hope. Billy Boy had never had a serious thing to say about anything. Everyone in the squad had guessed that if he had gotten serious, he would have broken down and cried, so he had never gone there.

Billy Boy had grown up in the Mission District of San Francisco. As a teenager, he had been faced with the Vietnam War and had thought it was disgusting. In protest, he had dressed up in his favorite tie-dye Native American pants and shirt, combed out his curly blond hair— which had cascaded over his shoulders, and walked down Mission Street, singing songs of peace. He had picked flowers out of people's gardens and handed them to astonished passersby. He hadn't known it at the time, but he had been the first "flower child." Janice Joplin had found out about him and infamized him with a song.

One delusional night, Billy Boy had fired up a joint of marijuana and decided to visit Southeast Asia himself to create peace through love. He had joined the army. Training had been wild, because Billy Boy hadn't taken any of it seriously. He had always thought it was a big joke, and when he had fired a right-handed machine gun from his left side by curling over the top and looking through the sights with his left eye, the commanding officer had caught him and told him he was nuts. Billy Boy had said, "If you can't take a joke, you don't belong in the army." That had been Billy Boy, and he hadn't been able to wait to get to Vietnam so he could spread his gospel of love and peace.

Actually, things had gotten better for him over in 'Nam, because he had found some of the wildest marijuana in the world, which had made his mission all the more feasible. Billy Boy had picked bigger flowers along wider street corners and had promulgated nonresistance.

How could he have realistically done this? His grandfather had been four-star General Michael Hayman, commander of I Corps in Vietnam. In spite of the wild stories about his grandson's antics, General Hayman had known that his grandson had the family's killer instinct, and the general had disregarded all rumors of the boy's treason. So Billy Boy had walked the countryside under the protection of his platoon, had collected wildflowers that lined the canals, and had dispersed them from a straw basket, to the left and right, as his platoon had marched through hostile villages and slaughtered gooks who ran around in black silk pajamas.

Billy Boy had said the silk was passion, reason was death, rice was deliverance, and men were not to be angered. So logically Billy Boy had gone after those little Army of the Republic of Vietnamese soldiers, ARVNSs, who he had been supposed to be training in the tactics of night ambush. Billy Boy had learned about love in a two-foot-diameter foxhole when the moon had been full, and the NVA had come out like red ants sprinkled with poison dust.

I just sat there thinking about Billy Boy, how he had looked with his long hair dangling around his battle helmet, flowers in the camouflaged band.

I stood up and looked around. A table made out of two-inch-diameter poles and lashed together with twine was strung between two tree trunks. Next to it was a broken three-legged stand, turned over, and a metal washbasin thrown into a clump of weeds.

I maneuvered my way back down the rickety steps and passed an outhouse with a half-moon cut out of the door. I explored a narrow deer trail that skirted north through a forest of poisonwood trees and manchineels, the barks and leaves of both trees poisonous to the touch. A pair of marsh rabbits, pint size with bulging eyes, flickered into the underbrush without a sound.

The trail opened into a large meadow of tall saw grass and fruit trees—lime, avocado, mango, grapefruit, and orange. I reached up and picked a grapefruit, peeled the skin, and tore off a section. It was dripping sweet. Chewing savagely, I picked two more and followed the trail through some eelgrass, finally stopping at a humanmade circular rock wall as tall as my waist. I looked over the wall into water as clear as a swimming pool. Healthy-size bluegills swam in circles, and freshwater shrimp hugged the rocks.

I thought of the Spanish explorer Ponce de Leon and wondered if he had stood here hundreds of years ago wondering if this were the fountain of youth he had so desperately sought. Now this freshwater was a fountain of life. Water percolated over the sides. The animal tracks around the artesian well were as varied as the species. A pair of Cuban sandhill cranes, perched in the bare limbs of the closest mahogany tree, twisted their necks in wonder.

Holy cow, I thought. We can stay here forever.

I ran back to tell John the good news, and when I burst into the clearing, John was standing there with his face on fire.

When I ran up to him, he blasted me with, "Where the hell are we?"

I backstepped, caught my breath, and replied, "You...you don't know?"

"How the hell am I supposed to know? I just went looking for town, and all I found was water and birds, not a person or house in sight. We're on a damn island. What the hell is going on?"

"Actually we are on an island. An island has a source for freshwater, and a key has no freshwater."

"What the fuck is going on?"

I told him about last night, about following Billy Boy from Sloppy Joe's and the canoe ride. John's jaw lowered with each and every scene until it was about to touch the ground.

"You got to be shitting me?" he asked.

"I'm not. I'm really not."

He sat down there on the water's edge and didn't move.

"There's a tree house here too," I said.

He didn't budge.

"Are you hungry?"

He grabbed his head and squeezed, stood up, and returned to the lean-to. He fell forward and assumed the fetal position.

I backstepped away, returned to that grove, and picked some oranges, grapefruits, key limes, and peaches. I returned to the tree house, emptied the fruit into a wooden bowl, and cleaned up the place, enough for us to eat and sleep. I knew it would be our new home.

There was a twelve-foot-long bamboo fishing pole leaning against the trunk of the baobab tree. Some fishing line was still tied to the tip. The other end of the line had a little rusted hook. I used a piece of coconut for bait and caught a mangrove snapper right there on the beach. When I cast out even farther the second time, my line got hooked on the bottom, and I had a heck of a time freeing it. Luckily I didn't lose that hook. I cast closer to shore the next time and caught another snapper. With enough for supper, I cleaned them and skewered them on a green stick, just like a barbecue. When John awoke again, I served the fish with oranges, coconuts, and bananas.

John was beyond anger and words. He ate in silence, disappeared into the tree house, and was asleep before sunset.

"Stand up straight," John hollered at me. He was definitely becoming himself again.

Sweating and taking a rest, I leaned on a shovel handle that had a bent tip, knee deep in the freshwater pond. John hadn't done much of anything since we got here, but he was sweating. He wiped his brow with his forearm and then wiped his arm on his T-shirt.

I replied, "This place is magical, and here it is."

"Here it is," he agreed. A bald eagle flew overhead. John's eyes drifted to the bird and then shifted the other way to a fluttering swallowtail butterfly. He said, "In all my years in the woods, I can't remember seeing so damn many birds and animals in one place."

"Yep." I felt proud of them all. I looked up at the overhead canopy of thick vines, air plants, and dangling old man's beard. I said, "This is what home is supposed to feel like." I quit twisting my ear and asked, "Do you think we're going to stay here, forever?"

John squirmed and whispered, "Aaaahhhhh."

I said, "I like it here."

He stopped and shot me a glance that could have downed a jet plane. When I retreated in silence, he sat down near the campfire where the bugs were the fewest and said, "We are not going to be together forever, remember that."

"But you told the judge you were going to be my guardian."

"And you were going to be my guardian too. But one of these days, you're going to find a girl and get married and have a family all your own."

I didn't feel bad about that. Not too much anyway.

"Just like you, John?"

"Yeah, just like me. I won't leave you. I just want you to learn to take care of yourself. We are partners for now, but not forever."

"That's because I'm a burden."

"You're not a burden, as long as you do as I tell you. Nothing will go wrong."

John glanced at the moon and said, "I've got to quit drinking."

"That's a good idea," I replied. "You always act so much nicer when you're sober."

"That's not the reason I want to quit drinking. I think it's driving me crazy."

"Crazy," I agreed. "It'll do that too."

He continued. "I'm going to have to get a job." He looked up at me and said, "And you are going to stay here, out of trouble."

I replied, "I won't get in trouble around here, because there's no trouble to get into."

"You're very creative, Bryan. Don't sell yourself short."

I guffawed, silly-like, rocking my head and rolling my shoulders like a buoy in a stormy sea. I asked him, "Was I a war hero, John? Was I?"

"Of course you were. Everyone over there was a war hero."

"What did I do?"

"You could carry more gear on your back than an army personnel carrier—a radio, a machine gun, ropes around your neck, bandoleers of ammunition across your chest. Everything short of an outboard motor."

"I like it when you tell me about myself, because I can't remember."

"You leave the remembering to me. You just do what I tell you."

John grunted and glanced deeper into my eyes. Sometimes he was so innocent, so full of love and trusting. He glanced at my temple where I had gotten shot. I felt it. It was flat, like it had gone through a buzz saw and grown back flat.

Sometimes I think John felt responsible for what had happened to me. I don't remember. He said before my accident, I had been playful, lighthearted, bright, and witty, the heavyweight wrestling champion in our battalion.

John looked me over and said, "Give me a hundred."

I grinned and dropped to the push-up position and started counting them out as if I were playing music, relaxed and cheerful-like. When I finished exercising, I stood at attention, smiling.

"Give me another hundred," John said, which I did even more easily and cheerfully.

"I like it when you give me orders too," I said. "It makes me feel good."

"Everything makes you feel good," John replied.

"It does, because I feel good. I'm happy here, and I don't want anything to go wrong."

He grew fidgety. "Then nothing will."

I picked up a coconut in my left hand, picked up a rock in the other hand, set the coconut on a boulder, and cracked it open. I drank the white milk, and some dribbled down my chest. I said, "I don't want to leave here. Those NVA soldiers are not chasing me away again. Come hell or high water, come death and damnation, come scurvy and starvation, I'm sticking this one out." I smiled so big, my whole heart showed through, but John looked anything but convinced. I continued. "Remember you told me about your first night in Vietnam, and you thought the VC were sneaking through the perimeter of our camp, and they were on the other side of that aluminum boat you were huddled against, and you couldn't sleep all night, and you lay there with your finger on the trigger of your M16, ready to shoot anything that moved? But nothing happened that night, except you didn't sleep, and you scared yourself nearly to death."

He smiled sheepishly. "Yeah, that was crazy."

"Remember in the morning what you said I told you about 'Nam?"

"No. Refresh my memory."

"I told you that the greatest enemy of any soldier was fear. President Roosevelt told that to America during the Depression. 'There is nothing to fear but fear itself.'"

"Thanks, Preacher. I'll remember that."

"John, I think you need me as much as I need you. At least for now."

"You could be right, Bryan. You could be right."

4

TROUBLE FINDS A FRIEND

My stubbornness delayed John's departure. However, the delay proved miraculous for John. Within a week, his body metamorphosed like a butterfly. His posture straightened, and the nervous twitch in his hands quieted down to a tremor. The skin on his arms and face turned olive in color, his voice smoothed, and his eyes deepened and sparkled. Most of all, his mental outlook improved. I guess with me not to worry about, he became cheerful and downright helpful. This was all in conjunction with a lot of hard work fixing up our home, healthy food, and fresh spring water. Mostly the water.

As a team, over a two-week span, we cleaned the rain gutters around the tree-house roof and then filled sand into the abandoned cistern at the base of the tree, thus depriving the mosquitoes of a breeding tank. We hauled freshwater from the artesian well in cleaned-out gourds and filled the shower tank with freshwater after letting it aerate for a couple of days in the sun. The frayed vines securing the tree house to the branches needed tightening and replacement. (I had to scour the shorelines for discarded ropes, and beachcombing became a daily adventure.) As all the timbers were fitted with mortise and tendon joints, they were rock solid, and the swollen wooden pegs were equally sturdy—definitely the handicraft of boat builders, probably pirates.

Daily there were fish to catch, fruit to gather, and meals to prepare, and the two of us became our own Robinson Crusoe family. Our diet became vegetarian creative. John liked my coconut pancakes the best with two gull eggs over easy (gull eggs were the most plentiful along the sandy shores of the north lagoon), fresh-squeezed orange juice served in a coconut-shell goblet, fried bananas, and an array of sliced mangoes. I dried bananas and made them into flour for pastries, crusts, and chip snacks. The longan fruit was dried and eaten like raisins. Fiddle ferns with passion-fruit dressing became a daily salad. For a stew, I mixed green plantains, bananas, coconut oil, cubed calabaza, and snapper. After a few days, our palates craved starches, but in spite of the craving, our waists slimmed down, and our energy levels escalated.

After much discussion, we concluded the camp was built by marooned pirates years ago. The pirates never would have survived without the artesian well, and that's why the well was elevated to the status of an altar.

There was a controversy about the name of our home. I called it Sanctuary Key, but John named it Hangover Key. I guess it would continue to mean different things to both of us. The water surrounding the key had probably been deeper hundreds of years ago, but storms and hurricanes filled in the reefs with sand and muck, and the aggressive mangroves spread their protective roots. The water depth was too shallow for larger boats to navigate, and the island was too remote from Key West for kayakers to venture into. We were definitely secluded by the mangroves that surrounded the outer island like a concertina fence.

Why we were there became a subject of silence, because John would cut me short whenever I mentioned the "the squad led us here" story. He preferred to think of it as haphazard fate. Time would pick the winner.

Without entertainment at night, we'd sit around the hypnotic campfire at the edge of the lagoon, and John would tell me stories about hitchhiking around the country, which he had done when I had been in the hospital, and about what I had been like in Vietnam.

"Tell me what's in that pouch?" I asked.

John looked at the black pouch on his belt and patted it proudly. He answered, "Like I said before, I'll show you when I'm ready."

I opened my mouth to reply, but I stopped myself. John was right. He'd tell me when he was ready, but at the time, I had no idea just how long that would be.

John told stories about the history of his family as professional soldiers. I knew he exaggerated sometimes, but I just loved to listen to him talk around the campfire at night. He told me about the Marley family fighting the invading Huns in northern Europe, and the invading Mongols in Siberia. His kinfolk sat with King Arthur as knights of the Round Table and drank wine with Robin Hood in the Sherwood forest. John said that recorded history did not document his family deeds, but the legends of his family were passed down through history in fables and allegories. The Marley family cherished and celebrated warfare.

The first recorded history of a warring American Marley was Buck Private First Class Daniel Marley, who had served in the army during the Spanish American War. Having had escaped the explosion aboard the battleship *Maine* in the Havana Harbor in 1898, Daniel had joined Teddy Roosevelt's Rough Riders, a diverse group of Indian fighters, students, lawyers, and roughnecks. Daniel had flown in the first reconnaissance balloon ever, drifting over San Juan Hill and waving flags to relay the movement of Spanish troops to Teddy himself.

The next famous Marley soldier was John's grandfather, Thomas Marley, an army colonel in World War I. Colonel Marley had spent sixteen months in the Marigot trenches, freezing in the winter and roasting in the summer. He had escaped death at the expense of a fellow soldier when a German hand grenade had been thrown six feet away from the two of them, the grenade landing in an open pot of boiling coffee. The brave enlisted man had thrown himself on the live fire, on top of the pot, and two seconds later had been blown to pieces.

After the war, Colonel Thomas had retired and returned home to Key West. He had thrown his hat into the political arena and had helped sculpt Key West's destiny. When the 1935 hurricane had destroyed Flagler's railroad, the only route to the Lower Keys, Thomas had lobbied Washington for a highway to replace the railroad. His undaunted efforts and unrivaled leadership had persuaded Washington to sign a blank check for the highway's development.

Thomas's second-oldest son, John's father, had been a buck sergeant in World War II. Samuel Privott Marley had served in the army supply corps. After the Battle of the Bulge, near the end of the war, he had drunk vodka on the outskirts of Berlin with the Russians. Samuel had become a politician like his father and had created an environmental coop in Key West that had saved the only American reef from sponge divers and overzealous fishermen. He had amalgamated the city's Bubbas to create environmentally friendly hotels—not the tall and ungodly buildings like in Miami, but plush and landscaped hideaways where tourists had felt privileged to spend their money. Money had flowed to Key West by the planeloads.

"What happened then?" I asked.

"My dad died in a car accident along the Eighteen Mile Stretch on Highway One between Homestead and Key Largo."

"I'm sorry." I lowered my head in respect.

He continued. "My mom was in the car with him, and she died too. They're both buried in the Key West Cemetery."

"I'm sorry to hear that one too," I replied. "So I guess it is just you and me."

"Yes, it is."

"You know I learned a lot about living with PTSD in that hospital, John, and I can see you are going in the right direction. The doctors structured our day and gave us lots of positive support, and we exercised and ate healthy, just like we are here. It all helps—it really does."

"Then I must be getting healthier, then, because I sure feel healthier. Besides, I'm getting too old to handle those hangovers."

"And I am here to help you. That's my job."

"And my job is to bring you back to reality so you'll quit hallucinating all the time and talking about the squad."

"But…"

"That is as much as I want you to talk about them."

On the twenty-first day in the sanctuary, John took a morning dip
in the freshwater pond I'd built near the artesian well. When he returned to our camp, I met him at the trail's end, my bare feet dancing
in the sand. I asked, "Can I keep him, John, can I? Can I keep him?"

"What the hell are you talking about now?" John asked as he ate
an orange he had picked along the way. "What?"

"I got a little fishy here. I never seen anything like it before. It's got
eyes on the top of its head, and it's got eyes in the back of its head. I
can't hold it anywhere where it don't see me. Can I keep him, John?
Can I?"

John shook his head in disgust and asked, "Where the hell did
you find him?"

"In the mud in the shallow water near our camp. It has little arms
that look like they belong on a midget, and it's got feet that look like
they want to walk out of the water too. Can I keep him? Please."

John looked into the can, and he squished up his nose like he saw
the most pathetic critter in the world. "What are you going to feed
it?"

I thought a second and answered, "Some bananas. Maybe some
coconut milk."

"No, Bryan, you don't understand. That is a mud-sucking fish. It
doesn't eat bananas."

"It doesn't eat bananas…What does it eat?"

He puckered his lips like he was sucking on a sour fruit and said,
"Whatever is on the bottom of the lagoon."

"Then I'll feed him some of that mud too. Maybe you can get me
some food from the fish store in Key West. You can bring some home,
and I'll feed him. OK? OK?"

John replied, "You don't understand. That poor little fish is wild,
and if you stick him in a can so you can look at him every day, he

is going to die within the week. I can guarantee it. Is that what you want? A dead fish?"

"No. I just want someone to take care of and to play with when you go to town."

"Don't you have enough animal friends on the island?" He spread his arms out like he was crucified. "I think you are going off again."

"Yeah, but they don't play with me."

"And neither will that fish, especially if it's dead. Now put it back."

I took a deep breath and realized that John was right, as usual. The can slipped out of my fingers, and the contents splashed on the ground.

John knelt down, scooped up the fish, and threw it back into the water.

I said, "When you go, I am going to get another one. I will. I really will."

Shaking his head, he asked, "I thought you were a caretaker out here?"

When I looked for an answer by digging in my ear, he said, "You are not here to capture or kill or make pets out of animals."

I replied, "I just want a pet of my own."

"Well, you are not going to get one from here."

I took a deep breath, looked down at the empty can, and stomped on it. John bent over, grabbed my foot, and tried to lift it, but I wouldn't let go.

"Now give me the damn can," he hollered.

"Not until you let me have a pet."

"Never." He struggled with my leg, pulling and pushing, but I wouldn't budge. Finally, he said, "You let go, or we move to town now. This minute. Now."

I let go and walked away to the nearest gumbo tree. I started to kick the trunk and scratch the bark.

"You cut that out, Bryan." John screamed. "You cut that out before I don't let you ever get a pet, wherever we live—never."

I stopped and turned around. "You mean I can have a pet."

John hollered, even louder, "You do what I tell you. Now give me fifty push-ups. *Now...now.*"

I huffed and ground my teeth, staring at him like a wild dog. I bounced toward him about as fast as I could.

John stood his ground. He wasn't afraid of me. He said I could crush him as easily as a peapod, but John wouldn't back down from me or anyone else. John stretched his neck in my direction. "Give me fifty. *Now.*"

I came to within two feet of John, pushed my face right up to his, breathed some hot air, and made him blink. I asked, "Should I use one or two hands?"

"Two."

I fell forward, did push-ups faster than ever before, and bounced back to my feet.

John had his hands on his hips, and he said, "It's about time you got off the island."

"I don't want to go," I said. "You might not let me come back."

"I'll let you come back, because Key West isn't ready for you yet. I'm going though. If I eat another coconut pancake, I think I'm going to puke."

"Do I have to go?"

"Yes. You are coming with me. I need a job to buy some supplies and some food. I don't want to leave you out here by yourself."

"But we have everything here."

"We are going to get some more then."

"I'll be OK here by myself."

"No. You are coming with me."

"But I don't want to leave."

"You come with me, and I'll let you have a pet, one of these days," he said slowly with accentuated lips.

I jumped up and down, opened my arms, and said, "I'm going to hug you. I really am."

John backstepped, splashing, and replied, "You go acting up, and you are going to hurt me. You don't know your own strength. You could break my ribs before you even know it. Now you stay put."

"No. I'm going to do it anyway. I just am."

I lowered my head, put my arms forward, and took real small steps toward him. Close enough, I grabbed John around the waist and lifted him in the air.

John shouted out, "That's enough now."

With a gasping smile, I set him down and replied, "See, I did what you told me to do, John. I'm a good boy. I really am, and I am going to be reaaaal good here. Real good. But I'm staying here because the squad..."

John stiffened and clenched his fists, and his lips curled inward. He just shook his head.

John said, "Well, I'll go to town myself and find us a place to stay so I can get a money-paying job and get you a little mental-health care at the VA center in Key West. That would be best for both of us."

I felt sad, but not too much, because I could tell he was getting happier, healthier, brighter, and calmer by the day, and as Bob Dylan once said, "Times, they are a changin'."

5

WHEN THE INDIAN WARRIORS TURN TO CHILDREN

After supper, John sat on his cedar stump on the edge of the campfire, picked up a poking stick, and rearranged the lighted logs into a tunnel of red-hot embers that sucked dry air and propelled crackling embers into the thinning darkness.

I asked John, "What's wrong?"

"I thought I heard something." He shifted his weight from his right cheek to his left, turned around, and inspected the perimeter of shadows. Naked branches and towering tree trunks hid his inner concerns. He leaned back, picked up the ax, and tossed the handle back and forth between his hands.

When a metallic sound came from the tree line, it reminded me of the sound of a shoulder strap swivel on an M16 rifle. I knew who that was. I grinned. "I know who it is, John. It is the squad."

John looked like he wanted to throw the ax at me. "Damn you," he said. "I told you not to talk about them anymore."

In defense, I spoke toward the tree line. "Come on out. I know you're in there."

John asked, "Who the hell are you talking to?"

"If I said his name, you'd get mad at me."

John clicked his tongue and nervously attended the fire. "I'm going to return you to Dr. Howe for a tune-up. You need some more time in that mental hospital," he whispered. A file of sparks spiraled skyward, changing ranks with the stars and losing their glow under the treetop canopy. John sniffled.

I was afraid the squad wouldn't come out and show themselves to John before he left for Key West, and I began that nervous twitch again, stuffing my earlobe into the inner ear, poking hard. I didn't want to see Dr. Howe again, ever.

John said, "You keep that up, and we are going to leave for town, now. Right now. In the dark."

"But they're our friends, John—they just want to help."

"You are so out of line. *Stop it! Stop* right now."

I hollered out over my shoulder, "Chickens." I pushed harder on my ear.

"Did you take your meds today?" John asked.

"Yes, I did. You gave them to me."

"You could have spit them out."

"You'll be all right, John," I said to him. "They won't hurt you."

John was freaked out.

There was a rustle of leaves, some footsteps, silence, the sound of a canteen unscrewing, lips sipping, smacking, and the metallic sound of the canteen.

"Chicken shit, is it?" a voice called out from the bushes.

John was on his feet in a flash, and, with the ax poised and ready to be thrown, he yelled out, "What the hell?" He darted in circles, kicking up sand. "Did you hear that?" he asked. "Did you hear that?

I called out, "I sure did hear that, John. I told you."

A body slowly moved out of the darkness, the face draped in shadows. The man wore green jungle fatigues and muddy combat boots. His brass belt buckle flashed in the firelight. It was Cameron Singleton. His eyes were sunken. A cigarette dangling from parched lips caused his face to screw up and his eyes to squint.

John stood as stiff as if General Westmoreland were inspecting his tonsils. "Cameron Singleton," he murmured. "You are alive. I'll be a son of a bitch."

"I told you," I said proudly. Cameron's dog tags jingled as he approached the fire and sat in the sand in the lotus position next to me.

Cameron hadn't aged one bit from his combat days. His tanned skin was still taut and youthfully shiny. Cameron had a bloody bullet hole above his left ear—the same wound that had caused his death years ago. I didn't want to embarrass him by stretching to see where it came out on the other side. Instead, I said, "Hi, Cameron."

Sergeant Cameron Forsyth had been the rifleman in the squad. Cameron had been more like John—serious and quiet. He had been a wiry young man with slightly stooped shoulders, quick to move and quicker to bet. He had been allergic to C rations and had survived mostly off cooked rice and Red Cross packages. He had done his soldiering job when he had had to, but he hadn't been looking for trouble. In his wallet had been a picture of his wife and four-year-old son. He had wrapped the wallet in plastic. Whenever he would take a smoke break, he'd sit down, light up, take out the wallet, unwrap the plastic, and look at the family picture. He'd shake his head. He had figured his odds weren't good to return home without getting shot or killed, and he had been right. Cameron had set odds on everything, and the day he had been killed, he had been betting on rain.

Cameron took a hit from his cigarette and threw it into the fire. "Hi, Bryan." He looked up at John and said, "Hello, Lieutenant." He exhaled.

"Cameron Singleton," John repeated.

"Sit down, Lieutenant. You make me nervous prancing around," Cameron said.

John searched the outer shadows of the fire for more bodies and then returned his attention to Cameron and said, "You don't have to call me lieutenant. Call me John, please."

"Whatever you say, J-J-John," Cameron replied sarcastically.

John asked, "What the hell are you doing here?"

"It's time. You are getting your life together, and we want to get our lives together, along with you, and with your help."

"What?"

"It's time, for all of us. Besides, if we had come for your help any sooner, you would have been so damn drunk, you would have thought we were apparitions."

"What makes you think I don't think that right now?"

"You are sober. We tried to contact you years ago, but you freaked out in a drunken stupor. We thought you might kill yourself, and then we'd all be lost, forever."

"I must admit I did see you before. But I thought they were dreams. I don't understand."

"You quit running, John, and you are ready to face your fears and start the journey of acceptance."

"I'm not afraid of anything."

He forced a chuckle. "You are afraid of your emotions. That's why you don't have any."

John huffed and puffed. "You're crazy."

"Someone here is crazy, but it isn't me. I'm dead."

John's head shook uncontrollably. Finally, he asked, "How long you been out there?"

Air exploded from Cameron's lungs. "Since 'Nam."

"Oh my God. I don't understand. What is going on?"

"Ask Bryan. He knows. It's no secret."

"Since they died," I replied. "I told you all about this before, John."

Cameron said, "Twenty years, three months, two days, four hours, five minutes, and twelve seconds. Make that eighteen seconds."

"That's when you died?"

Another gust of air exploded from Cameron. "No shit." He twisted around and looked at the tree line. Now I saw the other side of his profile—bony, gnarled, and sick looking. Blood dribbled down his neck.

John became thoughtful and said, "The day you died, I died as well, at that exact moment in time. Not physically, but certainly spiritually and emotionally."

"That's what I'm talking about," Cameron said. "We are all dead, and we all want our lives back, in one form or another."

"And you found me here?"

Cameron said, "No, we came here after we got tired of following you all over the damn country. We knew you'd return home when it was time. We came here first and have been waiting."

"You say 'we.' There are others?" John asked.

"Chickens, just like Bryan said. If I hadn't taken the first step, they never would have." He turned around and snarled. "They were afraid you might yell at them."

Chuckling erupted from the bushes. Even John recognized Billy Boy Blakeslee's laugh. Sure enough, Billy Boy staggered forward. In his right hand, he held his guts—steaming, white and crimson. He had that same shit-eating grin that he had always worn in 'Nam. Billy Boy changed his gait and walked like Miss America, hips swaying, his left elbow bent and wrist fading. When he reached the camp clearing, he fell to the ground, laughing. He said, "Cameron bet we'd scare the holy shit out of you, but I knew you wouldn't budge. You are sooo so cool…so cool, just like always, Lieutenant."

"And you are just as crazy, Billy Boy," John replied.

Billy Boy said, "This has got to be the funniest day of my life. I love it. I truly do. Love it. Love it. Love it."

Cameron shook his head. "Billy Boy is still the oddball. He hasn't changed one bit. He's been hell living with. I can't wait until it's over."

"Yes, sir. Yes, sir." Billy Boy jumped to his feet and saluted with his right hand. He whipped off half a dozen salutes before Cameron kicked sand at him. Billy Boy stopped saluting but didn't stop laughing. In 'Nam, Billy Boy used to push everyone's buttons until someone had gotten so angry, he'd wanted to kill him.

Only one time had the squad gotten back at Billy. I remembered that evening as if it had just happened, and the memory made me smile.

We'd been guarding a road outside of Nam Binj in the early evening, drinking beer, pushing each other around, and having a good old time. We'd been inside a safe perimeter surrounded by artillery and bob wire with no plans for a night ambush, so we'd felt as gleeful as a death-row prisoner might feel with a reprieve.

But the good times had come to a halt. Mortars had exploded in the rice fields, sending up gushers of mud and water, and then the explosions had started to move our way. Instantly, all of us had run for an armored personnel carrier about twenty feet away and scrambled inside. The last man in had been Cameron, who'd slammed the rear hatch shut. In silence, we'd counted each other's eyes. Billy Boy's smiley blue eyes had been missing. Friendly fire had pounded the distant tree lines, but the incoming rounds had come in just as fast, sounding even closer.

As dramatic as a grenade without a pin, there had been a knock on the back hatch. A voice had hollered out, "Say, guys, you forgot about me. I'm out here. Let me in. *Yoo-hoo.* It is me, Billy Boy."

We'd looked at each other, but no one had moved. If we'd dropped the rear hatch and a mortar had landed outside at the same moment, we'd have all died. The lieutenant had shouted, "Come through the top hatch. We're not dropping the back gate."

Billy Boy had sounded panicked and afraid. "What are you talking about? Let me in." Knock. Knock. Kick. Slam. "Son of a bitch. Little fuckers, you. Let me in there. Now. Assholes. Dirty little cocksuckers."

Mortars had played like background music.

We'd looked at each other and started laughing, and then laughed harder—gut-holding, sidesplitting laughter, insane folly in a moment of terror.

Billy Boy had cussed and hollered like a straight man, and that had gotten everyone inside to releasing tension in delirious abandonment. Finally, Billy Boy had climbed on top of the track, opened the hatch, and jumped inside. "What's so damn funny?" he'd asked as he eyed every man, who instantly grew silent. "What the fuck is so funny?"

Cameron had answered, "That's the first time you didn't talk like a faggot."

Even now, recalling the story, I smiled and chuckled. I thought of reminding Billy Boy of the story, but I knew Billy Boy would go off again, just like then—totally bonkers. He hated that story.

Cameron spat on the fire, bent over, picked up the coffee pot, and filled his tin cup. He set down the pot quickly and said, "Why the hell don't you get a damn kerosene burner instead of cooking over this flame. That pot is hot as hell."

"Let me kiss it," Billy Boy said as he gaily skipped closer.

Cameron leaned back and raised his hand to punch Billy. "You touch me, and I'll pull your head through your butt and tie a knot in your neck."

Billy Boy blew him a kiss.

"Where's Stuart?" John asked.

Cameron replied, "He back's there." Cameron nodded his head sideways. "You know how paranoid he is—making sure everything is tactically perfect. He is on high alert."

Billy Boy said, "Leave him there. If Stuart comes out, he might start a fight and kill someone. He hasn't changed one iota since 'Nam, John."

John asked Cameron, "What the hell is going on here? What do you want? Why are you here? Why am I here?"

"Oh my God." Billy Boy held his forehead. "No wonder we all died. He hasn't the foggiest idea what's going on. I told you we should have left him alone. He is totally insane. Asking us. Our fearless leader, asking us."

Cameron picked up a stick from the fire and lit another cigarette, flicking embers back into the pit.

Silence. They all looked at John for the answer.

John closed his eyes for a moment and then opened them and stared at Cameron.

Cameron broke the silence. "Lieutenant, we are here because we want some answers. Tell us what happened the day we died. We want some help so we can move on."

"Move on?" John asked.

"There are some unanswered questions in our lives, and that's why we are in this state of limbo, between life and death. When we died, somehow the Soldier's Code was broken. Someone was left behind. Someone didn't do his job, and now, only the truth will set us free."

Billy Boy said, "Let me explain. John, we are considered in the spiritual world as 'wayward' or 'lost souls.' We are trapped between worlds, and we need to stay close to you for guidance to the next level of spirituality."

"But why? Why me?" John asked.

Billy Boy continued. "Our situation isn't new, but it is new to you, because only you know."

"I don't know anything," John said.

Cameron said, "You know how we died."

"Yes…"

"And the truth will set us free," Cameron said. "Start from the beginning, and we'll tell you what we don't remember."

"You mean the ambush?"

Billy and Cameron nodded.

John shook his head in disbelief.

"OK. First of all, it was January 8, 1968. Right? It was dark, and we were going on an ambush." He looked around at the faces for confirmation, but they didn't move. John continued. "We were going out on an ambush. We split up into three patrols: Sergeant Mallory took one squad, Silvester took another, and I took you guys with Hank, my radio operator. I wasn't there when you died. What I know is from debriefing Hank. The NVA attacked so quickly, the whole fight was over in two minutes. You know that? Don't you?"

Cameron replied, "Yes, we just want to know why you, Hank, and Bryan ended up alive and we didn't—why we are roaming around, half-dead and half-alive. It's just not fair. We can't start new lives, and we can't end our last lives. We are in limbo. We need answers."

John massaged the bridge of his nose, closed his eyes again, took two deep breaths, and looked up. "I'll tell you what I know, OK? I'll tell you…as much as I can remember and the way it happened.

"Three days before you died, I remember the VC had retrieved an undetonated five-hundred-pound bomb from a B-52 air strike, and the VC had buried it under the road near the village of Can Tho. They ran an electric wire from the tree line a hundred yards away to the bomb and the electrical detonator. They set up two bamboo sticks in the rice field as sights and waited for someone to come by. On January 5, 1968, at about ten thirty in the morning, a convoy of American trucks passed that point, and the VC detonated the bomb under a deuce and a half truck full of C rations. The explosion dug an Olympic-swimming-pool-size hole in the ground and spread cheesed arms and crackered legs all over the Mekong Delta. That was the incident that set off the CO. The CO was so damn mad, he swore revenge. So instead of going out on platoon-size ambushes, the CO sent us out in as many small ambushes as he could muster. He figured it wasn't more than a half a dozen gooks causing all the trouble, and he wanted them dead."

"How did the whores fit in?" Billy Boy asked. "The girls." His upper lip curled.

John nodded his head. "OK. I'm getting there. Yes, and the whorehouse was Hank's idea. Hank had just returned from the hospital in Saigon after that cobra bite, and Hank wanted to take it easy. He wanted to keep that hand out of the mud and asked for a sheltered place for the night.

"I remember setting up inside that whorehouse, with you guys at different corners of the house, but something happened to me after my second watch. I was asleep and awoke to machine-gun fire, and then I was unconscious. What I know from that point on was what Hank told me, as we were the only survivors—and, of course, Bryan, who was so shot up, he didn't remember a thing.

"In the morning when I awoke, I had a knot on the back of my head the size of an apple, still in the whorehouse with all you guys dead and shot up. Hank was shell shocked and babbling.

"That's about it, because after that incident, I had to care for the wounded and dead and build my platoon back up manwise into a fighting team once again. There was no time to regret or worry or ponder. We went on another ambush the next night."

Billy Boy said, "It sounds like Hank has some explaining to do. That is what it sounds like to me."

I nodded my head and replied, "I'm going back into town tomorrow, so I'll get on it as soon as I can. Don't worry. I'm still watching out for you guys."

"That's right," Billy Boy said, "because we always watched out for you."

6

JOHN'S STORY

At the last minute—I'm not sure why—I left Bryan at Hangover Key by himself. The fact that the squad was there might have had something to do with it. Maybe when I talked to Hank, I didn't want Bryan to overhear the conversation. Maybe I thought I could accomplish more on my own. He wanted to stay, so that's what happened.

"Phew." That's about all I could say as I rowed the canoe in the direction I hoped was Key West. Bryan had said he'd rowed west when I was passed out drunk a couple of weeks ago, so now I was going east. Phew. I loved Bryan near to death, but what a responsibility I had assumed. I'd thought when he'd breathed some fresh air, withdrawn from all those drugs, and drank a six-pack of beer, he'd be a born-again human. But it didn't happen. That guy had problems, and he was giving them to me, and now I was seeing things—not like in dreams, but like for real…like real real. It was like Bryan was some type of shaman, a clairvoyant, or a psychic detective. A mediator! I don't know what. That bullet in the head dislodged something in his brain, so that now he was seeing more than one world at a time. I didn't get it. I had no idea he'd spend a quarter of each day either talking to the dead squad from 'Nam or chatting with the birds. I had no idea he was that squirrelly, and whatever mental problems he had, he was starting to give them to me. For real. And Billy Boy said he was watching out for me. I didn't get it. I was almost positive I had not been dreaming. Maybe it had been a lucid dream?

But I wasn't going to return Bryan to the hospital. That would kill him. Dr. Howe and Dr. Hensheman were right about some drugs to stabilize his moods, but the drugs did nothing for his hallucinations and these people he was seeing, and now I was seeing them too.

Bryan could go from elation to depression with the bounce of a ball, or talk like a scholar one minute and the next minute like a babbling baby. It all depended how that little bullet ball moved around in his skull. I loved him though. Bryan and I were partners, a team, just like in 'Nam, and, like I told that judge in court, having Bryan around was a daily Fourth of July celebration. Bryan's outlook on life was a hoot, and a day didn't go by without him making me laugh. He just saw the ridiculous and sublime in the ordinary. However, the responsibility of taking care of him was staggering, and it made me dig deeper within myself for answers. But I couldn't find any of the answers in my present life. Maybe the answers were hidden back there in my life before 'Nam—when I'd been popular, athletic, ambitious...a citizen-of-the-year kind of guy.

I needed civilization, and I needed some answers for my men, but most of all, I needed to arrange my life like railroad tracks—in order, with direction—and stick to it. Two decades after 'Nam, I was still running from life like it were an ambush. When I'd gotten back stateside and gotten out of the army, I'd been immensely relieved to sleep soundly throughout the night without worrying about some damn VC sneaking up alongside me to slice my throat. But then the nightmares had started, and that's exactly what I'd dreamed about—a VC in my face, holding a bloody knife. When I'd tried to scream, I hadn't been able to, because he had cut my throat. And I wasn't even sure if that encounter with the squad hadn't been just another nightmare, a real nightmare, like I'd still been asleep—some lucid dream.

In another recurring nightmare, I would be in a room full of people, and suddenly, automatic machine-gun fire would break out. I would run to avoid being shot, but once I would get shot and start to die, the peace would come to me. I would be eager to die and get out of that room. Unfortunately, just before I would die, I would awake again and start running from the machine-gun fire. Terror.

Like we used to say in 'Nam, "Shot at and missed and shit at and hit." In my case I couldn't have even said that was true, because I had been hit. 'Nam had been a bump in the road of life. I'd hit the bump and flown into another galaxy.

I needed stability in my life. I needed to quit running, and what better place than where I was born and raised? Key West. Home.

I rested the paddle on my lap and studied the horizon. Distant keys encircled me. I had a general sense of where Key West was located—approximately due east, maybe southeast—but since there were keys all around, I had to be careful that I didn't chase one key to the other and go in circles. Like a fool I brought no freshwater, so I couldn't afford to be too far off, or I'd be found dead in a couple of days, baked like a greasy slab of overcooked bacon. I looked back at Hangover Key and memorized its position on the horizon, a habit I would continue until I reached Key West proper.

In the far distance, I saw a line of charter boats, probably in the west channel heading south to fish for marlin, tuna, or sailfish in the deep Gulf Stream between Cuba and the mainland. If I followed them, I'd be swept north to the Bahamas in the swift currents. I headed east.

Within an hour of rowing, I saw the little white outline of houses on the verdant horizon. The sight made me want to eat something big and greasy and God-awful meaty.

I pulled my canoe ashore under the bridge at Garrison Bight and tied it off to the cement pillar, away from a bunch of kids fishing. I didn't have a lock, but I wrapped the line around the pier and tied a bowline knot. A peeling poster was glued to one of the pillars. The poster showed a great white shark with its mouth open. The header read "Send More Tourists to Key West."

I walked to Kim's Kuban restaurant on Roosevelt Avenue and ordered a soda and a spicy-pork sandwich with tomatoes, lettuce, and lots of onions. Yes, rice and black beans, please. No beer. When my teeth sunk into that fresh toasted bread and marinated pork, my taste buds danced the jumbo limbo.

I know I promised the squad I would contact Hank, but the first person I wanted to see was my aunt Wilhelmina on Loquat Avenue in old town. I walked across town, somewhat shy at all the changes. I remembered open lots, bogs, and fruit stands. Now, Key West was like Disney World but without the parking. Yet I pieced the places together like a puzzle. A Thai restaurant was now the lower floor of the home of my good friend Irving Warner, whom I fished with from the Trumbo seawall. We used to catch some huge snappers and black grouper. Frank's furniture store was now where I had bought my first pet turtle from Amanda's Pet Palace. I meandered up and down narrow lanes and backstreets and found my aunt's little cottage. The colors of her home were different than I remembered. The house was painted white with a cerulean-blue trim. The white picket fence was lined with roses.

As a kid, taking pit stops between play, Aunt Wilhelmina was always good for milk and cookies. Now, I was a little gun shy to knock on the familiar door, and I stopped, only to have the door and then the screen door open to reveal my aunt Wilhelmina Harvey. She recognized me right off, and we hugged and laughed and held each other at arm's length and marveled at the artistry of decades of living. She looked as wonderful and energized as I remembered her. Age blessed her with a grace of beauty and sparkle that could only be a gift from God. She was closer in age to a new century, and she wore her stature proudly. She was absolutely thrilled to see me. She was a people person, always had been, and she came alive with conversation and sparkling energy.

I sat at the kitchen table for tea and cookies, which, in spite of my age, I relished. She fed me news as she filled my belly. She was the Monroe County mayor emeritus.

"Why aren't you at work now?" I asked.

"I have to attend a Zonta dinner meeting this evening, and I came home early to get ready." As she pushed more peanut-butter cookies in my direction, I was reminded of all the times I had stopped at her house on the way to or from fishing, or from playing baseball or tennis, for just such treats.

I said, "Thanks for sticking up for me when that doctor called you from Miami."

"Whatever you want, dear. I didn't lie a bit to him about your character. You are going to stay in Key West this time, aren't you?"

"I think so, Aunt Wilhelmina. I think I'm home to stay."

"Well, good. It took you long enough, but I'm thrilled to have you back. I'm going to have a little family get together for you. I'm that thrilled, and everyone will be so excited to see you."

"Thank you. A friend of mine is with me."

"Is she pretty?" Aunt Wilhelmina sparkled.

"He's an old Vietnam friend. He used to be in my platoon. He's somewhat handicapped. I'll explain more later when you meet him. You'll love Bryan."

"I'm sure I will. The country is beginning to appreciate more what you boys sacrificed over there, and that makes me happy."

"Thank you," I replied. "It makes me feel better too."

"Now you know it's hurricane season, don't you?" When I didn't respond, she said, "It's hurricane season from June to November. Remember? And there's a weather system brewing up south of Cuba."

I remembered watching for hurricanes as a kid. Most of them would start as dust storms in the African desert and would blow west toward the United States, picking up speed and forming into hurricanes as they swirled over the warm summer waters. I would always envision the forming hurricanes as huge bowling balls headed for the States. It would take about a week for them to get here. Most of them would veer north toward the open Atlantic or the Carolinas, sometimes to Bermuda. Of course as a kid, I'd loved hurricanes. The streets would flood, and we'd splash through the water like a swimming pool in the backyard.

"How far off is it?" I asked.

"Way south of Cuba," she said. "It is two days away, and often the storms from Cuba are swept to the east by the Gulf Stream. I didn't mean to worry you."

"I'm not worried for myself. I just have to watch out for Bryan."

"We'll take care of him. Don't worry. So tell me, where are you staying?" She mixed a teaspoon of sugar into her tea, broke off a corner of a cookie, and placed it delicately into her mouth. Her whole face glowed when she chewed.

"I don't have a place in town right now."

"You talk to your uncle Dennis, because rentals are difficult to find. But I tell you what—he'll get you something." She spoke like that was an order for Dennis. She reflected a moment and continued. "It's so wonderful to have you back, just wonderful. Let me call over your cousins Ginger and Rachel. They live two doors down and would love to see you."

I smiled. The twins were both knockout teenagers, conchettes, vivacious, and the object of all the athletes' attention.

"Are they married?" I asked.

"Yes, they are, and they both have two children. Ginger's boy is named Timothy. He's about fourteen. The girl is Teresa. She's twenty...twenty-two. Rachel has twins about the same age as Teresa—two girls, Nancy and Samantha. They're adorable. Wait until they see you."

While Aunt Wilhelmina made a telephone call, I stood up and studied the pictures on the walls. There were pictures of kids at Disney World, young men holding lobsters, boys in sports cars, and girls holding pom-poms. Life and family were returning. I was home.

When my two cousins entered the kitchen, I felt an aura of gaiety fill the house. Both cousins were gorgeous, and they both looked like they had breast implants, but I didn't ask. They were euphoric to see me. After hugs and kisses, they took up coffee cups and positioned themselves around my aunt's kitchen table to get down to the business of questions and answers, and possibly gossip.

After I explained about Bryan and my wandering around the country, I asked, "How is Mary doing?"

They glanced at each other as if drawing straws to decide who would start first. They both caught their breaths.

I shifted to the front of my chair and asked, "Is she OK?"

"She's living with that asshole of a husband she married," Ginger said.

"I know, Hank Laser."

"Yes, Hank," Rebecca said. "He just turned out no good, neither for Mary nor for Key West."

Ginger said, "He's been a thorn in the town's side ever since you left."

"What's he been doing?"

"It's more like what hasn't he been doing? That man is into everything illegal that the devil invented, but mostly narcotics."

Ginger waved her hand in my direction and glanced around to see if anyone was listening. She whispered, "The worst of it is he smuggles those poor Cubans into the country. And last year two sacks floated ashore at Smathers Beach, and each sack had a dead body inside."

Rebecca said, "Everyone knows that Hank threw them overboard before the Coast Guard caught him."

Ginger said, "Everyone thinks that the Coast Guard was laying for Hank, and when they picked up his trail, Hank dumped his passengers overboard. When the Coast Guard finally overtook him, Hank was alone, but his pockets were full of dirty twenty-dollar bills."

"Nearly five thousand dollars' worth," Rebecca said. "Hank told them he won it in a poker game the night before."

Ginger said, "Could you imagine fighting to tear yourself out of a sack underwater?" She fanned herself.

"And there's more. He's always smuggling marijuana from Cuba. He's supposed to be a treasure hunter, searching for lost fortunes, but he hasn't found a piece of gold in all his years of searching, and he lives like a king. It's all dirty money."

"And Mary puts up with it?" I asked.

"The poor thing," Ginger said. "It's her religion. She's Catholic. You know Catholics don't believe in divorce, and that Father Murphy is so strict. It's scandalous."

"Is she OK?" I asked.

"Well, I guess. She spends all her time taking care of sick animals at the Indigenous Park shelter. She's just a saint who doesn't have the Catholic courage to divorce the man or leave him. If it weren't for their son, you wouldn't even have guessed that they slept together. It's just terrible."

"Oh yes. A fine boy named Terry. He teaches at the University of Miami."

Ginger said, "And they had another boy too, younger—Marvin—but he was killed in a plane crash during the Gulf War in 1991."

"That was a tragedy," Rebecca said. "A tragedy. I've never seen anything like that funeral for Marvin in my life, but, once again, Hank screwed everything up. Hank got drunk and made a fool of himself. Hank always favored Marvin over Terry."

"When Marvin blew his nose, holy water came out."

Ginger said, "It didn't matter that Terry pitched four years of high-school baseball for the Key West Conchs and won an average of eight games a year. It mattered that Marvin scuba dived and caught crawfish. It didn't matter that Terry became an environmental engineer and professor—it mattered that Marvin flew jet planes.

"At Marvin's funeral, Hank gave Terry the cold shoulder, which wasn't unusual, but at least Hank wasn't slapping him around. Then at the wake, Hank got to drinking scotch on the rocks. With a clinking glass of brown ice in one hand and a ham-and-cheese sandwich in the other, Hank turned on Terry. Hank's eyes became menacing and vengeful. Oh yes, there was an audience: uncles, aunts, cousins, nephews, conchs, and the preacher and devoted congregation—everyone shoulder to shoulder and within easy-listening distance."

Rebecca said, "Let me tell the rest of the story, Ginger. I have it memorized." Rebecca stood up and faced John. She warmed up her hands and hips, shook her wrists, and started to speak like an actress. "Hank, his lips swollen and creamy, teeth stained and filed down to points, screamed into Terry's face. 'I hold you personally responsible for your brother's death, you coward. While you were hiding behind your books and fucking your whores, your brother was on the other side of the world defending his country. You…you.' Hank was spitting now, the drool staining his shirt, getting caught in the crack of his chin, smearing across his left cheek, and staining the floor.

"'If you had a lick of sense, you wouldn't have come home, not while I'm still alive anyway. As far as I'm concerned, I hope I never set eyes on you again, because you are everything in my life that makes me want to puke.'

"Everyone was astounded. Morsels of food froze in locked teeth, and not a breath of liquor passed lips until Father Murphy came forth with the words that returned the wake to a whispering retreat. The dark-robed priest reverently displayed the full width of his white collar and exclaimed in a heavenly manner, 'I think I'll be going now.'"

Rebecca continued talking, but the story befuddled me, and I didn't feel emotionally involved. Finally, I interrupted her with a dismal non sequitur, "So Mary works at the Indigenous Park on White Street."

Silence. Then Rebecca commanded. "Now don't you go over there!"

"Why?" I asked.

The two girls looked at each other and smiled. Ginger said, "Eeekk."

Uncle Dennis had a furnished cottage across from Bay View Park, first- and last-month's rent free and no cleaning deposit. I told him I would pay up when the money started coming in, and he agreed. I could tell that Aunt Wilhelmina had had something to do with his generosity.

It was a historical cigar-maker's home, built in the late 1880s when Key West had been the cigar-making capital of the country and had boasted a dozen prime-cigar makers. Each cigar captain had been provided a tiny wooden cabin to call home.

The smell of linseed oil and pine pitch permeated the interior. The long hallway was scraped bare of paint, and the Dade County pinewood planks were pitted with decorative wormholes. Off to the left were two small bedrooms and a bathroom. At the end of the hallway was a "great" room with a kitchen, living room, and dining room. The back glass door looked out on a brick patio overhung with creeping vines, broad-leaved plants, and towering tree trunks.

I couldn't wait to show it to Bryan, but before I went anywhere, I did want to see Mary. I really should have married her. The chemistry had been there, but what had turned out to be the problem was that we'd been the best of friends. That had been our downfall. We'd cherished each other's opinions and advice and had overlooked the obvious infatuation with each other. We'd been hand-holding friends.

As a matter of fact, I'd introduced Mary to Hank Laser. That's the tragedy of life. In high school, Hank had been a jock—a pitcher for the Conch High School team. If you pitched baseball for Key West, it didn't matter if you were a juvenile delinquent; you were a special Bubba to the young and old.

So Hank had been this pitcher from Stock Island whom youth had blessed with a finely chiseled torso. Of course Mary had been interested in him, like the rest of the school, and, like an idiot, I'd set them up on their first date, since I'd played second base on the same baseball team.

I hadn't realized at the time that when I'd been telling her about boys and she'd been telling me about girls, we'd been telling each other about ourselves, and instead of being the I teenagers we'd been, we should have been dating each other.

Then when Mary had gone away to college and Hank had gone trailing after her, I'd felt a void like I had never felt in my life before. I'd had Susan Streep, whom Mary had set me up with, but Susan had proven to be just a pretty body with no answers beyond the color of her own makeup.

So I had run away and joined the army. I'd known Vietnam was going on, and I'd known that I would go there, but in reality, I'd felt like dying would have been medicine for my heartbreak.

I walked to the White Street Pier, crossed the street to the boccie ball court under the tall casuarinas, and turned toward the James "Sonny" McCoy Indigenous Park and Pavilion—"Wildlife Rescue Center for the Florida Keys." I had bought a small package of frozen silverback fish at a bait shop, and I swung the plastic bag joyfully as I strolled up the wooden stairs and down the wheelchair-accessible ramp that was flanked by potted trees and flowering plants. Bryan would have known all the names.

Off to the right was a cyclone fence cage. A colorful wood carving of a manatee, a pelican, and a dolphin was above the doorway. The three sea critters held their flippers and wings around one another in friendship. I heard movement inside, like furniture being rearranged, and the mumbling of voices. Feeling silly, I smoothed down my hair, tucked my shirt into my shorts, and smiled. My heart was racing, and I could feel my body temperature putting out some heat.

I walked through the door and saw the back of a woman sitting on a stump with a bird on her lap. Long blond hair screened her back.

"Excuse me," I said.

Her head turned, and our eyes locked. I remembered that hazel-blue color that had hypnotized me in my youth. I felt the dizziness of Mary's new spell.

"Can I help you?" she asked with a twinkle and a smile.

She didn't recognize me. I was dumbfounded. I used my hands to search for words, and my gesticulation helped me say, "I'm John Marley."

The bird on her lap, a pelican, flapped its wings and struck Mary on the side of the face, sending her hair fluttering. Mary struggled to take control of the bird, and she puckered her lips and rolled her arms around the pelican. Mary reached into a wooden box on the floor, fetched a sardine by the tail, and held it in front of the pelican. The pelican's long neck distended, its fatty mouth elongated, and the sardine disappeared with a gulp. Mary stood up, and the pelican flew to a nearby perch.

We stood there, staring at each other.

Her skin had darkened and matured, but she was still gorgeous.

"John," she said. "What are you doing in town?"

"I'm back, I guess you can say. I'm here to stay."

Her eyes did not gulp me in. Her magical twinkles turned to confusion.

"Oh my," she said, moving closer and giving me a handshake. Her hand was limp and moist and nearly as dead as the sardine she had given to that pelican. Her hand slipped away, leaving mine cold.

"What are you doing here?" she asked.

"I'm just in town. Back. Just back, and I thought I'd stop and see you. See how you are doing."

"I'm doing fine. Thanks. Just fine. I'm busy though."

I set the bag of silverbacks on a plywood table. Above the table was a chalkboard with a list of people's names under chore titles.

"How's your dad doing?" I asked.

"Mom and Dad are living in Fort Myers now. Dad retired five years ago." Her father had worked for the Florida Key's Aqueduct Authority, the government agency that delivered water to the Keys through a sixteen-inch aqueduct pipe that originated in Florida City.

"Great. I'm happy for them. I heard you have a son."

She smiled. "Yes. He's an environmental professor at the University of Miami. John…I'm sorry, but I'm just so busy now. I have to leave in ten minutes, and I'm not nearly done."

"Can I help?"

The question exasperated her. "John, not now. Some other time. I don't have time to explain."

"Sure," I said. "Need some help cleaning up?"

"Not right now. I'm fine. I really am." She stood in front of me with her hand outstretched and said, "Well, it's good to see you, John. Welcome back."

"Yes, it is good to be back. I guess."

She smiled. "Good-bye."

I sighed and walked out of the door, feeling a little clumsy and a whole lot awkward. I retraced my steps outside and up the ramp, and then I remembered the bag of silverback fish. I'd left them on the table and hadn't told her about them. I turned around and saw Mary sitting on her stump, her head in her hands, and she was crying.

I walked back in and definitely startled her with my presence. She stood up, sniffling and wiping her eyes with the back of her hands. She sniffled and said, "Leave me alone. Please."

I turned around and left. I was inundated with emotions and questions. Was she crying because she was happy to see me or unhappy to see me, or had that pelican hurt her? What was going on?

Per Aunt Wilhelmina's instructions, I visited my cousin Scott Rogowski, owner of the fishing tackle shop The Fly Fisherman on Simonton and Caroline Streets. Scott and I used to run the backcountry in fourteen-foot wooden skiffs. Mine had been powered by a twenty-five-horsepower Johnson outboard given to me on my thirteenth birthday by my father. Scott had a three-five-horsepower Johnson. (He said he still has it in the garage.) We'd sneak up into the shallow mangroves and catch baitfish: the blue crabs, sand crabs, shrimp, pinfish, silverbacks, or pilchard—a different bait for different fish at different times of the year.

"You gotta come home for supper tonight," he said. "Meet your cousins."

God, I wanted to thank my new boss by being hospitable, but I was worried about Bryan. "How is that hurricane doing?"

"It is downgraded to a tropical storm and supposed to be swept east by the Gulf Stream when and if it passes over Cuba."

"I really can't."

"Oh man. I give you a job, and you can't even visit my family. Come on, John. Loosen up. This is Key West."

"OK, but I can't stay long."

"Sounds good to me."

Scott had a comfortable house in New Town and a lively swimming pool, and while the kids played in the water, Scott and I watched them and talked fishing.

"Want a beer?" he asked.

"No. Not really. I can't."

"Man, has all that crazy living up north screwed up your head? A beer...just one."

"OK. Just one."

I awoke sometime the next afternoon in Scott's spare bedroom with a headache that felt like an ax blade was embedded in my head. I looked out the window. The wind was swirling and the rain gusting, and I said, "Oh shit. Bryan."

I got up, and Scott was already gone from the house, but his wife told me not to worry; the storm was barely a hurricane force and not going to hit Key West directly.

I trotted through the drizzling rain to my canoe. The wind was sucking from the south and devouring clouds as fuel for the oncoming hurricane. I found my way to the bight and looked to see where I had tied my canoe, and I'll be damned. It was gone.

7

BLACK JACK

I should have gone to town with John, because as soon as his canoe disappeared on the horizon, I was lonely. John didn't come home that night, and I got worried. He didn't come home the next day or the next, and I got scared. I knew he wouldn't abandon me unless he was sick, so I fretted that he'd had an accident. Maybe he was in trouble with the law and in jail. Maybe he'd returned to Stinky's, and Hank had finished him off. I was marooned without a boat, and even if I had one, I didn't know where I'd go.

I loved John. First of all, he'd sprung me from the funny farm. Second, he was just a very nice person. On the surface he was kind of grumpy, and he never let anyone get real close to him, except maybe me, and then only sometimes. He just didn't like people too much.

He didn't care much about worldly things either. If he had eight shirts and he didn't wear one for a month, he'd give that eighth shirt to someone who needed a second or third shirt. He never carried more than twenty dollars in his wallet. Maybe because he didn't work that much, but he said that if he got to thinking too much about money and needing too much of it, money would control his life and not vice versa. So whenever John had a wad of money, he found someone or some cause to share it with. John loved to make people happy with money, and that's what he said money was meant for.

He wasn't religious, because he said that the VC were praying to the same Catholic God that he was, and they were asking for the same thing: to live. John figured that the whole world was God. God was the air we breathed, the sun we adored, the breeze that softened our day, the water that cleansed us and quenched our thirst, and the sky that set our spirits to soar. God couldn't create anything he wasn't already, so God was everything. The universe was there to discover itself, and the big bang had been when the universe had patted itself on the back in congratulations. The American Indians who'd lived in America for twelve thousand years had had it pretty much figured out: a sustainable lifestyle and a spiritual gratitude for their existence.

Over the next few days, I noticed on my morning beachcombing that the water began to drop lower and lower, exposing more of the mangrove roots and making the island even more inaccessible. At the same time, the trade winds became still, and a cloudy silence hushed the trees. The birds thinned their ranks, and the ones remaining spent more time roosting. Then, very slowly, tumultuous, billowing gray clouds pushed northward, accelerating, whipping the trees, and pulling the earth into its vortex. The water slowly rose, inch by inch. When the wind started whipping, I didn't dare stay in the tree house, because I was afraid I'd be blown away. Instead, I huddled against a cedar trunk and held on. The water rose until it was up to my waist. My waterlogged skin shriveled up, so I climbed out of the water and onto the first limb of the cedar tree. I spent the night holding on and praying. It was the scariest night of my life, because the wind snapped tree limbs and hurled them like spears, and the water sent shudders through the roots of the cedar.

I don't think I would have made it through the night without John's help. I kept asking myself what John would want me to do. I knew he'd want me to remain calm, stay in the moment, and just tackle each problem one at a time. So that's what I did. I didn't panic. I didn't space out. I didn't hide. I didn't kill myself by trying to swim to Key West, or doing something so outlandish that I'd drown or hang myself from a tree. That's the type of person I was before John returned into my life.

I kept telling myself that everything was going to be OK, just like John had told me the day I'd gotten shot.

I started climbing that tree, but the higher I climbed, the closer the water came, until I reached the top of that tree and there was no more climbing to do.

I might have climbed a little bit higher, but the branches were getting so small that if I put my weight on them, I would break them off and float away.

I stopped at one branch about three inches in diameter and decided to make this the last stand.

The wind was whipping and the short waves crashing, and I started to pray. "Dear God," I said, "help me make it through the night."

"Yes" came an answer.

I caught my breath. I really didn't expect to hear a real-voice answer.

I looked around, and to my utter surprise, there was Billy Boy beside me, treading water.

"Follow me," he said.

"I'm not going anywhere," I answered. "I'm not letting go of this branch."

"Bryan, listen to me. Let go and follow me, and I will guide you to safety. If you stay here, the wind is going to blow you away, and you will drown."

"Where are you going?"

"Home...to my home...the squad's home...underwater...on a ship."

"But if I go under, I will drown."

"No. If you stay here, you will drown, because the water is still rising. Trust me. Like in 'Nam. Trust me."

I took a hold of Billy Boy's hand, took a big breath, and closed my eyes.

We both went underwater at the same time, but I didn't feel the pressure of the water against my ears. The sound of the wind stopped, and I could hear the sounds of tiny air bubbles gurgling to the surface.

We dropped feet first, and then we started to dive down head first, my eyes still closed. I had never done anything like this before that I could remember, but it felt totally normal. I didn't even feel like I needed a breath, but I held my breath anyway. As we dove deeper, I had the sensation of falling over a waterfall, and the sound of rushing water filled my ears as my body was slammed against something solid.

I gasped for a breath of air as I opened my eyes, and the first thing I saw was the light coming through the panel windows of a sunken ship. The squad, Stuart and Cameron, were sitting around a large wooden table, and they both stood up at the same time to avoid the water that Billy Boy and I had brought into the room.

I hadn't seen Stuart in forever. He still looked like the center-fold of *WAR* magazine. His massive black chest and shoulders were pumped and oily, and he had a bandolier of shiny bullets around his waist and right shoulder. His face was painted green and black. Reflective sunglasses hid his eyes, and a sweatband encircled his fore-head. Over his heart was a bloody wound, shredded and tangled, still dripping.

Both he and Cameron had a golden goblet in hand, and they spilled the contents on the deck, swearing and laughing at the same time. For some reason all I could focus on were the goblets they held—like I said, gold, but they were studded with some of the biggest shining diamonds and rubies and sapphires I had ever seen.

As I looked around, I realized we were inside the great cabin of a pirate ship, which in most pirate brigantines occupied the greater part of the upper gun deck.

A long teak dining table was elegantly carved and was a good twenty feet long. There were golden chandeliers, diamond-studded golden candle holders, and boxes of opened treasure troves dripping with gold coins.

"Why did you bring him here?" Stuart asked. Of course he would never dress up like a pirate. He was still in his Vietnam fatigues.

"He was going to drown up there."

Stuart shrugged like he couldn't care less.

A cabin door flung open, and a young pirate wench with a silver serving tray and a gem-studded silver pitcher walked inside and started filling the goblets of the rowdy squad.

I kept staring at her, because she was so beautiful, and I felt like I knew her. She just looked familiar. She wore black-and-white striped pants, a puffy white gauze blouse, and studded, pearl-wrapped black boots that were cuffed at the knee. She had the biggest gold hooped earrings I had ever seen. A gold chain belt held a puffy white skirt in place. A black scarf with the Jolly Roger on it wrapped her blond hair.

I caught my breath. I knew who she was. John had talked about her for years. He'd told me about her smile and her golden hair. This was Mary from Key West, John's old friend. "Mary?" I asked.

She didn't hear me, and nobody else paid me any mind. "Mary," I repeated as she placed a golden goblet with a cross of rubies in front of me. She filled it with what looked and smelled like grog.

As she stood close to me, I studied her smiling face. "Is your name Mary?" I asked.

"Yes, it is."

"John's high-school friend?"

"John? I've known a lot of Johns…" She laughed. "You are probably referring to one of my other lives. I have been a lot of Marys in a lot of times."

"That's because you haven't lived it," I said. "You haven't lived the life where you were John's friend yet. You haven't gotten that far."

She just laughed and waved her fanny at me as she went on to serve Billy Boy.

Well, this is about it, I thought. I'm crazy for sure now.

I really didn't want to ask any more questions, so I walked over to the paneled windows, sat in a royal-leather chair, and just watched the water outside.

I knew it wasn't real, because there was a big six-foot-long barracuda hanging there, and right alongside it was a lobster sitting on the ledge. They both seemed fixed on the shallow waters above, but under normal circumstances, that barracuda would have devoured that lobster in a second. Instead, here they just stood together, side by side in harmony as the other fish—groupers, yellow tails, and sharks—swam about like in a big aquarium.

I just sat there while the men behind me teased one another and listened to music from the 1960s, and Mary served the beer. The music lulled me to sleepy memories.

This was the first time I'd seen Private First Class Stuart Ippolith since I'd gotten to the Keys. Stuart had been the grenade launcher in the squad. He'd always made me feel safe, because he loved to kill people—short people, tall people, VC, NVA, anybody who posed a threat. Stuart was a gladiator-size black man with the vocabulary of a killer—swear words, hate words, bomb words, and sadistic words. He knew and loved them all. He was mean. He was crazy, but in a pinch, I'd always called out his name first. In a life-or-death situation, Stuart had been the best.

Of course some peace lovers might think of him as sick, but those same people wouldn't think so if they were pinned down by a handful of rice-eating VC shooting green tracer bullets through the jungle, breaking the sound barrier only inches away, branches splitting like flesh-eating ants. At moments like that, death had been playing peek-aboo. I'd been on that edge more than once, and when I'd call out, "Stuart" at the top of my lungs, he'd appear like the Lone Ranger on Silver, and he'd start making peace, at least for me. Stuart would fire a grenade launcher in one hand and an M16 machine gun in the other. He'd spit out grenades and toss knives with his feet. He'd jump over trees, firing away—firing between his legs, over his shoulder, under his arms, between his toes, with both hands, with one hand, and spinning. And nearly every single shot had been a bull's-eye. Or so he would say, because a lot of times, I'd been so scared, I hadn't been looking.

One time Stuart had explained to me that he'd wanted to be a soldier since the age of six, when he'd seen the John Wayne movie *Pork Chop Hill.*

Stuart had literally tried to clean up the world by killing everyone who'd disagreed with America, which had been quite a few people in Southeast Asia. I hadn't cared much for him when he hadn't been fighting, because he used to play a lot with dead people's ears and index fingers, making them stand up on their own, creating little castles and hallways out of them, or beading them into necklaces and rings. One time, he'd wanted me to play dominoes with them, but they had smelled so bad, I wouldn't touch them. The grossest thing he'd ever done was cork a bourbon bottle with a chopped-off finger. Toward the end, before he'd been killed, he'd started making mistakes. He'd caught a Cong strangling a woman one time, and he'd slit the man's throat. The trouble had been that the Cong had actually been a Chu Loi, a Vietcong gone straight and come to our side, and the Chu Loi hadn't been strangling the girl—he'd been...you know, doing something else to her. The company commander had said that Stuart was going to get in a lot of trouble for that one, and we'd waited for Stuart to be court-martialed, but he never was. Stuart had just returned to killing, and everyone had forgotten about that incident and loved him again.

Another time, Stuart had seen a platoon of NVA sneaking up the road, and he'd called for artillery. The artillery-battery commander had refused to fire high explosives (HE), because the commander had known that a three-man long-range recon patrol from the 101st Airborne Division had been in the same area. Stuart had knocked the commander to the ground, hollered, "Incoming," and charged. Luckily the recon patrol had recognized Stuart and hadn't shot his ass. Stuart had recognized them when he'd gotten up close, but he'd been so embarrassed, he had run right by them and run another four clicks before he'd met a Cong plowing a field with a musk ox. Stuart had decapitated the farmer and cooked the musk ox. Stuart hadn't come back for a month, until he'd eaten every last musk-ox steak.

Mostly, Stuart used to make me feel warm inside, like I'd been still in my mother's womb, and everything had been safe and happy and free of fear.

In spite of his fearsome outward facade, I'd wondered if there had been another deeper reason why he'd wanted to kill the world. Had it been the fact that he'd had to live with his last name, Ippolith?

In the morning when I awoke, I was still hanging on to that branch ten feet in the air, but now the wind had subsided and the water, although churned up and dirty, was gone. I looked down at the base of the tree, and I'll be darned—it was muddy, but the water was gone.

I was proud of myself, like I knew that John would be when he returned. But I decided to keep the story of my survival to myself, especially the shipwreck and Mary, because I knew there was only so much that John could handle.

I climbed down from the tree and surveyed the damage. There was more water than it looked like from above. The water was ankle deep, but the wind was dead calm. The place was a mess. All our personal belongings were gone, and the beach was filled with blankets of dirty kelp, tree trunks, limbs, and soggy leaves. I cleared off the beach and set all the debris in one pile. I didn't know what happened to our eating bowls and utensils, so I made two coconut bowls and two spoons with a file that was stuck in the trunk of the baobab tree.

Frustrated with the shambles and lost supplies, I went beachcombing. The coastline was filled with mounds of seaweed. I kicked around and found a five-gallon container half-full of gas, a plastic clothes basket, a coffee-filter holder, and yards of line. My apprehension and concern for John made me sick to my stomach, and I threw up in the bushes. To calm myself down, I walked to the freshwater pond, stripped, and soaked my feet. The water was brackish, but the freshwater bubbled to the surface, and I knew within a day or two, the water would be completely clear again.

I heard the sound of a canoe dragging over soft sand, and I quickly ran, naked, back to the clearing. Just as I got there, I saw Stuart step out of the canoe that John had taken to town, place the paddle on the seat, walk into the water, and disappear.

I ran toward him, hollering his name, but he didn't stop. When I reached the canoe, he was nowhere to be seen. "Damn," I swore. Now I was really worried about John. How had Stuart ended up with John's canoe? Was John dead?

The only way not to go crazy was to stay busy. Beachcombing became my favorite hobby. I could search for John and pick up goodies at the same time. I found a can of kerosene fuel, a galvanized bucket, a soggy Nebraska sweatshirt, a package of flares, and a mesh bag of rotting onions.

The water was always the prettiest after a summer storm, like a big bowl of smooth Jell-O. It was hard to believe that four days ago, winds had ripped the island apart. I wondered how it affected Key West. Where the hell was John?

As I walked back to camp, I spoke out loud to Stuart or to any of the other squad members who might have been listening. "Come on, guys. I need some help here."

No one answered.

I remembered when I'd seen the whole squad together three months prior in Bermuda, under the Long Tail bridge, where I'd dragged John's drunken body out of the weather. The squad had been sitting around a fire barbecuing wieners on sticks and boiling coffee. Although John hadn't woken up to see them, they'd asked me to ask the lieutenant what had happened the day they'd died. I'd told them I had once, but John had gotten real mad, and I hadn't wanted to bug John, because he might have left me.

They'd acted like they hadn't heard me and had kept talking among themselves and drinking coffee. Stuart had wanted to bomb the Bermuda Parliament building, because the Bermudians hadn't sent an envoy to Washington for Flag Day.

The next morning, John and I had eaten the leftover wieners, drunk lukewarm coffee, and caught the next bus to the town of Saint

George's, where we'd stayed for nearly a year. I never did tell John where those wieners had come from.

I found a bunch of fishing floats and a pair of new sneakers, the laces tied together, but four sizes too small. I kept them for John. I also found some fisherman-netting-wrapped green jars. The next day, I strolled around and counted wood storks, twenty-seven in all. I must have lost that much weight since John had left.

When I heard the whish of a paddle stirring up the water, I looked out the tree house and didn't see anything moving. I ran down the stairs to the water's edge and saw a green canoe headed my way with John aboard. I started jumping up and down. As he drew closer, I waved my arms and skipped in circles. I noticed what appeared to be something moving in the front of his canoe. I knew it wasn't another person, because John would never be that stupid. I might be, but not him. I looked closer and recognized the outline of a dog's head, a black one. When it saw me, it started tilting its head, swaying from side to side, turning around, and coming back to the same spot, lifting its ears.

"What do you have there?" I asked John, pointing at the dog.

"Bryan, I am so relieved to see you alive."

"You mean you got a dog for me?"

"It is the least I could do for leaving you out here in a category-two storm. I'm so sorry, and I promise you on my life, I will never, never drink another beer again."

"But I thought you said that before."

"But this time I mean it. I could have killed you."

I got all choked up with excitement, and I could tell that the dog was doing the same. Its tail thumped against the hull of the boat.

I asked, "What's its name?"

"She is a she and doesn't have a name yet," John replied. "I thought you'd name her."

"Where did you find her?"

"About a mile offshore from Key West. She was swimming in the same direction I was paddling, so I gave her a lift."

"Oh my goodness." I rushed over and stretched out my arms. She licked my hands. I picked her up in my arms, and she licked my face as I walked her back to shore. When I set her down, I thought I heard a squeak. She danced in a circle, hobbled over to me, and started licking my legs, my hand, and, when I knelt down, my face. "What's your name?" I asked her. But she wasn't interested in names. She was interested in how I tasted. Her tongue tickled, and I got to laughing and petting her on the side. Then I noticed something real peculiar about her. Her right front leg was missing at the knee joint, and instead of walking, she hobbled, like one-two-three-jump; the jump was so she wouldn't fall on her face. That didn't make me love her less. As a matter of fact, it made me feel compassion and love her more. I said, "I'm going to call you Black Jack, because you are my winner." She must have liked that name, because her ears twitched, her tail wagged, and she got to licking me more and more, so that I could hardly stop laughing.

"You've got to take care of her though," John said.

"If she's mine, I'll take care of her like she's my family."

Then John said something to me that made me feel very sad. He said, "But you know that she is a city dog. She knows her way around town and is best in town. She isn't staying out here. When I go, she goes. I'm just preparing you for the inevitable."

I took a deep breath and formed my mouth to say I didn't care if I moved to town. "What took you so long?" I asked.

"The good news is I lined up a job and a place to stay. The bad news is I got drunk, and I never did find or talk to Hank. I promise I'll never do that again. Promise. I was worried sick, but I knew you'd do OK. You're a survivor."

"I spent the night in a tree," I replied, "but Stuart brought the canoe to me the next day."

I pointed to the canoe.

"What the hell?" John said. "I thought someone had stolen that canoe and I'd never see it again. I had to borrow this one from my cousin. You're telling me Stuart brought it out here?"

"That's right," I replied.

"You're full of shit."

"Sometimes I am, but not this time. There is more too, but I don't want to tell you."

"I don't want to hear it. OK? I don't want to hear it. I'm just glad the canoe isn't lost. I am glad you are alive. Case closed."

"Thanks, John. Thanks for worrying."

"You are welcome. Just don't go hugging me anymore."

When John stepped ashore, he handed me a heavy package and said, "Steaks. Barbecue them up, will you?"

As I attended the fire and arranged the rocks around the hearth and the refrigerator shelf I used as a grill, Black Jack curled in a ball next to the fire. I asked John, "Do you love me and Black Jack?"

"What are you getting at?" he asked with his hands on his hips, sitting on a new stump.

"I just want to know why you won't let me call myself Marley, like you."

"Because you ain't my brother. We're not related."

"Then why did you tell the doctors at the VA hospital that I was your brother?"

"I said 'like a brother.' Besides, if I didn't say something like that, she wouldn't have let you out. You would have died within the year. Your spirits were going downhill. Burning up brain cells."

"It didn't feel like I was burning up my brain cells. It felt more like I was losing them."

"Either way, you were on your way. That's why I think they let me take you. They didn't want to deal with you dying."

"How do you know how to take care of me?"

"I was with you in 'Nam. You were in my platoon. I knew you like the back of my hand. I watched your every move."

"Just like now, which I really like, but I can't understand how come that means I can't change my name to yours."

"You didn't hear one thing I said, did you? You didn't hear a damn thing. All you did was waste my breath."

"John, when you get mad at me, you really aren't mad at *me*. You are feeling life's pressures and displacing your anger."

When he shot me a glance that could have melted a steel bar, I withdrew and muttered, "So you are saying that I can't just say that my last name is Marley."

"No, never, and if I hear you say it, I'll make you do so many push-ups, your arms will fall off."

"But I want you as my family."

"Give me fifty push-ups."

"You do that—you just try me."

"Do fifty push-ups," he hollered in my face.

"I'll do a hundred."

"OK. Well, then do a hundred. I don't care. Do a hundred fifty."

I smiled, fell to my stomach, and started pushing. When I finished a hundred fifty, I got up and asked, "Are you ever getting married?"

His head swung from side to side, his eyes shot down, and he replied, "My, you are talkative tonight. Do fifty more."

I crossed my arms and rested my chin on my chest. "I'm not gonna do it until you answer me."

"Do two hundred push-ups."

I shook my head and said, "I won't do another push-up until you answer my question. Because sometimes I feel like you are not having as much fun with me as you might with a girl."

He laughed. "Well, you are observant, aren't you? Very good! No. I don't have as much fun with you as I might with a girl, but that doesn't mean I don't consider myself lucky to have you as my friend."

I smiled. "Thanks. Sometimes I need to hear that from you. Do you think I'll get married?"

"If the right girl comes along, why not? Sure, you will too."

"Do you think my kids will be normal or like me?"

John's face tightened. "What happened to you has nothing to do with being abnormal. You got a piece of metal in your brain the size of a tooth. Before that happened, there was nothing wrong with you."

"I know. I just wish I could be normal."

"You are normal, for yourself. You are absolutely normal. I've never known a more normal you. If you have any kids, they will be as normal as you were before your accident."

"But in Vietnam, I didn't talk like this before the accident."

"No, you didn't, but now you do, sometimes. Not all the time, but sometimes. I'm hungry."

"Nobody ever talks to me normal. I say two words to them. Then they make a face and start talking to me like I wear diapers."

"That's their problem, not yours. You're normal."

"OK. I'm normal, just like you."

He gave me a quick and dirty look and sat down with a plate of steak and beans on his lap, grumbling.

"I haven't seen the North Vietnamese lately," I said.

"Good. Maybe they are gone for good."

I stopped eating, thought it over a moment, waved my fork at him, and said, "Yeah, maybe they have."

"I hope so, because I am tired of running from them all the time. Every time you see them, we run. I'm tired of that. I'd like to kill them all myself, whether I see them or not."

"You do that."

With the plate close to his face, slurping up the beans, he said, "Tomorrow I'm returning to town. Black Jack is coming with me, and if you don't come along, I won't come back here for you."

8

AN EASY PURPLE HEART AND A HARD ONE

They appeared again, but this time only one of them. It was, of course, Billy Boy, because he'd left his calling card—a bouquet of flowers—on a rock next to the fire pit. John was tired and getting ready for bed.

When John saw the flowers, he said, "Oh, shit…not again."

It was again, but this time Billy Boy spoke with indignation, an emotion he rarely expressed.

"What's wrong with you?" John asked. (John was getting used to talking out loud to Billy Boy now.)

"What's wrong with me?" Billy Boy asked. "The question is, what is wrong with you? You said you were going to help us get some information from Hank, and you go to town and spend a week enjoying yourself. All you did was visit old girlfriends, get drunk, and pass out. You didn't even look for Hank…"

"That wasn't my total plan," John replied.

"But that is what happened. Lieutenant, sir, John, ever since the squad died on the ambush, we have been watching out for your ass and saving your ass on more than one occasion, because we knew eventually you would help us. But you don't seem to be upholding your end of the bargain. You don't get it."

"I never made a bargain with you, and I really don't know what you are talking about."

Billy Boy huffed. "In 'Nam, we saved your ass more than one time."

"You were dead most of the time I was there. How could you do that? Like when?"

"Remember the day you got shot?"

"Yes, I do…and you didn't stop me from getting shot, and you had died about four months before that."

"Oh, you insolent, heartless man. You are still alive, aren't you?"

John started to act fidgety, annoyed, and maybe a little embarrassed.

Billy Boy said, "OK. Tell me the story, and I'll tell you exactly where we helped you."

"I don't like to go down memory road."

Bryan said, "But that's what they taught us to do in the VA clinic. They say the more you talk about traumas, the less important they become."

John started to tap his feet nervously. He looked around to see if anyone was listening and then said, "OK, well, maybe I will."

Billy Boy sat on a rock next to the fire, crossed his left leg over the other, rested his elbow on his knee, and then rested his head on his bent wrist. He just stared at John.

John took a sip of coffee and said, "The day I got shot was May 8, 1968, but I think I have to start a couple of days ahead of that so you get the feel for what was taking place. Remember, the squad had died in January. You were dead at the time I got shot."

Billy Boy rolled his eyes.

John continued. "After the January Tet Offensive in 1968, the North Vietnamese Army was physically defeated, but since the American TV coverage of the event took place on American news stations, Americans realized that this was more than a police skir-mish taking place—it was all-out war, because North Vietnamese soldiers attacked every American base in South Vietnam and won the propaganda war. The news coverage was realistically chilling for the American viewers, and damning to the politicians who wanted to keep us there. Instead of some local skirmishes, there was a bloody war exploding across the entire country of South Vietnam."

John looked at Billy Boy and said, "You guys had died about four months before this time."

"I know," replied Billy. "Of course I know. I was still there with you."

John took a deep breath and continued.

"After the first Tet in January, right after you were killed, I was assigned to a mechanized platoon. I drove around in army personnel carriers (APC M113), a.k.a. 'tracks.' Each track could carry about twelve men. Nobody rode inside the track, because if the track ran over a land mine, there was a good chance everyone inside would be killed. By sitting atop the track, it meant if the APC ran over a small land mine, the track would be disabled, unless the track ran over a five-hundred-pound booby trap—then the soldiers on top of the track would be thrown hundreds of feet into the air and land as body parts scattered over a large area of rice fields.

"The tracks had two fifty-caliber machine guns, one forward and the other aft. There was a place for two sixty-caliber machine guns on either side, but those guns were never there. Instead, that space was occupied by a soldier who sat on a sandbag for protection. We drove around a lot in the APCs, which is kind of like fighting from a Winnebago. If you have to do it, that's the way to go. We carried all our ammunition and supplies in the tracks—ice and beer, personal gear, Red Cross boxes of candy, and cigarettes—and we would drive from base camp to base camp escorting convoys of supplies to the camps. We were really close to supplies, and that was nice, and we didn't have to walk all the time, although we did do our share of walking and flying around in Hueys.

"But when it was my platoon's turn to be loaned out to a totally infantry battalion, I was ordered to report to C Company Thirty-Ninth Infantry on the other side of Saigon and help them with whatever they needed. At the time, they were guarding the fuel tanks outside of the city of Saigon along the Saigon River near Nha Be.

"I was happy to go. Since January Tet, I had increased my platoon size from two to four tracks and increased my men size from fourteen to thirty-three. Fully equipped and ready to go, we blasted up the road to Saigon.

"The problem was it was raining like a son of a bitch, and when we reached Saigon, it was getting dark. The city was deserted, and as I hauled ass through the empty streets with my map under my rain poncho, often I'd put my head under the poncho and use my flashlight to try and figure out where I was and where I wanted to go.

"We took on some small-arm fire around the city center, and I remember hauling my four tracks in a circle like the covered wagons used to circle in Indian country. I remember looking at the window spaces in this rather empty courtyard full of three- and four-story apartments, all with windows looking at us. I just dared someone to take a shot at us.

"I loved my fifty-caliber machine gun. Each round is about six inches long and an inch in diameter; each fifth round is incendiary, so you could see where you were shooting without using the sights. A fifty caliber could easily go through several brick walls without slowing down. There was nowhere to hide from a fifty caliber. It made me feel proud, and it made me feel safe and secure and kind of happy. It was the friend you always wanted to have in a fight. Nobody could argue with a fifty caliber."

"Getting off track here a little bit," Billy Boy said.

"The courtyard was quiet. I finally made it to Nha Be with a little help from some friends (soldiers near a bridge who knew the layout of the city).

"That night, we were served a hot meal and told we did not have to pull guard duty. We could sleep inside the company's perimeter and sleep all night, not having to get up every two or three hours to fight off sleep and look for someone who might be crawling inside the perimeter or turning our claymores around on us or harassing us, etc.

"I met an old friend from Officer Candidate School at Fort Benning who had a platoon in C Company. I remember him telling me that his men were like animals. He also told me that one time, he set up an ambush and watched as the VC walked right through it; he did not trigger the ambush. He just let them walk right through. (There has to be some grandkids out there somewhere in Asia who should cheer at that.)

"When we woke up in the morning, the radio was blaring with gunfire and the voice of an American major. He was attached to an ARVN Company (Army of the Republic of Vietnam, our allies). They had come under fire, and the major was wounded, pinned down in a rice paddy, and needed help. It was at the village of Xom Co Diem, on route two hundred thirty.

"Since I could get there the fastest, we headed off on our tracks. It would have been so much easier getting there using a GPS, but we found the place.

"The first thing I did was locate the major and his troops in the rice paddy. Then I called an artillery battery somewhere in our vicinity. I told the artillery radioman our location, and I asked for a burst of aerial smoke to make sure he had our position correct.

"The smoke burst kind of in the vicinity of where we were. I called for another smoke, and it got a little closer. I added fifty yards to that and asked for some high explosives on the ground.

"The rounds exploded along the line of the village, across the rice paddy—about two hundred yards from where we could see the major and his men lying flat in the rice paddy.

"After a few more suppressive rounds, I asked for some smoke rounds. When those started to land and fill the air with a ground-streaming fog, I moved half a dozen men with me, and we crawled up to the major and his wounded and dragged them back to the protection of our tracks. We didn't drag any of the dead ARVN back with us. We could pick them up later.

"The major was shot in the arm, not too seriously, but he quickly handed over the ground command to me, which I took.

"By radio, I ordered a medevac helicopter and had the wounded loaded into my last track. Then I drove back up the road about a quarter of a mile and waited.

"When the helicopter came into view, I popped some yellow smoke and waited for the helicopter to land.

"Of course, by now, things were getting crazy—smoke, dust, noise, wind, bodies moving about, a medic jumping off the helicopter, deafening noise.

"Richardson, a squad leader on my track, came up to me and said, 'Sir, one man is shot in the stomach. Every time we touch him, he screams.'

"I looked to where Richardson was pointing, and I said, 'Let's go.'

"When we got to the man, I saw him lying on his back, holding in his stomach. He was obviously in a lot of pain. I said to Richardson, 'You grab his feet, and I'll get him under the arms.' The wounded guy screamed bloody murder when we picked him up. We moved him to the helicopter and then heave hoed him onto the deck of the chopper. Things should improve for him from this point forward, I hoped.

"As the helicopter started to lift off, an ARVN soldier tried to jump aboard. I stopped him and asked him, 'What's wrong?' He showed me his hand. There was blood on his fingers. I waved him off the helicopter and gave the pilot the signal to take off.

"Back at the village, things were kind of quiet. We could see some VC moving from hut to hut, and my men were engaging them in fire, but there was no mass movement in our direction.

"We had our fifty-caliber pointed at them. My track was about one hundred yards from the entrance to the village, just out of RPG (recoilless propelled grenade) range. I was told over the radio that reinforcements were coming and to hold tight.

"A small loach helicopter flew over and engaged some enemy. Then the loach let the two Cobra helicopter gunships following him shoot some rockets and their mini guns.

"When they left, I wanted to call in some more artillery, so I needed another compass reading on a new target. The way it worked was that I had given the artillery unit—wherever the hell it was, miles away—my coordinates. They knew where they were and where I was, and if I gave them a compass reading from my position and the distance from where I was to where I wanted them to drop the ordinance, they could drop it fairly close to where I wanted it.

"Only problem was that I could not take the compass reading from my track, as it was all metal, and metal made my compass needle rotate out of control in circles. So I had to distance myself from the track.

"I crawled inside the track and worked my way up into the firing position for the fifty caliber.

"Around the fifty-caliber machine gun was a gun turret, all metal, which protected me from small-arm fire. Without the gun turret, I was a sitting duck.

"When I'd received this new track about a month before, it hadn't come with a turret. However, I had asked one of my men—I forget his name, but he was an ex-biker from California with a tattoo on his ass that read, 'Bury me face down so the whole world can kiss my ass.' I had never asked to see the tattoo personally, but the men in my platoon swore that it was there. I could not get the turrets through the normal supply requisition, so I'd asked my biker soldier to get me one for each track. He found them, and, without questions, I thanked him.

"I stretched my body a tad taller above the turret until the needle on the compass quit quivering. As I focused on the compass numbers, something hit me in the stomach, and, simultaneously, there was a loud whop. I fell back inside the track."

"Stop right there," Billy Boy said. "That is number one...strike one."

"What are you talking about?" John asked.

"You will figure it out soon enough," Billy Boy said. "Keep going. Go ahead...tell the story."

John touched his stomach and said, "I felt my stomach, looked down, and saw my shirt torn. A bullet had ricocheted off the gun turret and hit me a glancing blow in the stomach.

"'Look,' I said. 'Blood. I get a purple heart.' I smiled.

"Of course, the two guys inside thought that was a joke, but in reality, all you had to do was draw blood on a combat mission, and you were entitled to a Purple Heart, which basically means you were wounded on a battlefield. I had earned my first Purple Heart and my first combat wound. Even though I laughed about it at the time, since it really didn't hurt, there was something in the back of my mind that said, 'This is not funny. It really isn't.'

"I moved the artillery back and forth and up and down the village, but the artillery officer I talked to over the radio said that he could not move the rounds more than one hundred fifty yards into the village, the reason being that his map showed an ARVN (friendly) outpost where the village was.

"I argued with him over the placement of the outpost in the village, and although he probably believed me, there was nothing he could do about it. Orders were orders. I certainly saturated the area we were allowed to fire upon.

"About half an hour later, a Cessna 150 Bird Dog flew overhead. I knew that further up in the sky beyond my sight were a couple of F-4 Phantom jets with Sidewinder missiles and napalm bombs ready to drop their loads on the spot where and if the spotter Cessna dropped its smoke.

"I asked the spotter to drop some napalm on the area where we were getting fire, and after a pause, he said, 'Can't do it. My map shows an ARVN outpost located there.' I replied, 'But look, you can see the post isn't located there. The ARVN post is located near the river on the other side of the village.' He replied, 'I know that—I can see that outpost, but if I drop the napalm, I have to mark on my map where I drop it, and I'll have to put an X right over the ARVN outpost.'

"We argued to no avail. It did make me wonder who drew up the maps of Vietnam. Some of the Vietnamese soldiers who acted as our interpreters were probably working for the North Vietnamese. Their job was to make up maps for both sides—the maps for the enemy, which showed safe zones to hide from artillery and gunships, and the other set for Americans.

"About this time, the CO from Charlie Company comes walking up on the scene with his three platoons. Now he is a captain. At the time, I was a first lieutenant. He outranked me. He wanted to use the tracks on the road to hide behind and move forward against the village.

"I explained, 'We know they have RPGs in there.' (RPGs were designed to burn their way through the frame of a track and then explode an HE grenade, killing everyone inside. RPGs were bad news for tracks.) He insisted we go first as cover. He wanted to reach the front of the village and then spread his men out along the dike, moving forward from there.

"The way I saw it, there were just too many huts and fences and trees for the VC to hide behind and then pop up, shoot an RPG at us, and hide again. If a rocket hit a track, it would go sky-high, because our tracks were full of ammunition, rifle rounds, machine-gun rounds, fifty-caliber rounds, claymores, light antitank weapons (LAWs), incendiary grenades, and a couple of one hundred six recoilless rounds. I wanted to move closer to the village, just out of RPG range, and then cover the captain with fire from our four fifty calibers. Nope. He didn't like it.

"I just didn't feel right sending any other track ahead of me. If I ordered someone, and they refused, I probably would agree with them. So my track led the way. We did OK, actually, until we got to the village entrance. Then, all of a sudden, everyone on my left side started to open fire.

"I looked over, and I saw everyone pointing and shooting at a hole in the ground. Every American soldier within ten feet of that hole opened fire with automatic weapons. I mean all hell broke loose. I found out later that there had been a VC in there, and when he'd popped up, he'd been in for the surprise of his life.

"Up until that time, I'd been on the radio talking to the CO, who'd been behind the track behind me. When the firing had started, I'd lost all communications. It'd been too damn noisy to talk or listen.

"Then, all of a sudden, I was surrounded by a cloud of smoke. I could not see more than inches in front of my face, and then all I could see was dust—a khaki-colored dust, thick as a cloud, boiling.

"As the dust settled to the ground, I looked down at my body. The rifle I'd been holding in my left hand was gone, and the radio transmitter I'd had in the right hand was missing. Nobody else was standing around me. There was a lot of noise and a lot of rounds going past my ears at supersonic speed. I had no idea what had happened.

"I checked my body. I was still standing. That was good. I placed my hands on both kneecaps and started to move my hands up toward my thighs, stomach, chest, and face. Then I looked at my hands, and both hands were covered in running blood."

"Ding. Number two," Billy Boy said.

John looked annoyed and then continued. "I staggered over to the open hatch on the back of my track, and I saw the radio transmitter that was on a bungee cord. I picked it up, and then I moved inside the track and talked to the CO. I told him I was hit."

Billy Boy broke in. "And you weren't suspicious of why a ten-pound package of high explosives blew up in your face and you came away with scratches?"

"Not at the time, I wasn't. No."

"OK, remember that. Now tell us about number three."

"You know the story?"

"I told you I was there," Billy Boy said.

"As I sat there and waited for some type of response over the radio, I looked over at my new radio operator. He was inside the track looking scared witless.

"Anybody knows that being inside a track where the enemy has RPG rounds is not the place to be. But the radio operator had been in the country only a few days, and nobody had gotten around to telling him that—or if they had, he hadn't heeded the word.

"I felt like I needed to tell him something to remove the terror on his face, so I asked, 'What do you think of this shit?' He never answered.

"Before he had a chance to say a thing, I saw a ball of fire on the ground between my legs. If the Virgin Mary were about to appear to me, that is what I would imagine she might look like. It was just a glowing yellow ball of fire."

Billy Boy stopped him again. "OK, this is number three. In this one Stuart helped you out, because only he could enter that domain fearlessly."

John didn't like being interrupted, because he was in a trance. "My mind wanted to ask, 'What the fuck is that?' but I never had a chance to complete the entire sentence. I think I got as far as 'What the—' and then the ball of fire began to grow.

"I actually saw it grow in increments. It was like my focus had slowed down to a billion frames per second, and I experienced each frame."

Billy Boy said, "Let me finish the story. About the second or third frame, Stuart made his direct telephone call to God. The line bypassed Saint Peter and went directly to God. It was like the red telephone during the Cold War between President Nixon and the Russian President Gorbachev. Stuart said, 'OK, God, enough of this shit, OK? Abort...abort this mission now.'"

John said, "I saw probably about ten frames of the explosion. It approached my face, closer and closer each frame, until it just went past me.

"Now I don't know if I passed out or was knocked out, or whether I was conscious the whole time, but when I looked around and saw the doorway leading to blue skies outside the track, I leaped outside. For a second or two, I just stood there on the dusty road.

"My platoon sergeant, Sherfey, who'd seen me from the second track, later told me that he'd seen God standing there. Not me, but God. When he told me this story a couple of months later, I shrugged him off, but he probably had reason to think that way, because now that I've had time to think about it, I must have been a sight. Here my track explodes from an RPG. There is fire, smoke, flames, flying debris, and body parts flying. There's lots of dust, and as the dust clears, Sherfey sees my fifty-caliber gunner, who was firing from atop the track, now draped sideways over the side of the track in a seemingly lifeless position. His good leg is stuck around the track hatch, his other leg dangling inside the track half-torn-off.

"Then, out of all the smoldering, I jump out and stand there looking lost, as if someone had just taken my beer. Sherfey probably was experiencing and feeling the miracle of it all."

Billy Boy said, "And that was Stuart's help."

John said, "Then the bullets zinging past my head brought me back to the reality of the moment, and I realized I was once again the only one standing. I looked to the rice paddy on my left, and I did a swan dive into that paddy like I was diving into a ten-foot-deep swimming pool.

"I know I must have been a sight to see, because for some reason, my days from the seminary kicked in. I used to be on the diving team, and I remember one of my dives was a swan dive, an easy dive—graceful and arched, chin high and chest proud.

"I hit the paddy in a wet spot, and when I got to my hands and knees, I did the old body check again like I had after the first rocket exploded. My guts were not spilling out. Now mud was mixed into the blood on my hand. Fresh blood.

"My platoon sergeant, Sherfey, bless his soul, came to my rescue. Our plan had always been if I get hit, he takes over, but until I get hit, he stays in the background relatively safe until he has to take over for me. He was magnificent.

"Later on, he told me that even when I'd been hit, I'd still been giving orders and in command. I didn't see myself in command of anything, but from that rice paddy, half a dozen of my men gathered around me. I remember seeing all of them close by, and I remember seeing grenades exploding in the rice paddies, and I remember thinking, 'You guys have to spread out, because we are one grenade target right here.' That was one of my pet peeves.

"'Spread out,' I screamed. They did. Sherfey thought it was a grand idea, and I was still in charge. He didn't realize how scared I was. I crawled back to the next track and lay down inside on a bed of ammo cans and explosives.

"A crazy thought went through my head. The thought was, 'OK. I'm wounded. The fight is over. Everybody go home. No more firing. I'm hurt and have to be cared for. Quit trying to kill each other. Quit trying to kill me. It's over.' I asked for water, but there was none. I asked for morphine, but there was none. The face of my friend from OCS appeared at the door of the track, and he asked how I was. I said, 'OK.'

"He sobbed and left the scene. At the time, I thought it was weak of him to sob his eyes out, but as I found out later with problems with PTSD, it was much healthier emotionally for him to sob his eyes out. I had learned how to stuff my feelings by this time. I felt ashamed for his tears. I was stuffing it all, every feeling that previously brought joy to my heart. They got all stuffed with the fear. I stuffed too much. I stuffed things I never thought could be stuffed, like love, friendship, intimacy, and happiness. I was telling them to just shut up and not to come out until it was safe.

"On the way to the hospital, the helicopter touched down at a road accident on the way. As it touched down, I felt a moment of terror as I felt totally vulnerable to death. In the helicopter, I had grown somewhat relieved that I was no longer in harm's way, but now, I was right back in it. When the helicopter took off and got high enough to avoid ground fire, I relaxed again.

"When we touched down at the hospital, I got off the helicopter, and as I started to follow the guy ahead of me, I looked toward the tail of the helicopter, and I saw my squad leader, Richardson. I didn't even know he had been hit. He was walking like a wacked-out drunk zombie in the direction of the helicopter rear prop blade that was still spinning.

"I called out to him, and he stopped. I walked over to him and grabbed his arm. 'Where are you going?' I asked. He turned toward my voice with both his arms outstretched, and he looked right through me. I asked, 'What's wrong?'

107

"'I can't see. I'm blind.'

"'Follow me.' I grabbed his arm and ushered him in the direction of the staggering wounded. We were sat in a row of chairs. Those who couldn't walk were gurneyed past in stretchers.

"Richardson sat to my left. He was blind and shot up with shrapnel. I looked to my right, and a soldier sat right next to me; he had a hole in his neck. It didn't hit his windpipe. The hole just seemed to go through neck flesh, a small hole in and a small hole out. He sat there, motionless, with a stiff neck. He never said a word.

"When it was my turn, they laid me out on a stretcher and started to scissor my shirt and pants off—easiest way to remove them. When they came to my pants, I heard them holler for help. I had two incendiary grenades in one pocket and two HE grenades in the other pocket, and the nurses just found them. The nurses acted like the grenades were going to explode without removing the pin, and I remember smiling and thinking what idiots they were. They wouldn't go off until you pulled the pin.

"But the nurses got their revenge when they started to remove the shrapnel burnt into my right leg, right belly, right arm, and right cheek. I'd been pepper sprayed with metal—no pieces flying fast enough to kill me, but fast enough to burn themselves deep into the skin and crust over. It hurt like a son of a gun when they shot my body parts with novocaine and immediately started to pull out the steel.

"The ward I was on was a company reunion. The other part of my company had come into contact with the VC in Saigon, and there were many wounded and killed on both sides; we were all together. Richardson was blind for three days before his sight started to return. The radio operator was not there. He took a large chunk of metal through the stomach and literally never knew what happened.

"Then I found out that as my fifty-caliber gunner had lain backward, hanging over the track, when he'd called for help, Richardson had scrambled blindly out of his driver seat and had found refuge in the rice paddy, low and relatively safe. When he'd heard the gunner crying for help, Richardson had abandoned the safety of his rice paddy, stood up, and found his way blindly to his friend's aid by following the sounds of pain. Richardson had found him, pulled him off the track, and dragged him to the relative safety of the rice paddy. I felt guilty for my nonlife-threatening wounds.

"From there I was medevaced on a stretcher to the Two hundred forty-ninth General Hospital in Japan, and when the doctor asked if I was ready to return to Vietnam, I asked for one more week. He gave it to me.

"When I reached Saigon, as I unboarded the plane, I ran into, of all people, Richardson. He was going on a three-day in-country R and R to Vung Tau. Instead of going our separate ways, we went to the Continental Hotel in Saigon and spent the better part of a week drinking and whoring until we both ran out of money.

"Our last night at the hotel was July 4, 1968, and at sunset, the sky filled with tracer rounds, incendiary explosives, and bursts of color as parachuted lights filled the horizon with color and light. It was all the surrounding American bases celebrating the Fourth.

"As I watched from atop the hotel with a scotch in hand and a girl just as close, I felt proud of everyone in my platoon. Just proud. No forgiveness, no revenge, no hatred, just pride. Drunken pride.

"When I returned to my base at Binh Phuoc, nobody looked at my orders and asked why it had taken me so long to return after leaving Japan ten days prior. The battalion commander said that he'd flown over the sight where I'd been wounded, and he said that my track was still there. He said it was still at the front gate of the village. He said that the top had blown off the track, the rear wall was missing, and the engine compartment had disintegrated. All that remained were the two steel side walls."

Billy Boy stood up, took a deep breath, and said to John, "Three strikes and you are out, and you think it was just all a matter of luck. I swear to God, you are a thankless piece of shit."

Billy Boy walked into the darkness that surrounded the campfire, and John just sat there staring at the fire, looking exhausted and forlorn. "Those guys did that," he said. "They could do that?"

9

THE GUNFIGHT AT ROGET'S THESAURUS

In the morning Bryan and I rowed to Garrison Bight and tied off at the Pier House dock. I was still flabbergasted from the night before. It was just so bizarre and crazy. I knew that mental illness was not contagious, but now I had my doubts. Billy Boy was telling me that my dead men from another dimension had stopped bullets from hitting me and had redirected rockets in flight, like some type of supernatural powers. I didn't get it. But I did understand that they were pretty frantic about me talking to Hank and finding out what exactly had happened to the squad on their last day in 'Nam.

I wandered up Palm Avenue, mumbling to myself. I knew I wanted to find Hank and tell him about the squad, but my mind was so flustered, I expected Hank to just appear somewhere, probably just like the squad the night before. I'd look up a street and follow my nose and then look down another and go that way. Black Jack and Bryan were right behind me, as happy as ever, just enjoying the moment.

Exhausted, I rested on a black wrought-iron bench at Clinton Place, a small Union War Park across the street from the redbrick Custom House on Whitehead Street.

Bryan walked around the park for a minute before he stood in front of me and said, "This little park was dedicated to the memory of the Civil War Union soldiers, but the fence around the memorial was built by a Confederate sympathizer. Isn't that strange?"

I studied his perplexed countenance, realized the simplicity of his existence, and just smiled. "Yes, it is." He was as lost as ever, and now I was with him.

I stood up, took a deep breath, and asked, "Bryan, what say we head…" Bryan was gone. I looked around, and he was nowhere to be seen. "Shit," I swore. "Now where the hell did he go?"

It was evening, and a huge flow of people were headed toward the Gulf side of Duval Street. I let myself be carried by the ebb of warm bodies, as I was sure that Bryan had. The crowd flowed into Mallory Square and fanned out among the entertainers and vendors. The stage drop was the setting sun.

In the heyday of wreck diving in Key West in the 1840s, salvagers and wreckers would auction their rolls of silk and lace, cases of wine, and lumber at this time each day, right at this very dock. That had been a time in history when Key West had rightfully boasted being the wealthiest city in the country.

Now the tourists gathered on the dock to watch the sunset. This was as important an event in Key West as the changing of the guards at the Queen's Palace in England.

I didn't focus on the entertainers but looked through the crowd for Bryan and Black Jack. They had wandered off again. I wended my way past tank-top beauties, buffed chests, curious smiles, and inspecting faces over shoulders, all the time mumbling. The performers lined up along the water's edge. There must have been a half dozen of them. A blond girl in a pink crepe dress played her violin. Her violin case was open for donations, and there was a sign with her name: "Yana Britski from Yugoslavia." She wooed the crowd with Beethoven. The domestic-cat tamer was probably the most popular, as his small cats shook hands, bowed, jumped through fire hoops, climbed ladders, and danced in circles on two legs. The tightrope walker beckoned 100 percent attention before proceeding. It was a perfect picture for a photographer with the glowing red sunset silhouetting his outline. He acted like the sun was his partner, throwing oranges to it, twirling, and bowing.

The audience stood between the entertainers and a platoon of bead weavers, leather craftsmen, palm readers, and portrait artists.

There he was. Bryan was sharing a bag of popcorn with a flock of pigeons. When he turned over the bag and the last kernels fell to the ground, Bryan turned toward a fortune-teller sitting at a table only feet away. The fortune-teller sat with his arms folded, a tattoo on his bald forehead—sunset flames. His ears were covered with earphones. His eyes were shut, and he appeared mentally occupied. On his right forearm was a cobra tattoo, its neck bloated and ready to strike.

Bryan sat at his table and tied Black Jack to the leg of the chair. Black Jack sat and watched.

I started to say something to Bryan, but he was focused.

When the man didn't look like he was going to open his eyes in the near future, I sat down next to Bryan, and I nudged him to leave.

The fortune-teller peeked open his right eye and then the other. He acted like he had created us sitting there. His hands encircled the blazing sun on his forehead, and he spoke. "You are searching?"

Bryan's face perked up with surprise, and Bryan gave me an elbow in the ribs like, "Isn't he good?"

I had to maintain my sense of humor with Bryan. Sometimes he could crack me up. He was so naïve and trusting.

The fortune-teller bowed his head slightly, and his lips parted in an ever-so-slight grin. He asked, "In which language would you like to speak?"

Bryan answered, "The only one I understand is English, but if you could make me understand some other language, I'll speak that one too."

"English will be fine," he replied.

The teller took Bryan's right hand in both of his and turned the palms up. He used the fingers of his right hand to explore the lines in Bryan's palm, meticulously and softly, like a lost hiker reading a contour map.

Bryan wiggled like it tickled.

The teller said, "The man you are looking for is an old friend?"

"As old as they get," Bryan replied. "I even have his name if you want it."

The teller looked taken back, his sunset prematurely setting and his eyes turning into an ocean of knowledge. With little enthusiasm, he replied, "Go ahead."

"Hank Laser."

The clairvoyant chuckled and relaxed at the same time. He released Bryan's hand, leaned back in his chair, and let his arms dangle to the ground.

"Hank Laser. That will be twenty dollars, please."

"Of course," Bryan replied and looked at me. I pulled out a twenty from my wallet and handed it to him.

The clairvoyant made the bill disappear with a sleight of the hand and said, "Hank has a boat down at the Garrison Bight Marina. He's down there all the time. It's just a ten-minute walk from here. Hank spends a lot of time refueling his dreams at Sloppy Joe's or Rum Runners or Stinky's."

"You saw all that in the palm of my hand?" Bryan asked.

"Why not?" he replied.

"Where is he right now?"

He looked at his watch.

The crowd applauded, and we both looked up to see the last tip of the sun dip below the horizon. Then the crowd dispersed like a completed horse race.

"Happy hour at Sloppy Joe's or Stinky's, in that order. But I'd check the Marina first."

Bryan stood up and said, "Thank you very much, and you are very intelligent."

He touched the setting sun on his forehead and bowed his head.

Bryan was gone again, but I shoved my way through the crowd and saw the back of his head. I raced to catch up on the way to Garrison Bight.

Bryan saw Hank first and pointed to him standing at the bow of a thirty-foot-plus speedboat with twin outboard engines, outriggers, and a fancy flying bridge.

"You got a minute to talk, Hank?" I asked Hank, who balanced his weight on an outrigger and gulped a beer, throwing the empty bottle in the water.

I said, "The squad is back, Hank." When Hank didn't seem to understand, I continued. "Billy Boy and Cameron are here."

Hank belched and replied, "There was a time in 'Nam when I respected you, Lieutenant, but that was years ago."

"No. I saw them with my own eyes."

"I see things with my own two eyes when I'm drunk, but that's because my eyes get crossed."

"This has nothing to do with being drunk, Hank. I quit drinking. This has got to do with our lives. The men want to know how they died."

Hank's face grew taut, and he glanced around to see if anyone was listening. With no one in sight except Black Jack and Bryan, Hank returned his attention to me and said, "Well, I already told you that twenty years ago." Hank bent over, flipped an ice cooler open, removed another beer, popped the top, and threw the cap into the water. He smacked his lips and said, "Now don't go digging up the past. I don't want something that happened twenty years ago to bite me in the ass. OK?" He looked me over from head to foot and asked, "What was supposed to happen? Were they supposed to come back to life?"

"Sort of."

Hank rolled his eyes and took a long gulp of beer. He asked, "How long has this been going on?"

I took a deep breath and said, "I know what you're thinking, because I thought the same, but this is real."

"I'm sure it is, John, and I'm sure that's what all the patients at the De Poo Mental Hospital on Kennedy Drive say about their lives." He set a plastic fender over the railing and continued. "I don't believe I am having this conversation. I don't talk to you for twenty-plus years, and you are seeing things. Absolute garbage."

"Hank, I need you to release me from the pledge of silence we made with each other the day that the men died. It was a soldier's code of honor, between you and me, but what happened is coming back like a nightmare."

"Kiss my ass," he said.

"You don't understand how important this is to the squad, me, and probably even you."

"I know how important it is to me that you keep your trap shut, and that is what I expect. Now get out of my life, and take your friend. And don't come back."

"They know we are holding back information."

"They can think all they want. As far as I remember, nothing happened beyond what you say. Now get out of here. I got real business to do: *looking for treasures.*"

10

THE FAT LADY YODELS

My ringing alarm clock sounded like it was planted in my head. I peeked one eye open and saw the darkened room and windows, and I searched for the alarm with my outstretched hand. I came down hard on the button and got out of bed. Groggily, I sat at the edge of the bed and held my head. Pledge of silence…code of silence…soldier's code of honor…whatever that means. Was I the solution to the squad's problem, or was I the problem? If only these thoughts would stop haunting me and just go away, or find someone else to torment. I slipped into a pair of brown canvas shorts heavy from the knives and pliers and fly boxes I'd stuffed into the multipockets the night before. I buckled my belt decorated with a blue marlin arched in flight. I slipped into some Crock sandals, dragged a saltwater-fly-fisherman's T-shirt over my head, and picked up my wide-brimmed hat. When I walked out into the kitchen, I smelled bacon and heard eggs frying. I slumped in a kitchen chair and watched Bryan place a cup of coffee in front of me. The cup was steaming. Garfield was pictured on the cup asleep on a kitchen table.

Coffee in the morning is as sacred to me as a precious hair from the Lord Buddha is to a monk.

The thought of those bonefish in the trenches awaiting the incoming tides to prowl the flats for shrimps, crabs, and sand dabs boosted my spirits and masked my self-derision. Before I left the house, I

117

dabbed my nose and lips with sunscreen, since I usually forgot to do it later when the excitement of fishing kicked in.

My client was Roger Wagner, a CEO with REI headquarters in Seattle. Roger was impeccably groomed, right out of his catalogue: wide-brimmed hat, baggy vented short-sleeve white shirt, low-cut tennis shoes, and baggy shorts. He proudly held a cup of coffee, I'm sure envisioning the cup being replaced by a fish by the end of the day. While our deckhand, Clinton Provost, loaded my eighteen-foot flats boat with food and gear, Roger and I talked strategy for the day. He was new to bonefishing but was anxious to impress his team back in Seattle with his instant success, which meant he needed me, badly. The caffeine had kicked in, and the roar of the 125 hp Evinrude spurred me on. The bow slapped the water, and the wind dimpled the skin on my face as the adrenaline rushed.

Before we reached Marvin Key, I cut the motor, mounted the poling platform above the engine, and quietly pushed our way to the flats. The water was so shallow, the bonefish would spook at a touch of rain. But I had caught the grandparents of these fish, and these young whippersnappers couldn't fool me, no matter how fast they turned, circled, backtracked, feigned, or spooked.

Roger caught two bonefish that morning: a six-pounder near Rosemary Key and an eight-pounder off the north tip of Snipe Key. His marvel was my relief.

When the tide crested in the afternoon heat, we found a shady spot on Snipe Beach for lunch. We ate deli sandwiches from the Publix Super Market, drank bottled Canadian Blue Mist water, and ate granola bars as we watched a pair of naked women sunbathe. We finished the day on the Gulf side of Sandy Key, where Roger caught an eight-pound permit on a bonefish clouser.

On the return trip home, I pointed out to Roger two rare Florida birds: the gallinule and the palm warbler (I'd picked up their names from Bryan). He snapped off two quick shots with his Nikon camera and acted like he had never had so much fun spending $600 in his life.

At home, Bryan was bored. I bought him a bicycle, which was the preferred mode of transportation in town, and that helped for a while. He rode every day but complained that Black Jack had trouble keeping up with him. He rode the bike to the grocery store, to see me come in at the docks, and to the park, where he threw the Frisbee for Black Jack, but he definitely missed the adventures of beachcombing Hangover Key. He looked like he was getting into the "watch the paint on the wall change its molecular makeup mode" again.

As he sat on the couch next to the window and watched the raindrops falling from the rubber-tree leaves, I said to him, "Bryan, do you sit around all day long talking to the squad?"

"No, I haven't heard from them since we saw them at Sanctuary Key."

"Good. Maybe they know we can't help them and have gone away." Bryan's lower chin wrinkled in doubt.

"Bryan, I'm going to teach you how to tie some flies."

He perked up. "But, John, I don't know how to tie flies."

"That's what I said—I'm going to teach you."

I waved him over to the small oak table I used for tying flies. The table had a roll up top, and I flung it open with a rattle. "Here it is," I said. Bolted onto the tabletop were a Thompson hook vice and a basketball-size magnifying-glass light. I turned on the light and told Bryan to watch me tie a fly called "the bonefish clouser," a simple combination of chartreuse thread with a white-and-green deer hackle on a number-two hook. Finished, I removed the fly from the vice, set it in Bryan's outstretched hand, and said, "Now it's your turn."

He studied the fly for a good minute before he took my place at the table. He pulled the chair in and stared through the magnifying glass.

He really didn't know what the hell to do. He played around with the light and studied his hands under the magnification. The depth of field confused him. I talked him through opening the vice, clamping the hook in the vice by the shank, setting the bobbin thread, wrapping, knotting, whipping, and cutting. He glued thread and feathers to his fingers and, finally, glued his fingers together. I set his hand under hot water, lathered his fingers with soap, and yanked the fingers apart. His fingers hurt, but I wouldn't let him quit. That first fly was a mess. I made him tie another fly, which was a little better, with far fewer accidents. "Good job," I told him on his third try, and that was enough to gain his interest and attention.

For the fourth fly, I guided his hand through the movements, but he was all thumbs and knuckles. He had an especially hard time with the dumbbell eyes. When he would wrap the thread around the weighted eyes, the eyes would roll over backward or slip forward, always off center. Bryan spent two nights just tying that one fly over and over until he found the dexterity in his hands to hold, knot, and twist the threads. I wasn't going to let him quit until he became an expert. That notion settled him down, and he quit fighting his anxiety and relaxed. He moved his head real close to the magnifying glasses and moved his hands with the dexterity of a brain surgeon.

Every night I'd bring more supplies home until he had hooks size two to eight and nearly every color of the flat, waxed nylon thread—pink, green, brown, white, red, and black. He had everything from Krystal Flash and Flashabou to Mylar tubing and Sparkle Braid.

By the end of week one, I'd introduced him to tying the Ruoff's Absolute Flea, a more detailed combination of thread with winged feathers. That first absolute flea looked like it might scare a fish, but his second fly was crystal clear, and the third fly was downright awesome. The more I praised him, the more he blossomed until he was tying chartreuse Merkin with round rubber hackles, the Lefty Deceiver, the Tarpon Bunny, Whistler, Gotcha, Cuda Clouser, and Optic Eye Cuda Fly. By the end of week three, he was visiting my workplace and just studying the variety of flies in the little display boxes. He'd go home and make the same. Some flies took him about fifteen minutes to tie, like the Merkin and Absolute Flea, but others, like the Clouser and Gotcha, took him only about five minutes. The more flies he tied, the more organized he got, with boxes for hooks, plastic ziplock bags for the feathers and hackles, and plastic containers for the flies.

"Are you going to see that girl again?" he asked me.

"Who are you talking about?"

"You know who. The one at the Wildlife Center."

"I guess so; maybe not. She really kind of hates me, but I do enjoy the concept of helping pelagic creatures in distress."

"Let's volunteer as aides to help her," he said. "We'd both enjoy that, for different reasons."

I smiled and said, "You know, Bryan, I think you are a keeper." I thought about it. Maybe the best thing to do was to just be around Mary so she would start to see the person who used to be her best friend. Within God's given time, she might grow to like and admire me like she had as a young girl.

We volunteered to work at the Wildlife Center on stormy days or when the guiding business got slow. But from the start, things just didn't look too promising. Mary seemed more interested in Bryan than me. They hit it off right from the start when Bryan said, "I think I met you before, in another life!"

"What are you talking about?" Mary smiled.

"You were serving pirates grog on a pirate ship."

Mary laughed and replied, "You know, that does sound familiar. I have dreams every so often about being a wench on a ship."

"Wearing a head scarf with the Jolly Roger on it and black-and-white striped pants?"

"Shut up, Bryan...oh my God, cut it out. You are clairvoyant. I don't believe you."

"It is all good," Bryan said. "And it is going to get better with John and me around."

They walked down the path between cages while Mary explained the layout of the place.

There was this real squirrelly girl who followed Mary around and made it impossible for me to talk to Mary alone. This Sandra Elwood was probably in her late thirties, had straight brown hair, and was skinny. She hung onto Mary's words like those of a prophet. She always made this "hmmm" noise like she was indexing Mary's comments, which bugged the shit out of me.

During one of my first evenings there, we were all standing at the table, ready to start our assignments. I looked down the tunnel of cages filled with white-and-brown-colored birds and asked, "Where do all these birds come from?"

"Unfortunately," Sandra replied, "ninety percent of the birds have been injured, either directly or indirectly, as the result of human contact. The birds are victims of habitat destruction, cat attacks, oil spills, pesticide poisoning, car wrecks, fishing lines, and gunshots. Some of them wrap themselves around telephone wires."

"Wow! And where do you get the money to feed them all?"

"It costs over one hundred thousand dollars a year to run this clinic, and the money comes from volunteers."

"That's why you pay so well then?" I joked.

"Exactly," Mary said. "A big fat thank-you."

"I could use plenty of those," I said. "What do you want me to do first?"

Mary picked up the water hose and moved toward the cage. Swinging the slack in the hose toward her, she said, "Why don't you bring Nasty here for her evening medication."

Nasty, I thought. This does not sound good.

Sandra nodded her head down the row of cages, and I hesitantly walked down the aisle, reading the nameplates on the individual cages.

I found Nasty, a large-size barn owl, in a cage at the end of the enclosure. Nasty sat on a casuarina perch stripped of its bark. Of course Nasty probably did not chew it all off herself out of nastiness, but the thought occurred to me. Nasty was buzzard size with a pretty black back and white chest feathers. Nasty made eye contact with me, and I didn't get a warm and fuzzy feeling. Nasty had cold, dark eyes.

I entered the cage and shuffled toward Nasty. I talked to her as I got closer, introducing myself and explaining my intention and where my instructions came from.

I raised my right forearm and offered it as a perch for Nasty to jump aboard.

Her head reached out for my arm as to sniff me. She hopped aboard and sunk her claws into my bare skin.

My mouth opened in pain, but I couldn't bloody scream in the bird's face; it might have sunk its claws deeper. Nasty stretched her neck out and pecked at my face. I guarded her attacks with my other hand as wings flapped and feathers flew.

There was a shuffle in the cage, and I saw flashes of Sandra. Then a towel was thrown over Nasty, and Sandra slowly subdued Nasty and persuaded her to let go of my forearm.

Once my arm was free, I staggered backward and crashed into the cyclone fence, inspecting my bleeding arm. Blood dripped from half a dozen puncture wounds.

"Son of a bitch," I said.

"You're not supposed to handle Nasty without gloves," Sandra scolded. "And you should always keep her in the dark."

"How the hell was I supposed to know?" I asked.

"You were a friend of Mary's. I thought you knew, because you seem to know everything else."

"Holy shit," I said.

"Come on," Sandra said. "After I give Nasty her antibiotic, I'll take care of you."

Mary acted indifferent to my trauma as she hosed down the barn owl's cage and scrubbed the droppings free from the cement.

Mary asked, "Is he all right, Sandra?"

"Yes. He'll be all right."

"Thanks," I said to Mary.

Mary replied, "I mean Nasty...John didn't hurt her, did he?"

"No," Sandra replied. "They'll both be fine. Just a scratch."

My mouth dropped, and I whispered, "Just a scratch." I looked at my bleeding arm. "Just a scratch."

When Sandra got to me, she explained that if I ever handled Nasty again, or any of the birds of prey, that I should use the electrician's gloves in the desk drawer under the signboard. "And always keep the birds in the dark. They are much calmer. Hold their folded wings against their sides and point their feet away."

"I'll remember that next time," I said.

Mary was different with me than she was with the other volunteers. With me, she was just plain mean. She refused to make eye contact when we worked close together, and she talked to me like I was a delinquent child. Her voice was gruff, and her manners were impulsive and impatient. Still, I did what I was told, because even though she treated me thus, I felt like I deserved it. I'm not sure why I felt that way or what I had done to deserve such treatment. Maybe it was punishment for that soldier's code of silence. I don't know.

I always got the heaviest jobs dumping out the bird crap, and I didn't just hose down the cages—I brushed them.

And get this: Mary had Bryan, good-old Bryan, collect the plastic butter containers (thirty-two-ounce size) and make birdcages for the orphaned and feeble birds. Bryan weeded around the outside of the cages, planting, fertilizing, and picking flowers. He set them in a vase on top of Mary's desk every morning. Bryan collected money to feed the birds and to build new cages, and he painted.

You'd have thought Nasty and the birds of prey would have been the worst, but they weren't. Cormorants and anhinga were used to gobbling up and spearing with their sword-long bills, and they tried to gobble up my hands, my arms, and even my face when they got the chance. I had a hell of a time keeping those birds under control without completely strangling the breath out of the little shits. Mary saw my fear of the cormorants, and that seemed to be my daily assignment—care for the wounded cormorants. Cormorants hated me.

"Mary," Sandra would holler with her high-pitched, hysterical voice. "He's doing it again."

Actually, I never did anything. The damn birds were doing it to me. I think I was atoning for human sins against the bird world. Sandra told me the easiest way to handle those birds was to grab their beaks first.

Bryan put duct tape on the broken shells of turtles that wandered up on the streets and were hit by cars. Bryan fed crickets to the orphaned cardinals, moistened dog kibbles to the mockingbirds, grapes to the owls, and berries to the woodpeckers. Bryan worked in the flight cage to prepare cardinals and songbirds for release back into the wild.

Me? I handled the psychos.

Bryan mixed one hard-cooked egg yolk with a teaspoon of water, half a can of Ken-L-ration dog food, and three tablespoons of applesauce. He removed the cotton from a Q-tip and fed the baby songbirds every half hour. Bryan worked with the surrogate parents to avoid human imprinting on the young birds.

Sandra told me that birds have no sense of smell. If people called on the telephone and asked what to do with a baby bird that fell out of its nest, I'd tell them, "If the bird doesn't have feathers, return it to the nest. If it has feathers, leave it on the ground, because one of the parents will care for it even on the ground. If you return it to the nest, it will jump again and possibly hurt itself."

Sandra was actually a big help, but there was something about her high-pitched umpire's voice that screamed, "Mary, he's doing it again." That definitely bugged the hell out of me.

"He's doing it again, Mary." I'd been bitten by a bat and had to have rabies shots, but Mary was more upset that the bat had to be tested for rabies.

"He's doing it again, Mary." I was hearing it in my sleep.

I cared for one cormorant for close to two weeks before it was doing better than I was doing, and I went and complained to Mary about the way the bird was cutting me. Mary switched me from the cormorant to the peregrine falcon nicknamed Grumpy. Grumpy took over where Nasty had finished, and I dreamed about being on the lowest end of the bird chain.

One night I was working late with Mary, and I was in the back cage cleaning out the gutters when I looked around and realized that it was a bit too quiet. I put down my leather gloves and looked for Mary. She was on the phone.

Finally, we are alone, I thought.

I started to think about old times again and when her eyes and smile used to sparkle.

I heard a snap of the gate and footsteps. I put down the hose and looked to the front door. It was closed, and Mary was no longer at the desk.

"Mary," I said.

There was no answer.

I rattled the gate to get out of the cage, and I'll be damned if it wasn't locked from the outside. There was a padlock on the cyclone fence, and I was locked in.

I rattled the cage and hollered, and pretty soon a street person came over from the nearby park and came up to the cage, which was now only dimly lit from the White Street lights.

I told him I was locked in, and he looked at the lock like he knew how to open it. He looked me over, furrowed his forehead, and said, "I'm not calling the police."

"Could you call the number on the fence?" I pointed.

"Do you have any money?" His eyes brightened.

I found some change in my pocket, rattled around, and handed him a dollar or so in change.

"I don't think that is enough," he said.

"It only takes a quarter," I told him.

"But suppose I don't get it right the first time?"

"OK. OK," I said. "I understand." I gave him a ten-dollar bill and said, "Please."

When he didn't reply, I said, "Thank you," and he left.

I spent the whole night in that cage. I tried to unfasten the clips holding the wire to the bars, but I didn't have any tools, and I kept breaking sticks that I inserted in the clamps. I could have worked my way under the wire if there hadn't been a bar along the ground that the fence was wired to. Finally, dejected and despondent, I just sat on the chair in front of the table, put my head on my arms, and fell asleep fitfully.

I was so happy when dawn finally came and the roosters started crowing and pecking around the cages. The streetlights went out, and people started moving around, taking walks and walking their dogs. Mary got there at 0600, and when I saw her walking toward the gate, I put my fingers through the loops and said, "You locked me in last night."

She didn't even act surprised. "Why didn't you say something?"

"You were gone before I realized you had locked me in. Didn't you get an emergency call last night?"

"Yes. Someone did call."

"*And?*"

"I told him I'd attend to the problem in the morning."

"Why, you little…"

"Yes," she said as her eyes turned to one glowing arc of fire, certainly hot enough to melt the fence.

"Are you going to open the gate?"

"Of course."

She opened the gate, moved to the table, and acted annoyed that I had pushed some papers around, that the chair was out of place, and that my sandals were under the table.

"What's wrong with you, Mary?" I asked.

"Nothing," she replied. "Nothing."

"OK, nothing. OK." I was steaming mad. "I come here religiously to help, and I pull the crappiest jobs you can think of, and what do I get? Not even a thank you. I've just about had it."

"Then quit," she said.

"Well, I just might do that."

"Well, good."

"Then again, I just might not."

I stormed back home and realized that I was late for work. When I reached the dock, my Canadian client was upset, because the sun was already up, and we were still on land. It took me two hours to make him a happy customer. He hooked a nine-pound bonefish at the Content Keys.

Mary was beginning to remind me of Hank, at least the way she treated me. I saw the young and vivacious Mary when she talked to coworkers or to the birds, but to me, her voice was gruff and her manners short.

Just to bug her, I kept returning.

One night I was sloshing out the birdcages on the far end of the compound when I heard a scream, and I recognized it as Mary's. I dropped the hose and, without turning off the water, ran down the lane toward Nasty's cage, where I heard the screaming.

There in the cage, bent over, was Mary, and on Mary's back was Nasty prancing in circles. I ran back for the glove and blanket and removed Nasty from Mary's back. I took her arm, led her outside the cage, and sat her down. She was not crying, but she was in pain.

I asked, "What happened?"

"I bent over to turn off the water, and before I knew it, Nasty was on my back."

I put my hand on the back of Mary's neck, and I bent her forward and inspected her T-shirt. There were dots of blood on the shirt.

I pulled her shirt out from her shorts and saw a good dozen marks on both sides of her back where Nasty had repositioned her claws. The punctures were not deep, nor were they bleeding profusely.

I moistened a cloth and cleaned her wounds. Next, I got the first-aid kit and cleaned the wounds with peroxide. I started to massage her shoulders.

"What are you doing?" she asked.

"Just circulating the blood," I replied. "How does it feel?"

"I'm in pain. Thank you."

"You're welcome."

She said, "John, leave me alone."

I was taken aback. "What do you mean?"

"You've been after me since the day you returned to Key West, and I don't want anything to do with you. I'm a married woman."

"I know that, and I don't know how much I'm really after you anyway."

"Don't give me that. You're around here all the time. You're on me whenever I turn around. You're right there."

"And it's not like you appreciate my help?"

"I would appreciate the help if your intentions were honorable, but they're not."

"Well, excuse me."

Before she stormed off, she gave Bryan a kiss on the cheek.

He stood there smiling at me.

"Youuu," I said.

"Well, John, are you ready for my help now?" Bryan asked.

"Your help?"

"Exactly."

"*You* are going to tell me how to get along with women?"

He smiled. "Exactly. I learned a lot at the hospital in Miami, and one of the things I learned was about relationships and about how guys like you with combat experience deal with relationships. When you get into a situation that you lose control of, you get scared and then angry, and that is the end of the relationship or marriage or casual acquaintance. You want to solve all your relationship problems like you did in 'Nam—by stuffing your feelings.

"I've been watching you, not just with Mary, but also with the other women in your life, like that Sandra in San Francisco and some of those other girls. You treat women like sexual objects. You act like you want them for just one thing, and you are the platoon leader, the decision maker, the king. You have to learn about having fun with them as equals. John, you need to learn about intimacy and communication—the essence of a relationship. Right now, when you speak, you talk to people like they are enemies that have to be conquered. Either that, or you treat them as members of your squad who need direction. You have to relax and let your feelings out and learn to communicate your feelings, and then as a team, you will move forward in a direction on life. Don't be afraid of your feelings."

"Sometimes I just feel like I am going to get angry and then want to kill someone, like maybe you."

"Remember what you told Dr. Howe at the courthouse: 'Your killing days are over.' And remember what I said about displaced anger."

My mouth was glued shut.

11

THE RIGHT DOOR OPENED INTO THE WRONG ROOM

When we returned home that night, Cameron was sitting at my fly-tying workbench, inspecting my work through the magnifying glass. He wore the same clothes as always; his M16 rifle was leaning against the table.

Billy Boy stood in front of the sliding-glass-door window, admiring his reflection. He wore a white double-breasted suit and white oxford shoes. On his head was an Australian bush hat with a fluffy peacock feather in the red hatband.

Black Jack was OK with them, like she had already accepted them as part of our dysfunctional family. She didn't bark, but she didn't wag her tail either. She just sat a foot and a half behind Bryan, her eyes fixed to their every movement.

I felt off guard. Here they were, making themselves at home in my house, uninvited. They came and went as they pleased, the self-centered little jerks. Annoyed, I asked Billy Boy, "Where did you find those clothes?"

Billy Boy giggled and twirled, flicking his wrist. He replied, "History is my wardrobe. It came from England—a nobleman, Sir John Duval. I traded him an Amazon pygmy's necklace for it."

"A gay nobleman," I replied.

His lower jaw twitched. "Does it matter? Just because I have so much to choose from. Would you like a new wardrobe? Maybe Wild Bill Hickok's cowboy hat, holster, and six-gun?"

I replied, "I think I'll pass this time."

Cameron interrupted. "Let's cut to the chase, John. Things are not getting better."

"What now?" I replied, flopping on the couch and setting my feet on the coffee table. I really liked the domestic life I was creating for Bryan and me.

"Since your talk with Hank, he's taken a ninety-degree turn in his shipwreck search. He's headed right for us. Although he can't follow you directly to Sanctuary Key because of water depth, he is headed in that direction. It is like a sixth sense or something...the way we used to read each other's thoughts in 'Nam when things got tense. He is picking up our vibes."

Black Jack pointed her tail.

I'd begun to observe a peculiarity about Black Jack. Bryan was forever talking to her, but I noticed a turn in Black Jack's behavior toward Bryan's dialogues. Black Jack seemed to be answering him. From my observations, when Black Jack pointed her tail, she was agreeing. Sitting was a no. When Black Jack wanted Bryan to repeat himself, she wagged her tail. Squatting was a fervent no. Black Jack lying down and covering her ear with the one good paw was "I can't handle this any longer." It was like the two of them were creating a new language.

"Hank is going to find where we live," Cameron replied. He took a drag from his cigarette and blew smoke rings.

I asked, "Am I supposed to be upset?"

Billy Boy wagged his fanny, extended his right arm, and flicked it at the wrist. "Didn't you ever wonder why that pond at Sanctuary Key is so bright in the middle?"

I thought a moment. "No." The pond was serene and reflective. It was dark at the perimeter, turning pastel and transparent toward the middle. I'd thought it was the color of the sand. "Not really," I said, shaking my head. I removed my pocketknife and cleaned my fingernails.

Billy Boy said, "Bryan, you explain to John. I took you there the night of the storm. Remember?"

Bryan's eyes darted toward mine and then back to Billy Boy. "I didn't want to tell John about that, so I think I forgot about it."

Billy Boy puckered his lips and said, "There are more gold coins down there than there are BBs in a 106-canister round. I mean, gold, baby, all from the sunken ship *La Cruz*—the one Hank is looking for." He did a little jig, twisting his ass in circles and grinding his hips. When he stopped, with his arms around the coat rack, all eyes in the room turned on me. I stood up and went to the refrigerator. I got out a soda, popped the top, and closed the door. Shrugging my shoulders, I returned to the couch.

Billy Boy said, "If Hank finds our home, he will destroy the place, and we will be homeless...no place to go...straight to hell."

"You guys are playing with my mind so much, I feel like I don't want to know you. I really do like just being a fishing guide and a volunteer at the sanctuary, getting paid every Friday and watching the sports channel on TV."

"Kill him," a voice bellowed from the hallway. "Kill the son of a bitch."

We all turned around as Stuart walked down the hallway. He still sported a bandolier of shiny grenades around his waist and right shoulder. His bare chest was oiled and sweaty. His reflective sunglasses freshly cleaned. Moving forward, he watched the placement of each footstep, stopping and crouching. When he got to the couch, he said, "Hello, Lieutenant."

"Please, Stuart. The war is over, and I have a real name."

"OK. Lieutenant John...Lieutenant John Beckwith?"

"You guys are having problems," John said. "Definite posttraumatic stress problems. Mind-boggling stress! You are blowing me away. You are not supposed to be here, and now you want to kill people."

"Don't you love it?" Stuart asked.

I replied, "God, help me. Please. God, help me."

Billy Boy said, "Stuart is one scared black man. He do fear the Lord Jesus. Oh, he do that. But now he is ready to kill. Just like always. Take the law into his own hands. Kill."

"Shut up," Stuart hollered at Billy Boy.

Billy Boy caught his breath, turned sultry, and then giggled, covering his mouth.

Stuart said to me, "Shove Hank out in the middle of traffic on Duval Street during Fantasy Fest. Knife him in the back. Take him to Hemingway's house, and drown him in the pool. Drop him off the deck of a tourist ship. Hang him from the lighthouse. It's our only way."

"But that is murder," I replied.

"If you don't stop him, Lieutenant, our lives will be lost forever."

They all stared at me again.

"Save you from what?"

"From wandering around the world for the rest of our lives like big idiots," Billy Boy pleaded. "It's bad enough that we can't get on with life, and I have to live with these barbarians, but if Hank kicks us out of our home, there will only be one place for us to go." He looked at the floor. "John, we are crying out to you for help from beyond the grave."

"Clear our names," Cameron said.

Billy Boy said, "Justice."

"So you are telling me that you live on this underwater ship?"

"Exactly."

"How did you find this ship?"

Billy Boy explained. "When a person suddenly dies, his soul is frightened and lost. To rescue a lost soul, you have to coax it forward with the truth. We knew you'd eventually sober up and return to the Keys. This is your home. After following you around for years, we decided to come here and just wait."

"Can't you find another home?"

"Can you find another Key West?" asked Billy Boy.

Cameron said, "We had one pick, and that was it."

I shook my head and downed the soda. "What have I done wrong in my life to be talking to you people? Is this what happens to people who quit drinking alcohol?"

Cameron said, "We are like the souls of dead and unburied Indians. Our spirits won't release us. We are spiritual failures, crippled legends, dead spiritual bodies."

"Refresh my memory. How does Hank fit in?" I asked. "And me?"

Stuart said, "Hank is crossing the line. He is sealing our coffins with his greed. If he gets his way, we will be lost forever, evicted from Sanctuary Key, and he won't tell you, or us, the truth about our deaths. So there is nowhere for us to go."

"Maybe if I talked to him again?" I asked.

Billy Boy lisped, "Oh my Gaud. We are in sooo much trouble. So much." He fanned himself quickly. "You already tried that, and nothing happened...nothing happened. Now you won't kill him."

"What good would it do for me to kill him?"

Stuart replied, "He will be on our side then. We can deal with him from where we are."

Billy Boy turned and faced the others, saying, "The lieutenant thinks we are crazy. He probably doesn't even believe we exist. We are in deep doo-doo."

Cameron turned to me and said, "Straighten Hank out, Lieutenant. Just like in 'Nam. Straighten his ass out."

Stuart said, "We have been watching your ass ever since we died. You didn't know it, but we have."

"Billy Boy did remind me of the day I got shot and how you might have helped me not get killed," I replied.

"Is that all he told you about? There's more too," Stuart said. "Lots more."

"Remember the day you got ambushed on the way to Can Tho? Remember?"

"Of course I do...of course, but you guys were dead..." My voice trailed off into silence.

"Tell us, John," Bryan asked. "Tell us the story."

Billy Boy said, "Tell us, and Stuart will tell you exactly where we were."

Bryan said, "Tell us, John."

John took a deep breath and sat at the kitchen table. "But you guys had died two months earlier."

Bryan said, "This is like a group session at the VA counseling center. In the thirteen-week workshop, if you didn't tell a story, they wouldn't let you go home for the weekend pass. Tell us."

I took a deep breath and started. "Around dusk, during the dry season, the three tracks in my platoon were returning to a base camp in the Delta area, south of Saigon. The whole battalion was camped in a rice paddy. During the day, it was our mission to keep the road open and safe to travel between My Tho and Can Tho.

"The VC and NVA had been ambushing a lot of supply vehicles and convoys between the two towns, and the VC were mining the roads at night and then, during the day, detonating the mines under American resupply vehicles. It was late afternoon, and as we headed toward a little village, on the other side of which was our camp, I saw a lot of the Vietnamese standing in the road, looking our way. I was curious, and then, just as suddenly, there was an explosion in the road right in front of me but behind the lead track right in front of me. It was an RPG round, or maybe a land mine—I'm not sure—and when it detonated, it created a cloud of smoke, mud, and debris in the air, nearly blocking the view of the APC ahead.

"I kicked my driver in the back of his helmet, which was the signal for him to stop, and as he stopped, he turned the APC to the right in the direction of the firing. There was a line of hooches about one hundred yards away and half-hidden in the green undergrowth of the jungle. While my men returned fire into the tree line, I called up the front track and told them to stop and return fire, because they were still hauling ass down the road.

"This was an extremely precarious position to be in, in the middle of an ambush. So after a few minutes of returning fire, I spoke into my radio headset and told the tracks to move out, as the track behind me was stopped and returning fire.

"My track started to move down the road, but as we fled, I saw enemy machine-gun fire coming from the doorway of a hooch, and I kicked the driver's helmet to stop. The fifty-caliber machine gunner couldn't swing the barrel of the fifty caliber around far enough to take out the machine gun, because I was in the way. So I took the grips of the fifty caliber and shot a short burst, which made a huge stream of water in the flooded field. I adjusted my short spurt and shot low again, but the third time, I was right on. I shot a long consistent spray into the doorway. Meanwhile, another RPG round was fired, but now at my track..."

"OK, right here," Hank said. "Tell it nice and slow. What happened next?"

I continued. "As I found out later, this RPG hit the handle on my engine cover, ricocheted, and exploded over our heads."

"Bingo," Billy Boy said. "It hit the handle on the engine cover and ricocheted. And how big is this handle?"

"Maybe about four inches square," I said.

Stuart asked, "And what if that RPG hadn't hit the handle? What would it have done?"

"It would have borne its way into the engine block, into our ammunition cache, and blown us all sky-high."

The squad was silent as they watched me.

"You guys had something to do with that?"

"Tell the rest of the story," Bryan begged.

I continued. "I looked around, but once again, I saw no targets and thought it foolish just to sit there, a big fat target in the middle of the road, so I gave the command over the radio to move out again.

"As my driver gunned the engine and swirled in the direction of the village, I looked behind to see the track directly behind me, and it was not moving. I radioed the platoon sergeant, but there was no answer. I tried again. No answer. I was stressing. The track was right in the middle of the ambush. I found out later from the platoon sergeant that the VC had been running toward the track, and the track had been motionless, no firing coming from it.

"I called again to the driver of the track, and finally the platoon sergeant answered. 'Move out,' I shouted.

"'I can't,' he yelled into the microphone. 'The driver has a bullet in his head, and he is slumped over the controls.'

"'Pull him out of there, take the controls, and get the hell out of there.' My heart nearly exploded with relief when I saw the track moving. We got back to camp in about five minutes, and on the way, I was instructed to stop and talk to the battalion commander about what had happened. We drove into camp and headed toward his post.

"The battalion headquarters had a rain tarp protecting a huge area map pinned up against a track, and that's where the battalion commander stood. As I showed the colonel where we had taken fire on the map, the body of the dead driver was unloaded right in front of us. The men in my platoon drove away, leaving the dead body alone on the ground as I explained to the colonel what had happened. I didn't show it, but I was falling apart inside. I wanted to cry and scream for my driver, but I just didn't feel it would be appropriate. The colonel seemed nonplussed.

"After the briefing, I left the body there and returned to the platoon area. I told the men to prepare for a night ambush in about an hour. I felt like the men hated me, like they were talking behind my back about how I had gotten the driver killed and how I was going to get them all killed.

"A couple of days later, in the same area of the ambush but with more tracks with me, I heard firing, and I looked into a field close to where I had been ambushed. I saw a bunch of farmers in black pajamas and coolie hats stopping their work and looking my way. I quickly grabbed the fifty-caliber gun on my track and emptied it into them. My men just watched, aghast. Nobody else fired. They looked at me like I had gone crazy. I picked up the radio and told the commanding officer that I had returned fire on the enemy contact. It was a lie.

"When a religious service was held for the killed driver and three other men from other platoons, I didn't go the ceremony. I believed that there was nothing to mourn for; they were just dead. I couldn't weep for him or them, nor did I feel a tinge of compassion. I had completely stuffed all feelings—all feelings except hate."

Stuart said, "Lieutenant, that ricochet was no accident, believe you me. Just believe me—it was no accident."

Billy Boy said, "Yeah, you weren't just lucky *again*. Every time you escaped a catastrophe, you claimed you were lucky, but in reality, it was us watching over you."

Cameron said, "Remember that time you were pressed up against a booby-trap wire connected to a hand grenade? It was pitch black that night, and you froze in place until the ARVNs, who had set the trap, came from their little village and cleared the wire. John…you didn't even see the wire, but you froze in place like you knew it was there and that if you did move, you would have blown yourself to pieces. I was the guy who told you to freeze. It wasn't another one of your lucky stories."

I looked around at my battered men and said, "I love you guys, but I can't stoop to Hank's level and kill him. I'd be no better off than he is. It doesn't make sense. I can just imagine explaining killing to the police. 'You see, Officer, there are these three dead guys who told me to do it.'"

"OK. If you won't kill him, we want you to get the truth out of him," Stuart hollered. "We'll desert. We'll go AWOL. We'll disobey a direct order."

Cameron and Billy Boy gasped and stood back.

Enraged, I moved toward Stuart and stood toe to toe with him. I stared into his sunglasses, motionless. Finally, I said, "You'll do what I tell you and when I tell you. You'll desert over my dead body."

Cameron said, "See, he's still the same-old lieutenant. He'll stick up for us, just like in 'Nam. Right, Lieutenant?"

I said, "OK, men. If that's what you want and need, lieutenant it is." I studied each and every one of them and asked, "Stuart, what do you remember about the night you were killed?"

Stuart shrugged his shoulders, removed his Ka-Bar knife, and started to shave with it. He said, "Cameron and I were pulling watch on the north corner of the house. Cameron was asleep when the NVA came in. I thought it was Bryan or Hank or Billy Boy moving in my direction, because the NVA didn't approach from outside, or from a door, but from within the house, so they caught me off guard. They knew exactly where I was and started shooting right off, before I could even put my finger on the trigger of my M16. I remember seeing Cameron lifting his head off his helmet. I remember automatic gunfire riddling his body. I went blank that fast."

"I don't remember even that," Cameron said.

"And you, Billy Boy—where were you?"

"Bryan and I were in the other corner of the room, near the balcony where Hank and you were upstairs. I was asleep, as it was Bryan's watch, so I awoke to automatic weapons firing all around me and people running around like shadows, and then I was asleep again, but dead asleep."

All eyes turned to Bryan. "Bryan, how about you?" I asked.

"I don't remember anything," he replied.

Stuart said, "If anyone is hiding something, it's probably Bryan. He's using his stupidity to hide his guilt. It's him."

Bryan replied, "No, I'm not. I really am stupid. I just remembering seeing shadowlike ghosts running around me, and I had no idea who they were until I was dead."

"Well, that is remembering something then," Cameron added. "Isn't it, Bryan?"

"And you, Lieutenant? How about you?" Stuart asked.

"Hank and I were upstairs. Something happened, and I didn't wake up until the morning. I might have gotten hit in the head or something, but I was not awake during the firefight. Hank said the NVA didn't know that he and I were upstairs. Hank said he looked through the rails, and the downstairs room was full of NVA regulars. Hank said that your bodies were on the floor, and the NVA were going through what was left of your pockets. Hank said he stood up and fired. The NVA went for their AK-47s and pistols as Hank emptied his magazine. He reloaded and didn't stop firing until they were all down. After the pandemonium, Hank said he walked around and put a bullet in each and every one of the heads of the VC. That's why I put Hank in for the Silver Star Medal for bravery."

"And that was it?" Billy Boy asked.

"That was it."

"In the morning, I had a big knot on the back of my head that was the size of an apple."

Bryan looked shocked and said to me, "That isn't what you told the doctors in the Miami VA what happened to me. You told them we were surrounded by VC and I came running to you all bloodied and fell on top of you."

"Well, I didn't tell them everything. You did come running out of that house the next morning when I gained consciousness. You were shot up, close to death."

"So you got knocked over the head, or something happened to you?" Stuart asked me.

"Yep. That was it."

Billy Boy said, "I think Hank knows something more about this disaster, and for some reason, I feel like the lieutenant is trying to protect Hank. Protect him from us."

Stuart said, "Somebody is lying about something, and it could be any one of you guys." He challenged each man with his eyes, but not one rose to the challenge.

12

THE GOD OF FATE DID A NASTY

There were some things I wanted to hide about the night the squad had died. I couldn't tell the squad 100 percent of the truth. I had hoped by being 99 percent truthful, the other 1 percent would go away. But that 1 percent was coming back like an infection—a mold. What had happened was that, under the stress of war, I had made a soldier's pledge to Hank the night my squad had died. Since we were the only survivors (well, Bryan was a survivor, but he didn't remember anything), I had hoped that the story we told could and would be believed and life would go on. A pledge is a pledge, and if Hank wouldn't release me from the pledge, I was helpless.

Ninety-nine percent is a good score, but sometimes maybe not enough.

I kind of believed the squad about the sunken ship, and there had been a lot of "luck" that had kept me alive in 'Nam, but then again, I kind of didn't believe them, especially about this sunken ship, so I decided to do some historical research at the city library before I returned to Hangover Key. I wanted to authenticate what the squad had told us about this shipwreck, *La Cruz*. I didn't want to go looking for something that wasn't even there.

The city library was located on a quiet section of Fleming Street, and the historical research room was located in the far-right back corner, open daily from ten o'clock in the morning to noon. There, the books could not be checked out, only read at the centrally located wooden conference table. An elderly, suspicious-looking librarian sat at a desk by the doorway, surreptitiously reading.

My research took me first to coral reefs. The only living coral reef in the United States is located in the Florida Keys. This reef stretches 250 miles from Key Largo to the Dry Tortugas Islands, which is 70 miles southwest of Key West. Thousands of different corals exist in distinct shapes, with names such as elkhorn coral, mushroom coral, brain coral, and stringy feather corals. Coral consists of individual polyps approximately half an inch in size. Colonies of corals have grown on top of each other for millions of years, providing an underwater forest of colors and food for fish, crabs, crustaceans, and sea anemones. The decomposition of coral provides the snow-white sandy bottoms. Each coral covers itself with a limestone shell for protection, and no matter whether these coral are alive, dead, or dying, they have one thing in common: they are cement hard.

Throughout Spanish history, the reefs had been the demise of many a sailing ship, the most famous wreck being the *Nuestra Señora de Atocha*. This royal-guard galleon had been the flagship of the Spanish armada and, because of its size, had always contained the most precious jewels and gold of all the ships. In 1622, the armada had been on its return voyage to Spain and had run into a hurricane. *La Atocha* had been blown toward the shallow reefs of Key West and had never been heard from again. There had been no survivors.

Mel Fisher, a famous wreck diver who had scoured the reefs for twenty-three years in search of *La Atocha*, had finally found the ship on July 20, 1985, twelve miles west of Key West. *La Atocha* had struck a reef, opening the bow like a gutted pig. As she'd foundered, she'd spilled a trail of gold and silver coins, precious stones, and necklaces for two miles before she'd sunk.

Mel's discovery had been the richest find ever recovered since the opening of King Tut's tomb in 1930. The federal government had estimated the worth of the precious emeralds, doubloons, gold and silver bullions, chains of pure gold, and seventy-pound blocks of gold to be $700 million.

The *Atocha* armada wreck had not been alone in the Keys. In the Spanish annals covering 150 years of shipping precious metals from the Americas to Spain, the chroniclers had registered over five hundred shipwrecks in Florida, which in 1850 had made Key West the treasure hunter's capital of the United States. Included in this list had been seventeen ships in a treasure fleet of twenty-one that had broken up on reefs along the Keys in 1733. All these ships had been plugged with gold. One of them had been named *La Cruz.*

"I got it," I told Bryan. "I got it." But when I looked up from my book, only the librarian looked at me over her reading glasses. Bryan was outside sitting on the library wall, talking to Black Jack.

We left for Sanctuary Key later than we had planned, because Bryan couldn't find Black Jack's leash, which had been left in the crook of a tree the day before while the two of them had been playing Frisbee at Bay View Park. So we waited for the cover of night to row to Sanctuary Key. We unloaded our supplies and spent the night in the tree house, enjoying the silence and peace of our sanctuary.

When I awoke, I heard noise from the camp area and looked out the opening to see Black Jack hobbling down the beach after a flock of egret. Bryan was working at the blazing fire pit.

I joined them and sat on my log, poking at the fire and staring at the lagoon. It was a good hundred yards across and colored different shades of green and turquoise. There was definitely one spot close to camp where the water was light turquoise. It was the same spot where we had fished and lost several fishing hooks, so we'd quit fishing there. That is where we would check first, just like the squad had said. If we didn't find anything, I'd fan out along the shoreline and work my way around the lagoon, going into deeper water. I'd end the search in the middle of the lagoon.

Bryan made a wonderful breakfast: sliced pineapple, toast (slightly burnt), a glass of tomato juice sprinkled with bacon bits (which I preferred instead of pepper), scrambled eggs, and bananas. We ate silently. Bryan and Black Jack were on vacation. Bryan was throwing sticks, and Black Jack was splashing in the water, retrieving the sticks. One thing about those two was every day was a celebration of the joys of living.

"You ready to go for a swim, partner?" I yelled out.

Bryan trotted closer holding a stick and asked, "We're not leaving already, are we?"

"No. We're not leaving. We came here to dive in the lagoon and check out the squad's story."

"That's what I meant," he replied as he picked up the pot of coffee and, holding the lid on tight with his other hand, poured me some, stopping halfway.

I looked at the cup and asked, "Tight on the coffee this morning?"

"I didn't want you to spill it."

Shaking my head and then smiling, I said, "Give me some more, please."

He did so as proud as an Olympic swimmer recently decorated with a gold medal.

Invigorated by the caffeine, I said to Bryan, "You do the dishes first and then follow me."

I slipped into a bathing suit, donned a diving mask, picked up the fins out of the canoe, and walked toward the water's edge. I slipped on the fins, lowered the mask over my eyes, and waded into the water deep enough to swim. The water was brackish and colorless. I dove to the bottom, about eight feet deep. The sand was rippled. I surfaced and looked back at the beach. Bryan was tossing all the dishes into the clean rinse bowl and running after me. At the water's edge, he kicked off his sandals and walked in the water, splashing, not even bothering to change into a swimsuit. I took a deep breath and dove under the water again, found the rippling bottom, and headed directly offshore. My ears hurt, so I grabbed my nose and blew until I heard a pop. When I reached a drop-off, I ran out of air and surfaced.

Black Jack had followed Bryan into the water and was trying to climb on top of him. Bryan was moving away, splashing and giggling.

In a circle of turquoise water, I took another deep breath, reached the bottom, and saw what looked like waterlogged timbers, and more timbers, jutting from the sandy bottom.

I came up hollering. "Bryan…Bryan…I think I found something."

He stopped long enough to push Black Jack away and then came swimming toward me, holding his head high and squishing up his face as the water splashed.

When he reached me, he asked, "Can I try?"

"Sure," I replied.

He dove under and came up with a black sea cucumber about a foot long, all balled up and spitting ink in Bryan's face. I told him to put it back. He spat out some ink, took two deep breaths, and shot back down to the bottom. When he surfaced again, his hands were empty, and he sputtered, "I put him back where I found him, John."

I moaned into the snorkel.

I dove again and reached the timbers, grabbed a hold of one to stabilize myself, and reached into the sand. I could feel my fingers curl around something like a rock, but the sand was stirred up, so I couldn't quite see what it was. I put a death grip on whatever it was and shot to the surface. When I came to the top, I spat out the snorkel, looked at my hand, and saw the sand spill through my fingers, revealing a handful of coins. "Oh my God," I said.

"Well, I'll be a dirty mudsucker," Bryan replied. He was frowning like he was unhappy that he hadn't found it first.

"I got it," I repeated. "I got it. The squad knew what they were talking about." I swam to shore, washing the sand from the coins. "Gold," I muttered to myself. "Gold…I can't believe this. It was so easy. Just like they said. Just like they said."

I collapsed on the beach and watched as the coins played out of my hand. Bryan sat next to me, and then Black Jack came over, kicking up sand and licking the salt off my leg. She wagged her tail at Bryan, which was her way of asking that he explain again. Bryan did so, and she replied with a curled tail, which meant, "No kidding."

I said to Bryan, "Just like Cameron said." Panting, I handed a coin to Bryan, and we both inspected the same one. Apparently the Spanish had refined and minted the gold before sending it home. On one side was a single-masted sailing ship with hand-scribed letters. Neither Bryan nor I could make a word of it out. I flipped the coin over and saw a woman in a royal, fluffy dress and jeweled crown sitting on a throne. She was scowling.

Bryan said, "I can't wait to show Mary."

I licked my lips and said, "Now don't you go getting any crazy ideas. This gold is staying put, and nobody is going to touch it, including you. If we go flashing those coins around town, every treasure hunter south of the Yukon River will be sniffing us out."

"Can't I even keep one to play with?"

"No," I barked, "and if you have one, you better throw it right back where you found it."

Bryan sulked, cuddled the coin I had given him, and replied, "But it feels so smooth to touch, and it's so heavy."

"Yes, it is, but it doesn't belong to us, and I haven't figured out what I'm going to do with it yet."

"Please."

I thought a moment, looked Bryan straight in the eyes, cocked my head slightly, and replied, "If you go messing with that gold, I'll disown you and never make you do another push-up your entire life. I mean it too. You stay away from that gold."

Bryan moved the coin away from his pocket and gave it a hard look before he turned his back to me and threw the coin over his shoulder, back into the water. When it splashed, he asked, "Don't you want to know what I wished?"

"No."

"I wished that you'd let me have your last name."

I held up my hands like a referee splitting apart two wrestlers and said, "I don't want to hear it. OK? I just don't want to hear it. It's not good luck to tell someone your wish."

Bryan was miffed, but I didn't have time to baby him.

Now what the hell was I going to do?

Bryan convinced me to stay another night at Sanctuary Key, and I agreed, since it would give me time to figure out my next move. That evening, I expected the squad to appear around the campfire, but they didn't. I was really looking for some direction. But no one came forward.

Mary was on the phone at the Wildlife Center when we arrived. She quickly hung up the phone, picked up her cup of coffee, and took a sip when she saw me. Sandra was there, and her elongated neck was stretched out and her lips puckered.

When I got close enough, I asked, "What's going on, girls?"

Mary turned toward Sandra, who pursed her lips and glared at me. Sandra's face was flushed with anger.

"What are you doing?" I asked Sandra.

Sandra whipped the hair out of her face.

Black Jack stood on the fence with her one good paw, panting and lapping. She jumped down and licked the joint of her missing leg. We didn't let Black Jack inside the cage, because she harassed the birds.

Bryan entered the cage and closed the door in Black Jack's face.

I moved toward the coffee pot and got a better glimpse of Mary's face before she twirled away from me. Mary's right cheek was swollen and black, her eye nearly closed.

"Mary, what happened?" I asked. When she didn't answer, I continued. "You need more attention than your birds." Her good eye shot between Sandra and me, and for once, she didn't fight me. Studying the broken veins and the ruptured blood vessels that spread across her face, I winced and asked, "What happened to you?"

Her eyes turned away, and she answered, "I...I...I'm having a terrible day. When I grabbed Oscar, he head butted me and nearly knocked me out. I should have known better."

For a split second, I believed her, until Sandra said, "Bullshit. It was her asshole husband. He treats her like my ex treated me—a punching bag for his frustrations. I don't know why she stays with the jerk."

"Sandra, that's enough," Mary said.

"If he treated you decently, I wouldn't say anything. But he's an abusive alcoholic asshole. He's a sick man."

"It isn't that bad," Mary said.

"It's worse than that," Sandra said. "Sometimes I feel like killing him. Mary won't press charges against him either. One time I filed a report myself, but Mary wouldn't sign it. She just lets him abuse her with impunity."

"Where is he?" I asked.

Sandra said, "As usual, he's hiding on his boat, totally inaccessible except by float plane. He works feverishly every time he screws up, looking for his dumb treasures at everyone's cost."

I asked, "It looks like he backhanded you." I could feel my neck swell and the veins in my temple strangle my rationale. I was slow to anger, but the gap between anger and rage was small.

Bryan said to Sandra, "Hank was our radio operator in 'Nam. John was our platoon leader."

Obviously Bryan was starting to lose it.

Mary's face turned skyward, and small droplets of moisture dampened her eyes.

"I'm trying to get Mary to move up to Miami with her son, but I know she never will. Not unless she can take her birds with her."

By the time Sandra had finished telling her story, Mary was sobbing her eyes out. I lightly placed my hands on Mary's shoulders. Vietnam had destroyed our relationship and sent our lives in a spiraling tailspin. Yet here we stood, years later, in a birdcage in Hurricane Alley, at the southernmost tip of America, bruised and battered and hysterically alienated from each other.

"Why did he hit you?" I asked.

Sandra replied, "You don't even want to know, because it doesn't matter. Last time he hit her because she dropped his breakfast on the kitchen floor and he had to wait. The time before that, he smacked her because he couldn't find his sandals on his way to the bar. It really doesn't matter."

Mary looked at me with a bowed head and tearfully embarrassed eyes. "He's still my husband," she said.

I rattled the coins in my pocket and realized that they could wait.

Mary looked fearfully at me and, reading my mind, said, "No."

I said, "I'm not asking your permission."

Sandra smiled.

Bryan broke in. "Where is Black Jack?" Bryan rattled the cage.

Everyone looked around, but Black Jack was gone.

I need a leash for both of them, I thought. God help me. I'm the guy who needs some medication from Miami.

Bryan started calling for Black Jack as he ran outside.

Fuck, I thought. I didn't like Bryan running off hysterically after Black Jack. Bryan might run in front of a car and get hit, or he might do something else equally disastrous, but there was a fire in my heart. All I could think about was what Hank had done to my friend Mary, and I knew there was only one way to quench that fire.

I found Hank at Stinky's, and as soon as we made eye contact, he knew what was going to happen. He took a swig of his beer and then grabbed it by the neck of the bottle. As I got near, he took a swing at me with the beer bottle.

I feigned backward, and he missed. As he drew back to take another swing, I stepped forward and threw a left jab toward his face. I didn't make contact, but Hank stepped backward and set himself off balance. That is what I was hoping he would do. I stepped in closer, came over and around with my right fist, and came down on Hank's left eye. Hank went down like a shot put, and I stood over him waiting for him to move, but he didn't.

Then the power of the squad took over, and I realized for the first time what they were talking about. I could feel their energy warning me.

I threw back my left elbow at about eye level and made contact with something. When I turned my head to see what I had hit, it was the jaw of Eduardo, Hank's first mate. Eduardo still had the beer bottle cocked back in his right hand and ready to come down on my head. The surprised look in his eyes told the whole story. Eduardo fell backward and laid beside his friend Hank, both motionless.

"Thanks, Cameron," I said as I stepped over the two bodies and left.

The fight was over so quickly, the bar did not have time to pick sides, get all excited, and start a free for all. In silence, they stared at me as I walked out of the door.

13

HOUSE CALL

I ran hard. Black Jack usually listened to me, faithfully, but now she wasn't even in earshot. I roamed down the dock at White Street, checking out the shoreline in both directions. I sniffed the air and looked back toward the bay grape trees, the shallow mangroves, and thickets of sod grass. No signs of Black Jack. I trotted back to the dock and followed the shoreline east, looking in the yards of the condominiums. When the beach ended, I entered a garden area at the Atlantic Shores condominium complex. The air was alive with the scent of ornamental flowers.

There she was, standing on her good paw on the block wall overlooking the swimming-pool pavilion. She was sniffing the air.

I ran toward her, past the swimming pool, where several tanned beauties in skimpy bikinis glistened in the baking sun on chaise lounges.

With all the people around, I didn't want to cause a scene, so I whispered her name, but that didn't work. She kept going. Although Black Jack might have smelled it first, I saw it first. It was right under the redwood picnic table: a hardened rawhide doublewide dog bone.

Black Jack innocently moved toward the bone with her mouth open, neck extended, and head low to the ground, tongue sprinkling the pavement with saliva, her eyes focused. Just as she licked the bone, a splash of black fur attacked from her left. A Doberman pinscher clamped its teeth on Black Jack's neck, tossing and swinging its head from side to side. Even though Black Jack growled, she wasn't getting close to freeing herself. The Doberman had its forelegs spread, claws sunk into the sand, and eyes glazed with hate.

If I hadn't rushed up there and put my face right in that dog's snout, that dog might not have let go of Black Jack until she was dead. I buried my face into the Doberman's whiskers and growled like a polar bear making its last sound before pouncing on a defenseless hair seal. The Doberman unclenched its jaws and retreated with bloody teeth, its claws bared like knives and its lips quivering. Black Jack was all crunched up, and her neck sat at a particularly obtuse angle. A woman screamed, and a man grabbed the Doberman by its choke chain, but the Doberman didn't want to give up, leaping and snarling and choking itself nearly unconscious. I lifted Black Jack into my arms and returned to the beach, talking to her softly, encouraging her to get better. Her brown fur was covered with blood, and her bad leg was open to the bone with a gash so deep that the meat hung limply like shedding snakeskin.

Black Jack didn't move. Her head rested on my forearm, and she whimpered as her heart pumped pain through her fading consciousness.

I knew the only place I could save her was Sanctuary Key. I wanted to bathe her in the freshwater pond, let the hoot owls sing her to sleep at night and the cooing doves awaken her in the morning. If anything in the world could cure her, it was the power of love and the sacred waters of the artesian well. That's where I headed.

At home in Sanctuary Key, I removed Black Jack from the canoe, took her to the tree house, and set her on my bed. Then I lay down beside her, placed my hand on her side, and prayed to the forces of nature that owned the universe's healing power to share a bit of grace with my friend. I prayed to the god of love and the god of animals and promised my daily devotion if Black Jack survived.

Black Jack battled the demons in her sleep, whimpering and twitching and jerking in a restless coma. I watched her for the longest time until I couldn't keep my eyes open any longer. I fell asleep after placing my hand on her side again, hoping to infuse my life into her.

The next morning, I heard a canoe paddle slicing the canal and looked up to see John rowing his way to shore. When I met him at the beach, I asked, "Where did you get the canoe?"

"Scott let me borrow it again. How is your dog doing?"

"Not too good," I replied.

"Next time, don't leave me in town alone. At least ask if I want to come back out here with you."

"OK, but I was so scared."

"I understand, but remember, we are partners. I have to return to town. I have a half-a-day charter starting at one. I just wanted to see if you were OK. You know I worry too."

I asked, "Do you want some breakfast?"

He smiled and nodded, so I fixed him some sliced pineapple, tomato juice, and eggs.

Sitting there all alone, I felt sorry for John. He just looked lonely. I asked, "Did you fix Hank?"

He replied, "Does a bear shit in the woods?"

"And Mary?"

"You've been there. You got two eyes."

"I know. In the VA hospital, we took classes in grieving and relationships. Vets with PTSD fail miserably in relationships, because they are always barking orders, making rules, and demanding compliance, just like they were still in battle. When a man suffers a painful traumatic experience like in 'Nam, he feels like life is meaningless and not worth pursuing. Hate and anger become so strong that the man stuffs all other feelings. He just hates—hates life, hates himself, hates everyone. By grieving, layers of feelings surface, and you become human...again."

John said, "I think I'm in for a relapse." John took a quick shower, advised me to do the same, and left for work, fading into a dot on the horizon in the direction of the rippling ocean.

Black Jack didn't get any better. I began to learn the meaning of "sick as a dog." Black Jack wouldn't eat or move. She just lay there, faintly breathing, in a near coma.

I didn't know what I was going to do.

I needed to take a shower like John had told me. I climbed up the ladder to the tree house, picked up some clean shorts and a T-shirt, climbed back down, and walked past the fire pit toward the bushes where the bathroom and shower were, alongside a gumbo-limbo tree. I was worried to death, in spite of John's consoling words. Usually when John gave me an order, I obeyed, but this time, I just couldn't stop worrying.

In 'Nam, I used to worry, but I didn't cry. It was an emotion that had escaped me, because John explained that it was the last step before giving up. John said that while I grabbed on to my mother's skirt and buried my face in tears, the VC would take advantage of me, bend me over, hump me from behind, steal my wallet, and cut my throat. John was always right in matters of war and fighting. Even now, he strategized and planned his moves like a sniper.

With Black Jack as motionless as a baby quail, a flood of grief overwhelmed me, and I balled my eyes out. It was silly, ridiculous, and insane, but, after all, Black Jack was my best friend. John was my best human friend, but John was different. John didn't need me now, but Black Jack sure did. Here I was, weeping, hardly able to breathe, and choking on my own gasps of air as I worked out of my clothes and turned on the water.

Black Jack's innocence is what did it—innocence in the face of brutality. Courage responded to love, courage outsmarted fear, and fear was the bait that death was a sucker for.

Black Jack's health headed toward the South Pole. I showered real fast, as the water supply was low. When I turned off the water, I opened my eyes, but soap stung them, so I closed them real tight. I groped for my towel on the nearby tree branch, but I couldn't find it.

I peeked one eye open and looked over the top of the branches. Not seeing anything, I pulled down the leaves with both hands and continued my search. The only thing white around was half a dozen ibis pecking their way along the water's edge.

I felt a touch on my right shoulder. I jumped in the air and let out a whoop as I turned. There stood Billy Boy in silk underwear. If it weren't for his gut-dripping stomach, he would have looked handsome. His chest was white and hairless and shiny with oil. His blond hair was groomed pertly, and his blue eyes twinkled.

"Hello there, big boy," he greeted.

Of course I was shocked, but I didn't want him to know it. "Good morning," I replied, catching my breath and acting normal.

He handed me the towel and said, "You're so fun to watch take a shower. Aren't you even going to give me a hug?"

I didn't answer him. I noticed that his blond hair had a little curl that danced across his forehead when he moved, but I wasn't going to let him know I saw it. I took the towel, hid my privates with a corner, and used the other part to dry off.

He eyed me like he was interested, but I didn't want him to get the wrong idea.

"You always were so modest," he snickered. "I've seen you naked before, and to be honest, I liked what I saw. I watch you a lot."

"Well, you are not going to get any of me, if that is what you are thinking."

"Big boy, if I did, you'd die faster than I did. The difference is that you'd have a smile on your face."

"I'm a good boy," I replied.

"And so am I, especially when I'm bad."

I looked around nervously for help. John was long gone, and Black Jack couldn't open her eyes.

"Who are you looking for?" Billy Boy asked.

"Nobody. I was just looking around. What are you doing here anyway?" I asked.

"I just wanted to spend some alone time with you, that's all. This is where I live, you know." He eyed the pond quickly.

"Well, I'm a good boy."

"Congratulations. I have a question for you."

"Uh-oh."

He fluttered his eyebrows and said, "How come you never stayed in the same foxhole with me in 'Nam?"

"I didn't think we could fit."

"We'd fit all right, just like a wet suit on a chilled body." He wound his index finger through the loose corner of my towel and twirled it around, making it shorter. "You'd get in a foxhole with everyone else, but not me. Did you know that hurt my feelings?"

"More than your feelings would have hurt if you had tried something."

"OK," he retreated. "I promise I won't try anything."

He said something under his breath, and I asked him what it was, but all he said was, "Let's talk."

"I am," I replied.

"But more intimately."

"I think John is coming. I think I hear him."

Billy Boy laughed, slapping one hand on his knee. He said, "I just saw John leave, and I saw him in town last night. He found Hank at Stinky's bar and knocked him and that Eduardo out so fast that the bar didn't have time to erupt in a free for all. That's one thing John doesn't believe in, hurting women, and heaven have mercy on the bully who picks on John's women friends."

"You were there?" I asked.

"Saw every punch thrown, and let me tell you, John is getting me worried. He has fought more since he got to the Keys than he has the last thirty years. This is totally unlike him. In the past, he always ran for it."

"I hope this is a good sign. He didn't look hurt this morning."

"The lieutenant was on a mission. He never got hurt on a mission. Don't worry about him. Worry about me. I don't like wasting my time in this God-awful, boring limbo. I just can't do anything. I can't commit myself emotionally. I can't be myself."

"You seem busy enough to me."

"That's because you are half-dead, big man, and you need my help. Your dog needs my help."

My ears perked up, and I replied, "John told me that she will get better."

Billy Boy shook his head and winced. "If I help you, would you help me?"

"You just said you couldn't do anything."

"I can give advice."

"Like what kind?"

"You have to promise to help me first."

"Help you do what?"

"I want a piece."

"Of what?"

"Of Hank!"

I wiped the sweat from my brow and sighed. "That sounds better than a piece of me."

"Well?"

"I don't care. We can give it a try. Sure, I'll help."

Billy Boy clapped his hands together and danced a little jig. When he stopped, he got real close to me. I looked down to make sure he didn't drip any blood on my feet.

He whispered, "Why don't you take your poor dog to town before it dies. I can feel her spirit growing stronger, which, from your side of the world, isn't good."

Gasping, I asked, "Black Jack is not going to die, is she?"

"OK, OK, calm down." He beckoned with his hands. "You big hunk, you. Calm yourself. Calm yourself, and then take your dog to town, and take her to a veterinarian."

"John doesn't want me to."

"John doesn't want you to," he mocked. "And do you do everything John tells you to do?"

I thought a moment and replied, "Yes."

"Oh God, you are such a slut. You'll let your dog die because John told you not to leave. Isn't that rather strange?"

"Not for me," I replied. "Besides, I don't have the money."

Billy Boy laughed a moment, twirled his eyes, lifted his right arm, bent the elbow and then the wrist, and pointed his forefinger at the lagoon.

I started playing with my ear, twisting and turning it inside and out. I knew what he was getting at. Veterinarians cost money, and I had none of that, but Billy Boy was reminding me of something just as good as money, if not better—gold. I had a sudden flashback. It was the night before Christmas, and I was a child in a room full of presents around a Christmas tree. My mouth watered with guilt. Then the picture disappeared, and I was back with Billy Boy. If I took the gold, I would be defiling the sanctity of what I had been entrusted to safeguard. I would be defiling the very rules that I lived by and which I had sworn to follow. I would be defiling myself and betraying my best friend. What kind of advice was that? No wonder I grieved so, but my love for Black Jack was awfully strong. "Oh God," I said.

Billy Boy said, "It is the only way, believe you me. You do what I say, and your dog will live. Come on now. Think on your own."

"If I think too much on my own, I will be on my own," I replied.

"That's the risk you have to take," was the answer. "Now come on—let's do it, down and dirty, wallowing in carnal pleasures, humping and rutting. Do it."

I asked, "Can't you do it for me?"

"I'd like to, but I can't."

"Why not?"

"There is only one way a dead person can interfere in the life of the living, and every dead person, including Stuart, is afraid to take the chance, because the consequences could be eternal damnation in hell." Billy Boy circled nervously, wagging his finger, and continued. "It's Dante's *Inferno*, and that's no shit. Dante didn't make up all that fire and brimstone he wrote about, standing in shit up to his neck and all. The god of creativity allowed Dante's soul to experience one second of hell and live to write about it. The devil is real. Can you imagine pleading for mercy from Satan? Death would be unbearable. Unmerciful pain and more pain."

"How do you take that chance?"

"Nobody has ever taken it, but from what I understand, you go before a court of good and evil, in your own soul. It's a self-trial. The judge, jury, and lawyers are made up of your worst nightmare. It's impossible. It's doom. The odds are better of winning the Florida lottery three times in a row."

"But..." I said. Billy Boy was gone before I could finish. I glanced around quickly, searching for him. Nowhere. The coward! He wasn't risking eternity for me.

I remained naked for the baptism of betrayal of John's instructions. I moved to the water's edge, stared at the light in the middle of the pond, and stepped into the water. As the water rippled around my ankles, the sanctuary began to change. I felt a chill run through my veins, and I knew that I had made a decision that would change my life forever.

I walked deeper, up to my waist, to my belly, and finally, I was swimming toward the sinful light.

I swam to the center of the glow and looked down. Without a mask and at such close quarters, all I could see was the brightness. I took a deep breath and dove. Sticking my feet into the air, my weight pushed me deeper. I reached out as I groped forward. The visibility was unpronounced and evasive. I grappled forward, feeling for the hardened round coins. But the throbbing pain in my ears made me return to the surface for another gasp of air. I realized I was going to challenge my diving ability to the max, so I took concentrated deep breaths, which started in my belly and ended with a bloated chest. I took three full breathes and then five quick ones to fool my inner self, and I dove again—hard, fast, and deep.

I kept my hands in front of me and used them to pull my way deeper, rotating my jaws to clear my ears from the mounting pressure. Finally, at last, my hand struck bottom, and I heard a jingle. My fingers snaked through round and heavy objects, deeper and deeper until I was satisfied that whatever I would bring up would be pure gold. My fingers closed like the jaws of a trap, and I sprung to the surface and exploded from the water. Quickly, I opened my hand, and there were perfectly preserved coins, as golden and pretty as the day they had been minted.

The sanctuary changed at my resurrection. The gumbo-limbo tree painted with scarlet ibis exploded with color as the birds became airborne and disappeared into the stratosphere. The Florida panther that squatted at the water's edge kicked up a paw full of sand and darted back into the green shelter, pouncing on a key deer and ripping it to shreds. The heads of loggerhead turtles sank under water as fast as a shot. A pair of wood storks stretched their necks, displaying the full extent of their wings, and noisily flapped out of sight.

I dropped all but four of the coins back into the water, moved three of them to my left hand, and held the last one up like a Communion Eucharist. I held Black Jack's life in my hands, and the hell with the rest of the world.

14

IS THERE A DOCTOR IN THE HOUSE?

"I'm a good boy. I'm a good boy," I repeated to myself as I walked up Caroline Street with Black Jack in my arms. Her eyes were closed and her head drooping over my elbow. Her body moved with my rhythm, but only with my rhythm, not hers. This was not good.

Fearfully, I looked around for John. If I saw him, I'd start running and possibly not stop until I reached McGrath, that Indian village up in Alaska. I didn't think John would believe that Billy Boy had made me take the coins, and I didn't want to face John's wrath. I felt like I was walking into VC territory. My pucker spasmed like it had diarrhea and was trying to hold it back. It kept dancing—one of the subtle side effects of terror. With my free hand, I began to twirl my ear, nervously and ostentatiously, with my elbow out at a ninety-degree angle. I felt terribly confused and fearful.

There he came, walking up the street toward me: President Harry Truman wearing a colorful Hawaiian shirt and puffing on a cigar, his head cocked back slightly to see through his wire-rimmed glasses. Four secret-service men trotted to keep up with him. As the president passed, he nodded his head at me and said, "Morning, Bryan." I stopped in my tracks and watched him pass. He entered a smoke-filled bar where conchs were playing dominoes at a short-legged wooden table.

I ran up Caroline Street to Duval Street and stopped. I didn't want to look inside the open-air windows of Sloppy Joe's Bar, but when I heard a guffaw, I whipped my head around and saw Ernest Hemingway sitting on the last stool at the end of the counter. I'd have recognized his broad, square-jawed face and fluffy white beard anywhere. He toasted to me with his tall glass of rum and slammed the glass on the counter with a roar.

Not one of my best days, I thought.

I looked to the right down Duval Street and saw the Havana Madrid Nightclub, and there in the street danced Sally Rand. She held her famous pair of goose-feathered fans, her pet python around her neck. As she twisted and turned, her body remained hidden behind those luscious feathers.

I stopped at the first phone booth I came to, set down Black Jack so that her head lay on my right foot, and flipped through the yellow pages. I almost lost my ability to read—my mind was that flustered. I wanted to find a veterinarian, but I just couldn't think of how to spell the word. I reached into my pocket for phone change, but I couldn't find any. A lot of good this gold was doing me. I replaced the phone book, picked up Black Jack, and continued my search, telling myself, "I'm a good boy. I'm a good boy." I walked up Duval Street looking for signs of animal doctors, pictures of sick dogs or cats, anything.

I focused on the world of T-shirts in motion, with a lot of them on women, stretched real tight across huge breasts that flopped like puppy ears. A voice hollered to me, "Spare a buck."

The words hit me in the side of the head and made me look down at a small set of eyes clouded behind a massive beard. A tiny mouth appeared. I wondered if this was Captain Black Caesar, Captain Morgan, or some other pirate ghost wandering the streets of Key West. I looked around for Black Caesar's harem of beautiful women in knee-length fluffy dresses and low necklines. Seeing none that fit the bill, I decided that this man before me was a street person. I stared closer at him and saw inside that beard a row of chipped black teeth. I drew back my head and looked him over. He was dirty and didn't have any legs.

He repeated, "Got a buck?"

"Ohhh," I replied. "What happened to you, sir? Did you lose your legs in 'Nam?" (I knew a lot of guys in the VA hospital who had).

The man looked down at himself, chuckled, moved his legs out from under his bottom, and replied, "Hell no. There's nothing wrong with my legs."

"Then why do you want a buck?"

"'Cause I want to buy a steak sandwich. I'm hungry."

I shrugged my shoulders. "I don't have a buck."

As he scrutinized me, I didn't move. I played with my ear.

He asked, "You got anything you can give me that is worth something?"

My free hand rushed to my front pocket, and I replied, "Maybe I do, maybe I don't." I hoped that was enough for him to leave me alone.

His eyes shifted to my pocket, and he asked, "What you got in there?"

"Not a dollar," I replied.

"Is it worth more than a dollar?"

I felt cornered. "Yes, I think so, but I'm taking my dog to the hospital to have the doctor fix her up."

"What are you going to pay the doctor? He won't do it for nothing." He peered at me with one squinting eye, the other eye closed.

I was trapped. I pulled a coin from my pocket and showed him.

At first he sneered, and then his eyes got real big, and his squinting eye got closer. He asked, "Can I touch it?"

"I guess you can touch it," I said as I let him lift the coin from my palm.

He weighed it in his hand and shifted it to the other. He said, "This feels awful heavy. Where did you get it? Did you steal it?"

"No, sir. I found it."

"What's it made out of?"

"I think it's made out of gold."

"Golllld." The word rolled from his lips like honey. "I don't know much about golllld, except for a Rolex watch a tourist donated to me one time, but this coin feels an awful lot like it. This ain't lead or stainless steel, is it?"

"No. I don't think so. It's gold," I replied. "Old gold, if you know what I mean."

The guy looked up the street one way and then the other way. He drew closer and asked, "You going to give this to a veterinarian?"

I nodded my head. "If he makes Black Jack well, I will."

"How many of these coins do you have?"

"A couple more." My hand returned to my pocket defensively as he licked his lips. I explained, "I got a sick dog, and I gotta take her to the doctor. I sure hope the doctor knows what is wrong with her. *Say*, do you know where a doctor is?"

The man's face cracked with a smile, and he said, "I most certainly do!"

I shifted my weight from one foot to the other before I asked, "Are you going to tell me?"

"Most certainly."

"OK. I'm ready."

He stuck his chest out proudly and took a deep breath. "I used to be a doctor."

"Really? What kind of doctor?"

"A dog doctor...or animal doctor."

I gasped. What luck, I thought. "Do you think you know what is wrong with Black Jack? She got in a dog fight and won't wake up." I held her out at arm's length.

"Sure. I probably do, but if I take a look at her, it is going to cost you a coin."

I nodded at the coin he was already holding and said, "You already got that one. You can keep it. No problem. Now what do you think is wrong with Black Jack?"

"The first thing wrong with her is her name."

When I looked horrified, he replied, "I'm just kidding." He looked at me for a long moment and then turned to Black Jack, opened her mouth, and said, "Her tongue is white, so she could probably use something to drink."

"But she can't wake up to drink a thing," I replied. "That's the problem—she won't wake up."

"Well, then, let's look for something else. Let's take a look in her ears."

He flipped up the right ear and spied inside. "Looks pretty clean to me. Real clean. I think the problem isn't there." He dropped the ear and placed his index finger on his chin and said, "Let's see her eyes." He bent over, placed a forefinger and thumb on one eye, and opened up the lid. The eyeball had rolled over, and there was no pupil. He let go of the lid, frowned some, pondered, cupped his chin, and continued. "I think she's getting plenty of rest. I'll tell you what. I'm going to have to look a little closer at this dog…under her tail. But if I do that, it is going to cost you another coin."

"I don't know," I said. "I've given you more than I thought I was going to have to spend, and you haven't done a thing for her yet. What's under her tail?"

"The beginning of her insides. The big bang of the universe. No other way can I do it for anything less. That's my practice. I charge according to the scale of problems. The sicker a dog is, the more I charge, because when the dog gets well, I've done more for her than I would have done if she weren't real sick."

That made sense, so I gave him another coin. He put it in his pocket and pulled out a piece of candy-striped candy. He said, "Here, have a piece of candy while you wait. It will help kill the smell."

"No," I said. "I can't eat candy. Besides, I've smelled her before, and she isn't bad."

His brow furrowed. "What? You can't eat candy?"

"No. It makes me sick."

"Hey. I'm the doctor, and I tell you what makes you sick. Now eat the damn candy before I make you drop your drawers and I look up your pooper for your problem."

I unwrapped the candy, put it in my mouth, and let it melt on my tongue. He was right again about that taking away the smell, because that sugar set my tongue on fire with flavor. I'd never tasted anything so relaxing in all my life. Plus, the taste made me feel very happy.

He walked around to the left of her, lifted the tail quickly, and dropped it. "She don't have the runs or anything like that, which is good. Real good. There's only one other thing I know that I got to do."

"What's that?" I asked, crunching on the candy. "It didn't seem like you looked up her pooper long enough to see anything."

"I've seen enough assholes in my life to know when I see a healthy one. What I am going to have to do next is bleed her."

I gasped, cocked my head sideways, and stared hard at the man as I swallowed. I asked, "You mean you are going to cut my dog?"

"I'm afraid so. The lack of tension on the cell's membranes will relieve the pressure on her eyes, and she will be able to open them and see again. Then when she can see, she can eat, and then she'll get thirsty and so forth and so forth."

"You mean that is all that is wrong with Black Jack? She can't open her eyes?"

"That's the beginning."

"How much blood are you going to take?"

"Just enough to perk her up. That's what I learned in veterinarian school."

"Will it hurt her?"

"Does it look like anything can hurt that dog?"

I looked lovingly at Black Jack. Her fur was so soft and clean, so tenderly brown, except around her neck where there was a lot of dried blood. I replied, "If you cut my dog and she doesn't get any better, I'm going to cut you."

The man shook his head and winced. "Well, I'll do my best."

"If you don't fix Black Jack, I'm going to hurt you real bad." My neck muscles bulged and made my ears ring. With every breath, I pumped myself bigger, so that my arm muscles started to stretch the ears of the monkey on my T-shirt.

He looked hard at me and replied, "That's Doctor to you, Mister."

"OK, Doctor, and hopefully you'll be a doctor after you fix Black Jack."

"That's OK with me. Sure, why not."

He took a deep breath and held out his hand for my last coin. I took it from my pocket, gave the coin one last squeeze, and placed it in his hand. The doctor pocketed the coin, turned around, screamed, "Help" at the top of his voice like he had just been mugged, and ran down the street.

At first I was shocked, and then dazed, horrified, and then very angry. I felt like chasing after the doctor and retrieving my coins, but I felt too embarrassed to admit what I had done. By the time I quit thinking about it, he was nearly out of sight except for a clump of flaring hair that bobbed above the tourists' heads. I looked down at Black Jack and said, "I'll find someone to cure you, Black Jack. Don't you worry."

I wandered out of town, sat on a park bench, and stroked Black Jack's head. Black Jack's left eye opened. For a split second, I thought that doctor might have done her some good, but when her eye closed again, I knew it was all a hoax. "You're going to be all right, girl," I said. "You're going to be just fine."

I looked up, and there in front of me was a carving of a green turtle with its arm around a blue dolphin and a white egret. The animals smiled at me, and I smiled back. It was the entrance to the Sonny McCoy Indigenous Park.

Mary was inside. I had forgotten all about her and the animal hospital.

I told her my predicament and that John would kill me if he knew I was in town and how sick Black Jack was and how I had been robbed by a fellow who'd said he was a dog doctor and how he'd given me a piece of candy that had tasted real good at first but now it was giving me a stomachache. I didn't know what I was going to do.

Mary didn't say a word. She just got to work.

"Bless your heart," I replied.

Mary gave Black Jack some antibiotics and an IV for dehydration and wrapped her in warm blankets. She held Black Jack in her arms, sat in a rocking chair by the bulletin board, and rocked Black Jack like a real baby. After a while, I cradled Black Jack, which I did until my stomach hurt so much, I could hardly breathe without twisting over.

I started to hallucinate, and I told Black Jack about the squad and how Cameron and Stuart and Billy Boy were guarding over the hammock and that Stuart was meaner than I ever could be, and he might kill someone who invaded the place. I told her about Billy Boy liking boys more than girls and Cameron wanting to bet his life away. She smiled like she understood, which made me feel good.

The pain in my stomach spread to my head and thumped my brain like a shovel. My 270 pounds pressed down on my feet so hard, I felt like fainting. I stayed as sick as Black Jack all that night, and then some into the next day or the next, when we both got better about the same time.

I tell you what—there was some truth to what that doctor who'd stolen the coins had said about Black Jack. Once Black Jack opened her eyes, she started to eat, and then she got thirsty, and then she started to hop around in her familiar way, and that brought joy to my heart.

When I returned home that night, John didn't say a word to me. He had probably talked to Mary, and she had probably explained all that'd gone on. He scolded me with his scowl and put me to work right away tying flies.

It was kind of like that soldier's code of conduct that John had been talking about. Now I had a secret with Black Jack that we could share. A harmless secret between living beings is just that—harmless, and life can go on without the whole world knowing about some little episode and falling apart.

15

THE SECOND HAND ON THE CLOCK DIDN'T HAVE THE ENERGY TO MAKE THE UPHILL CLIMB

John wanted to talk to the squad, and he was sure they would come forward if he returned to Sanctuary Key. I didn't want to go there, because I was afraid that if they did appear, Billy Boy would blab his mouth about the coins. But John was in charge and adamant.

When John drank his morning coffee, I removed a cube of sugar from the cupboard and ate it. Within minutes, I had a stomachache. John asked what the hell was wrong, and I told him it was because of that sugar cube. He called me an idiot and said I was going to kill myself, which actually made me feel kind of good. I didn't like this little code of silence that Black Jack and I had formed.

John said we were going anyway.

That evening, when my stomach cramps subsided, we rowed to our second home. Within shouting distance of Sanctuary Key, the water was stirred up and muddy, hiding the upside-down jellyfish, the feather duster worms, peanut worms, and the sea biscuits. The amount of sedimentation wasn't enough to kill the sea life, but it was a start. I felt responsible. My disobedience was polluting the ocean.

"What the hell's going on here?" John asked.

"I don't know," I answered, holding my stomach and moaning with dread. The plankton that lit our way home shed less light than usual, and our voyage reeked of depression. My belly ached, and that was my excuse for not talking. Innocence nurtured my courage, but now my self-esteem was dead. My body was following, running scared from the world of my newfound silence. I was a liar, and worst of all, I lied to my best friend.

Even my body labored to row, which had never happened before, because never before had rowing been a chore. Black Jack lay in the bow, her head resting on her paws, her eyes averted.

"How are you feeling?" I whispered.

Her chocolate-brown eyes blinked once. Her tail thumped once and stopped.

"Where did I go wrong?" I whispered. "I was only trying to help."

She covered her ears with her paws. She wasn't going to talk to me. I looked to John. If the squad appeared at Sanctuary Key and said anything to him about the stolen gold coins, I'd be uncovered for disobeying a direct order. John might return me to the hospital in Miami. He would never trust me again.

Black Jack started licking her paw, between the toes. As she continued to lick, she became more intense, the tongue pressing harder and longer into the crack, vengefully, savagely, without compunction. She couldn't stop. I leaned forward and offered her my sandal. She didn't take it, but now she was distracted enough to start licking her other paw.

When we entered the channel to Sanctuary Key, my head became entangled in spider webs that stung me with confusion. I pawed the air with both hands. The scene was totally riveting, nearly as shocking as the first day I had set foot on the hammock. Now, the landscape had become dark and foreboding. The trees were bare of birds, and the shoreline was ghostly cold. The pond was no longer transparent, and the overhead umbrella of trees was nude of leaves. The sky was open to the stars, which was pretty enough now, but if a plane flew over during the day, our sanctuary would certainly be uncovered.

I didn't watch where I was rowing and smacked into a red mangrove root. The canoe came to an abrupt halt, and I fell forward and caught the gunwale with my right hand. My other hand splashed into the water. Before I could withdraw the hand, it felt on fire with pain. I yelped, cradled my hand, and inspected the fingers, covered with flea lice. I rubbed my hand up and down my shirt and on my pants until the stinging subsided. About the same time, a cloud of horseflies and mosquitoes surrounded my head and dive-bombed me, biting and crawling. I got to swatting and scratching until I found the bug repellent and squirted myself, the air, and myself again. I was choking.

John was already out of the canoe and headed for the tree house.

A hum filled the air, and I listened closely. I heard, "Bryan stole the coins. Bryan stole the coins." I started humming louder than the sound of betrayal, kicking up sand and barking at the moon. The fear of change, of confrontation, of intimacy lost, of bare-bone defiance, and of idolatry muddied my thinking. I could tell I was going off, but where else was there to go?

When I walked closer to the camp, the vibration turned to music, 'Nam music, loud and adulterous, carnal and lascivious. "Louie… Louie…come on, baby—we got to go now…ah, Louie, Louie…"

"Son of a bitch," John swore as he started to run.

I strained to see what he was after, and sure enough, it was up in the trees, in our bare-bone dwelling. I knew I was in deep shit. People were inside, swirling—girls laughing, giggling, hooting, and howling lecherously.

Stuart appeared in the lighted window, sunglasses in place, his right arm wrapped around the waist of an oriental girl. She was sucking on his neck. It was the first time I'd seen Stuart without his rifle, but he was still invulnerable. His right hand moved to her booty and grabbed it like it were a bowling ball, his fingers buried in flesh.

"No," John screamed, pointing at Stuart and waving his finger derisively. "Cut that out. I won't allow that here."

Stuart flipped us the bird. The little oriental girl climbed up Stuart's body, wrapped her legs around his waist, and buried herself in his lips.

My nose followed a rotten smell to the fire pit. The stench came from conch shells, broken open, with decayed and rotting meat. I ran around the desecration, raced up the ladder, stopped behind John, and looked over his shoulder at the wild party.

There on my bed was crazy Billy Boy on his back, naked. He sucked air passionately through gritted teeth. Kneeling alongside him was the naked back of a shiny-skinned, bare-chested youth who was going down on Billy Boy.

About five feet away from them, on the bamboo kitchen table, was a woman, the top of her dressed dropped below her chest, exposing her chest and flat belly. She held up her skirt with both hands. Cameron's head was between her legs. When she looked at me, she licked her lips with her tongue. She dropped her skirt, and then her facial expression turned to passion as Cameron's head moved under the dress. I pointed at her, but I didn't know what to say. I just gurgled.

Stuart moved to the window frame, and the little Vietnamese girl with big chocolate-brown eyes sat, naked, on his lap. Stuart's pants were down around his boots. He just held on to the little girl, who was doing all the work. Stuart looked heavenward and pointed the .45-caliber pistol at the girl's head. It was cocked and ready to fire.

"*Ssstttoooppppp*," John screamed. "*Stttoop.*"

Nobody did.

They didn't even slow down. John looked at the radio on the shelf, ran for it, and tried to turn it off, but he couldn't find the right dial. Finally, he picked up the radio with both hands, lifted it over his head, and slammed it onto the floor. Plastic and dials, resistors and transistors spread across the deck like grenade fragments. Sexual tomfoolery screamed with orgasmic delight. The music slowly faded away like a passing car radio at high speed. The orgy ended with intimate groans, slipping away.

"You know what I told you about women and parties," John screamed. "I won't allow it."

"I don't remember," Billy Boy replied, smacking his lips.

"What the hell are you so uptight about?" Cameron screamed back.

"I won't allow it. Not in the sanctuary. At least not here. Not like this. Not with these whores. Not now."

"What do we have, a war to fight?" Billy Boy teased. His companion stood up and displayed a mountain in his underwear where there should have been a valley.

"I want these women to leave," John shouted.

Tapping John's shoulder, I said, "John, I don't think they're all girls."

Billy Boy's companion giggled.

John said, "I don't care what they are—just get them out of here."

Stuart moved to the table, picked up a bottle of bourbon, and pressed it to his lips. His dog tags jangled. The bourbon in the bottle exploded with bubbles as his Adam's apple choked it down.

There was movement under the table in front of Cameron, and I bent over to see the back of the head of another woman with her face buried in Cameron's crotch. Her head moved like a swan's neck while it swims. Her right hand rubbed herself between her legs.

I stood up straight, pointed my finger under the table, and said, "John, there's one more under there."

John ran over and threw back the cover, but no one was there.

I looked again, and sure enough, no one was there.

"What the hell is wrong with you?" Stuart demanded.

"This is not a whorehouse," John screamed. "They're not allowed here. They can't be here. This is a place of silence, solitude, and sanctity. Not a fuckin' whorehouse."

"Bring back bad memories?" Cameron asked.

Everyone listened to the silence.

"What are you talking about?" John asked. "What?"

"Like the night we died. Were we partying like this?"

"No...no," John screamed. "It was nothing like this. You were on an ambush."

Stuart said, "We're on an ambush here, and we just captured ourselves some pussy."

I stepped forward and began to explain. "The Russians really didn't know how to build a rocket until Einstein died. Then they copied us."

"OK," John said, pointing his thumb to me. "Tonto here is getting all riled up. Now would someone please explain what is going on here?"

Billy Boy stepped forward, hips swinging, elbow cuffed, and wrist swinging freely. His dainty little finger pointed at me. Billy Boy said, "He took four of the coins."

All eyes turned on me.

"I did?" I asked.

"Yes, you did, you little twerp," Billy Boy continued. "You expect us to live by all the rules, and what do you do? Just what you tell us not to do."

I took the biggest breath of my life and pointed back to Billy. "You told me to do it, and, you little cocksucker...how do you expect a parrot to learn to talk if you don't turn on the radio?"

Stuart's finger shot forward as fast as a bullet. It stopped at me. He said, "You violated one of the laws. You removed something from the sanctuary. You gave us away, you pinpointed our position, and we were the guardians."

I gulped. "I didn't blow anybody, and I'm not blaming anything on you. You knew what happened. It couldn't be helped. It was Black Jack."

"What's going on?" John asked.

I started to recite the rosary with my eyes squeezed tight and fingers in ears. I hummed so that my mind couldn't hear what he was saying. I peeked my eyes open halfway and saw John arguing with the squad, Cameron throwing dice, Stuart swinging a machete, and Billy holding his companion's erection behind his back. I shut my eyes again and spoke my prayers out loud, and then just a tad louder. I could feel John's finger wagging at the back of my head. I squeezed my eyes shut.

When I said the last amen, I peeked one eye open, and John was standing right there, his scowl ripping through me, his tongue as long as a tootsie roll. He barked, "You rewrote the rules, you idiot. That always was your problem. You rewrote the rules."

Billy Boy said, "Yes, dear. That's why we are all here. That's why we are all trapped in this world of transition, because of you rewriting the rules. We're exhausted. We want to have some fun too."

"It is a lie!" I screamed. "It's a lie!"

"It's the truth," John screamed back, "because Billy Boy saw it all."

I sat in a chair, leaned forward on the table, placed my face in my hands, and rubbed my forehead. My fingers ran over my cheeks and through my hair. "I guess maybe I did."

John said, "Get rid of the girls, and we'll talk."

I said, "John, I tried to tell you before. One of them is not a girl."

Billy Boy blew me a kiss.

"Oh God," I said.

John barked, "Get rid of them. I won't say a damn word in front of them. Understand?"

There was moaning and groaning, but the men did as they were told. Cameron helped the young girl to her feet, let her have a swig of beer, and then slapped her on the booty as she walked out the window, giggling.

I jumped to my feet and ran to grab her before she fell to the ground, but she disappeared in my hands. I searched for her between my fingers, but when I didn't find her, I played with my hands, chasing the fingers around the knuckles and backward like race cars.

Billy Boy hugged the young boy and cried on his shoulder. When John told them to hurry up, they faced each other, touched each other's faces, embraced again, and then the boy left. I didn't make a fool of myself again.

Stuart slapped his girl on her booty, and she hopped out the door. He twirled the pistol and snatched it by the grip.

Billy Boy sat on the bed in the lotus position like an anxious young boy ready to hear a bedtime story. Stuart sat on the windowsill, looking outside, pistol in lap. Cameron turned the back of his chair around, rested his arms on the backrest, and faced the lieutenant.

In a way, I was glad I was sick. Otherwise, the tongue-lashing would have cut my heart out, but not now. My wrenching stomach took all my concentration. All I wanted to do was puke.

Billy Boy said, "He gave three coins to a street person on Duval Street, who sold them to Sun Lion Jewelry Shop, who in turn contacted Hank. Which means Hank is on to us, and if he finds us out here, we'll never...never transform into another life form. We are up shit creek."

"Is that right?" John asked me.

"Do you have the phone number of the Miami veterans' hospital?" I asked. "I think I'm ready for the fourth-floor tie down."

"I can get it easy enough. Just answer the questions."

"I'd feel safer there."

"And you can go there once this is over, but for now, answer the questions."

Billy Boy swung his hips and said, "Honey, Hank already has one, and it's just like a French tickler in a whorehouse—he wants more."

Stuart said, "Bryan is probably lying about the night we died in 'Nam too. He's not as dumb as he acts."

"I am too!" I screamed.

"What'll we do?" Cameron asked.

"Kill Hank," Stuart screamed, "just like I said in the beginning. If he were dead, we wouldn't be in the fix we are in now." Stuart fired off a burst of gunfire into the stillness of the night. When the slide locked in the open position, the clip was empty. His face was as red as the smoking barrel.

"You're so silly," Billy Boy replied with a wave of the hand. "We can't kill him."

"Beat him at his own game," John replied. "Let's beat him at his own game."

But none of us could have guessed, even in our wildest dreams, what that meant.

16

HANK GOES FOR THE JUGULAR

Hank caught up to me Sunday morning when Bryan and I were paddling the canoe toward Sammy's channel. We were ready to disappear amid the mangroves when a very fast speedboat entered the channel about half a mile back, kicking up wakes at every turn.

"That looks like Hank's boat," I said as I nodded my head in its direction.

"What should we do?" Bryan asked.

"Put on your life vest."

"But I already have mine on."

"Then start praying."

Hank's boat carved a wide wake of white sea spray, approaching us at ramming speed. We had only one speed, and that was slow.

Bryan asked me, "Don't you think he's going kind of fast?"

"Especially for this channel." The closer the boat got, the taller it looked. If it continued on the same course and same speed, it would cut us in half. I couldn't tell who was driving the boat—I could only see two heads.

The engines quieted down, the boat came off plane, and the wake overtook the limp transom and splashed water on the engines. The boat slowly limped toward us.

Hank was at the wheel and wearing oversized sunglasses, but the swelling in his left eye was still apparent. The discoloration spread down to his cheeks. Eduardo stood alongside him. In the bow appeared a dark-colored man, square jawed, wearing a sleeveless T-shirt, identity unknown. When the boat got within spitting distance, Hank tipped his hat to us and, with a smile, turned the controls over to Eduardo. Hank hollered out, "Good morning, mates. You interested in a cup of Java?" He was all self-serving smiles. Cotton balls filled his nose, and he spoke with a nasal twang.

Hank cleared his throat, leaned closer, and said, "John, I'm ready to talk."

"Does your timing have anything to do with your needs?" I asked.

Hank laughed nervously. "I've drawn back my fangs. I'm a tamed lion. You always had that way with me. I could be totally out of control in 'Nam, and you could calm me with a stare."

"I don't have any reason to stare at you, Hank," I replied.

There was a black space in Hank's smile where there should have been a tooth.

"I've got some important news that you might be interested in," he said. "It's about Mary."

I perked up a bit and turned my head. Bryan noticed my enthusiasm and lifted his eyebrows.

Hank continued. "She and I worked things out. Come on aboard, and I'll tell you. Come on aboard," Hank repeated. "We have some things to attend to before we go killing each other."

I back paddled until I was alongside the speedboat. I nodded for Bryan to go aboard first.

Once aboard, standing face to face, Hank asked, "How many years has it been since we were in 'Nam?"

"Enough years for me to lose my hair, pop a gut, and dissolve the better part of my brain with alcohol."

He roared with laughter and replied, "It shows, but not many people our age look that much better." Hank held out his hand to shake mine. "Peace—like we used to say back in the '60s." He raised his other hand in the peace sign.

I looked at the hand and then the face. I looked at Bryan, who was smiling, and, without making eye contact with Hank, held out my hand. Hank grabbed it firmly and shook with laughter. He continued. "It's my turn to reunite us into the slick team we were in 'Nam. There was a time when a Cong couldn't pass within a hundred yards of us without us sniffing and snuffing him out. We were a hell of a team."

"The timing was definitely right back then," I said as I stumbled. I looked down at my tennis shoes and saw a lace dragging. I bent down, tied my shoelace, and stood up.

"Let's try and make it that way again," Hank said. "Mary and I both agreed that I'm just not the marrying type. I spend all my time at sea and the other time drinking and making new female friends. I admit I'm a lousy husband, and I probably never would have married her if you hadn't been so interested in her. Back then, I guess I was just jealous of everything you wanted. But now, I'm giving her the house and the property at the Wildlife Center, and I'm keeping the boat and my salvaging operation. We're going our separate ways before we kill each other."

I said, "You mean before you kill her."

Hank nodded and winced. "Whatever you say. I'm not here to argue. I'm just telling the facts."

I thought a moment about why Hank was doing such a ninety-degree turn. I figured that if he were a single man, and if he did find the treasures from *La Cruz*, he would not have to split it with an ex-wife, whereas if he were still married to Mary, half would be hers.

Hank acted all cheerful-like and waved us forward as his sandals slapped the fiberglass deck. "And another thing. That pledge of silence we made with each other in 'Nam—forget it. I release you from your silence. You can tell whomever whatever you want about me. I don't give a shit. Never really did. No strings attached. You are free."

When my mouth dropped open, he laughed and said, "Let me show you around the place. Come on."

I couldn't remember ever meeting a more hospitable person than Hank as he showed his boat. It was a Thunderbird Formula 303 with twin 525 hp engines. It was rigged for deep-sea fishing with a live well, tackle cabinets, and outriggers. Inside the three-sided cabin was a TV, VCR, stereo, radar fish finder, and refrigerator.

Hank was all grins, but the years had not been good to his teeth. Those teeth were crooked and bent, different lengths, and various colors of yellow and brown, stained to the bone. His recent loss of a molar didn't help.

"How long would it take you to motor to Cuba?" I asked.

"If I ever went there, it would probably be under an hour."

"Rumor says you transport illegal aliens from Cuba to the United States for a price."

"Don't believe everything you hear in this small town. Come on— let's have some coffee and pie."

As we sat at the small galley table, Bryan asked for some water, and that's what Hank served, with lots of ice.

So far Hank had not mentioned the coins, and that made me curious, but not enough to bring it up, although I knew that was what it was all about. I had made a year's worth of mistakes over the last few days, and I had been slow to improve the record. I said, "I can't spend too much time here. I have to meet my aunt Wilhelmina at Mallory Square at sunset."

"I can get you there from here. Relax. I've heard about you guiding all those executives from up north. You're the talk of the town, in more ways than one. You're a real conch success story—a Key West hero."

"Thanks. I feel like I am finally getting my act together. Being home helps."

"Indeed you have. But let me show you what I've been up to. It's only a few minutes from here, and I can save you time by dropping you off in town. You've still got an hour of rowing from here, and I could have you out and back to town before that."

When I shrugged my shoulders, Hank's deckhand dragged the canoe over the stern and set it on the open deck.

Hank manned the wheel, gunned the engine, and made a donut in the water. He headed west toward the open sea and the Dry Tortugas. After a twenty-minute ride, a stationery vessel appeared in the water, and Hank headed right for it. It was a dredging barge anchored in the middle of the sea. Hank tied up alongside it and said, "This is my pride and joy." He got right to the point and showed us the heart of the operation—how he uncovered the sand from the bottom of the water. He had welded together a five-foot-diameter culvert and placed it over the prop of the metal tugboat tied alongside. When the engine revved, the prop blast shot water down through the tube to the ocean's bottom to blow the sand away. Hank said that he could dig a fifteen-foot-deep hole in the sand in five minutes.

Hank had three dark-skinned workers on the barge, but none appeared very professional. They were dirtier than the dirtiest engines I'd ever seen, skinny, and mean looking, with facial expressions that held in a lot of hurt, like they wanted to pass the hurt on to others. They reminded me of Hank's teeth.

After talking and fussing for a while, Hank finally came to the point. "What do you say we become partners again? I can't offer anything better."

Pumps, hoses, steel cables, and makeshift iron gadgets littered the deck like a rusting junkyard. I asked, "What exactly are you looking for?"

Hank had never smiled as much in his whole life. "The *La Cruz*, a Spanish shipwreck with a reported booty worth at least fifty million dollars."

"And you think I could help you find it?"

"I know you could help me find it." Hank dipped his right hand into his pocket and pulled out a clenched fist. He rotated his wrist upward and opened his hand, revealing the gold coin.

Bryan covered his face with both hands and moaned.

I didn't flinch nor move my stare from Hank's face. I said, "I'm not interested in gold, nor am I interested in becoming your partner again. Now, if you will, please take us back to the Marina."

Hank said, "But don't you understand what I'm offering you?"

When he read my expression of disdain, Hank's smile turned stone cold. Just as quickly, he changed his attitude and grew giddy. He said, "I need your help."

"Let me think about it."

"OK." Then Hank looked at Bryan and said, "And I'll tell you what. As partners, I'll tell you everything I can remember about the night the squad died in 'Nam. The more I've been thinking about it, the more I realize I do remember some things that might be of interest...to whomever. And, John, like I said before, whatever code of silence we made to each other, I would give you my permission to speak and say whatever you want to whomever." Hank held his breath a moment before he continued, "No hurry, no hurry. I'll take you to Mallory Square now and give you time to think it over."

When Hank brought us back in sight of Key West and dropped our canoe into the water, we boarded, and Bryan moved forward to his spot while I sat in the stern. As we started to paddle, Hank sped off to parts unknown.

Bryan asked, "Are you going to do it?"

I shook my head, shrugged my shoulders, and stared at the Key West coastline.

Bryan continued. "But the squad would be released from their living hell if you told them what happened. They wouldn't have to stay on that ship any longer, because their souls would be set free."

"I know that," I replied. "I just have to figure the consequences of it all...just the timing...timing."

As we approached Mallory Square, there was an unusual amount of activity, considering it wasn't sunset. There must have been four to five hundred people on the dock looking our way, waving banners and streamers and throwing confetti. I wondered why they were all cheering.

When we got to within a hundred feet of the lively crowd, a banner went up in the air between the tightrope walker's poles. The sign read "JOHN MARLEY FOR FANTASY FEST KING."

Bryan asked me what the signs meant. I acted like I couldn't read. I wanted to hide.

I thought that Hank had headed back to his barge, but instead, I saw him on shore right next to the banner. Hank helped us ashore with an extended hand and said, "It looks like John is going to be the new king of Fantasy Fest."

Bryan asked me, "Are you?"

I couldn't talk. I was reminded of that monkey cage at the San Francisco Zoo when Bryan had told me about the NVA regulars. Fantasy Fest was a week of celebration held the last week before Halloween every year. The purpose of the celebration was to raise money for local charities and the fight against the dreaded disease AIDS. Of course the locals thought it was just another excuse to party and get naked in the Keys. The king and queen of Fantasy Fest were the couple who raised the most money.

Aunt Wilhelmina was there to greet us, and all her relatives surrounded her. There was Uncle Dennis, Scott and his family, the twins and their kids, and some other faces I recognized from pictures at Aunt Wilhelmina's. We disembarked where the cruise ships docked, and the people were going crazy—I mean everyone.

The performer with a long sword threw back his head and sucked down the sword. A woman in a tutu spat fire in the air. An acrobat flew ten feet into the air on a trampoline and waved a banner with my picture on it. I felt like a stretch man tugged ten feet long.

Aunt Wilhelmina took my hands in hers and, smiling, said, "I told you we were going to have a family reunion. And this Saturday night, we are having a fundraiser at the Hemingway House. Five hundred dollars a plate to support your bid for the king of Fantasy Fest."

From the expression on my face, Aunt Wilhelmina probably thought I'd forgotten how to talk. Now I felt like a pincushion coming alive.

Black Jack kept jumping in the air in my face. Bryan said, "This is what Black Jack and I were planning with Aunt Wilhelmina all along. It was all Black Jack's idea."

A dog is my downfall, I thought. When I saw Black Jack jump up and look at me at eye level, I thought of a carnival shooting gallery.

Uncle Dennis pulled me through the crowd, introducing me to people, shaking hands, waving at people, calling out names, and pulling me along like a celebrity. I felt comatose and near dead. That just gave the crowd more time to blow their horns and shout and chant and toast. We marched through the parade, which formed into a cheering, banner-waving line that led to the entrance of the Marriot Hotel, where a tent had been erected around the pool, the barbecues were smoking, and the live band was playing. More cheering voters were waiting, and the celebrating ran into the night, with me gaining more and more votes by the hour. Half of the people didn't know what they were cheering about.

My years of isolation were turning into celebrity.

Mary would practice playing the pipe organ at Saint Paul's Episcopalian Church on Duval Street every Tuesday and Thursday after sunset. I loved to sit in the last row of the church near the exit door and listen to her practice. Most of the time, she wouldn't even know I was there.

Around eight o'clock that evening, I snuck away from the festivities, walked up Duval Street, and made myself comfortable in my reserved back-row seat.

Mary's music filled every corner of the church with a vibrancy that elevated me from my earthly problems into peaceful tranquility. If ever a humanmade structure had been dedicated to a superior, supernatural being, it was this white church that spiraled skyward in points of light that attracted sinners and worshippers to its magnificent front portals. The interior of the church was darkened with heavy wooden pews and dark walls. The sanctuary was lighted with colorful wall murals. The pipe organ had a five-keyboard console and a digital four-keyboard console that played five thousand pipes.

When little Mary mounted the organ, touched the keyboard with her fingers, laid her feet on the pedals, and began to play, a tidal wave of powerful heavenly sounds filled the cathedral with a vibrating resonance.

Mary appeared trite and humble, and certainly the loft of the sounds made me wonder in admiration, because here was a human reaching for the stars. I was so proud of her.

When she finished practice, I met her at the front steps as she exited the church. She acted a bit startled to see me, but not angry or upset with me.

"Good evening, Mary," I said.

"Hi, John."

"Are you feeling better?"

"I always feel better after playing the organ," she replied.

"Mind if I walk you home?"

"For a little ways, anyway."

As we proceeded up Duval, Mary kept her distance and, without eye contact, said, "You shouldn't trust Hank. I've heard him talking, and whatever is going on between the two of you, watch your back."

Her right eye was still black, and it made me feel close to her.

"Hank told me he was leaving you…divorcing you."

"He left me a long time ago, but yes. Finally, he had me sign the divorce papers. I'm not contesting a thing, so it should all be over in thirty days. All I want is my freedom and my sanity back. Hank is more interested in treasures than anything. I don't know why he ever married me."

"I decided that I am going to help him find his treasures. But you know what I want?"

"Me?" She looked at me.

I smiled and just sighed.

She said, "John, we were always the best of friends growing up, and it would be fun to be your friend again. But right now I am not ready to exchange a psycho alcoholic treasure hunter for a fishing guide."

I took another deep breath and said, "I'll take whatever I can get. Sounds like a deal. But guess again."

"About what?"

"What I want."

"I haven't the foggiest."

"You know about my bid for Fantasy Fest king?"

She finally smiled. "Yes. Aunt Wilhelmina has been planning that for you since the day you returned home."

"Well, what I want right now is for you to be my Fantasy Fest queen."

She smiled again and shook her head. "I'd be upset if you asked anyone else."

"Let's go fishing then."

17

WHEN IN DOUBT...FISH

Before I started the boat motor, I said to Mary, "I just have to be straight with you. Everyone I take out fishing goes home with a good fish story, but for you, I don't even care if you catch a fish. That's a first for me."

"You take fishing that seriously?"

"It's embarrassing, isn't it?"

She was pretty with her little brown shorts, white shirt, broad-brimmed hat, and oversized sunglasses. I had to stop myself from gawking at her.

I discovered that Mary was an avid fiction reader, and two of her favorite authors were John Dufresne and John Cormack. Two of her all-time favorite books were *One Flew Over the Cuckoo's Nest*, (I loved that book), and *All the Pretty Horses*, my second-favorite novel. I was glowing inside.

"Mary, I just wanted to thank you again for taking care of Bryan. Of course, you know you have Bryan's unconditional devotion for the rest of his life."

She smiled and said, "He is just a wonderful person to be around. He reminds me of the simple joys of living."

"I feel the same way. I don't know what I would do without him. What do you do in your spare time?"

"As you know, I love to play the organ, and I'm a student at the community college on Stock Island. I'm completing my undergraduate work for a degree in biology. How about you, John? How do you like working for your cousin?"

"I love it. I really do. It is more like working for myself since I love to fish."

I donned my sunglasses, stretched taller, sniffed the wind like a hunter, and said, "Let the adventure begin." I untied the clove hitch from the dock cleat while the motor warmed and pulled in the plastic fenders. When Mary sat in the bow, I slowly motored under the Garrison Bight Bridge and, once clear of the shoreline, sped on plane northeast toward the backcountry. Zigzagging around shallow shoals and darting through channels between narrow keys, I navigated by distant white markers. Mary's blond hair circled and danced with the wind.

The water in the backcountry glowed with shades of breathtaking blue. The water was the lightest blue over the white sandy bottom that reflected the ultramarine-blue sky, shimmering in the heat. The bottom turned a deep green over grass beds teeming with sponge and short whip coral. Every so often an eagle ray would explode from the bottom and dart across the surface, diving and leaping like a porpoise. Three dolphins rolled in our wake, and the birds painted the sky with their flapping wings.

I swung the boat toward a large white sandbar covered with a foot of azure-colored water and backed off on the throttle, eventually killing the motor and lifting the prop out of the water to prevent the fish from entangling themselves and snapping the line. I said, "OK, Mary. We are about there. You'll fish from the bow, and you have to be quiet on the flats. No talking."

"Can I point?" she asked.

"You can point. As a matter of fact, you can talk too. What the hell. I'll do the poling, and you do the fishing."

"I've never done this before, John."

"Then let's practice first."

I jumped off the platform, moved toward the control panel, and removed my favorite beginner's pole—a nine-foot Penn with eight-weight line on the Garcia Diplomat reel. I withdrew the pole from its nylon sock and handed it to Mary.

She acted as perplexed as if I had handed her a surgeon's scalpel.

"Here, I'll show you."

She stood next to me on the fishing platform, and I showed her how to shoot line on the back cast and cast forward. Then I stripped the line from the reel and cast again. I told her that if she cast and the fish did a quick ninety-degree turn away from the fly, she should do a short, quick flick and set the fly in front of the fish again—never wait for the fish to return to a sinking fly. Finally, I gave her the pole, and I had her hold the pole higher on the forward cast and then double haul and shoot line on the back cast. She was a natural angler, and, with the quality of the heavy line and pole, casting came easy for her. Within half an hour, she was ready to fish.

"When you get your chance, you have to set that fly right in front of the bonefish, let it settle, and then give it a twitch. Make it appear like your bait has just seen the fish and wants to get the hell out of there. You'll only get one chance at each school of bonefish. If you don't catch one, that's it. Bonefish are spooky, and we'll have to find another school."

She asked, "Why don't I pole the boat and you fish?"

"Because you're the lady today, Mary. Make it happen."

"But I'd hate to make a mistake."

"Just relax. That's the key—relax and enjoy and feel the love." I mounted the platform above the motor and started poling toward the flats.

Mary appeared nervous as could be. She looked around at me, and I pointed my head toward the bow. She mounted the casting platform, took the bonefish clouser fly in her left hand, and searched the horizon.

I didn't see anything moving out there, but it was hypnotically peaceful.

The heat added to the intensity of the overwhelming beauty. Searching for fish in this now-turquoise reflection was mesmerizing. The only thing that could have made it more exciting would have been spotting a school of bonefish.

I poled abreast of the mangrove trees, and about fifty yards off to the right, a black movement on the white sand caught my attention—a sting ray about two feet wide, its whip tail about three feet long, leisurely cruising. It calmly swam within twenty feet of our boat and continued swimming until its black shadow joined with the shadows of the distant rippling surface. Later, a bonnethead shark about two feet long meandered by the boat, swimming in wide circles with its mouth in the sand. But no bonefish.

We tried the flats around Johnson Key without any luck, and then I said, "Let's take a break at Marvin Key." So, with the wind at our backs, we anchored in azure-colored water about eighteen inches deep. I pulled some deli sandwiches, marinated olives, and water bottles from the cooler, and then we jumped in the water and walked to a sandy shore, where we sat in the shade of a mangrove tree and ate our lunch. Although we didn't bring our bathing suits, we immersed ourselves in the water and cooled off. When Mary stood up, her shirt stuck to her chest, and she shyly freed it. When she let go, the cloth went home again. Mary let it go. She got aboard, laid on the deck, and, with one hand in the water, closed her eyes. Physically, she was gorgeous.

"Time's a wasting," I said.

We continued to fish the inner and outer banks. I had Mary practice her casting on some mangrove snappers in three feet of water, and she caught a couple, which I released. Next was a foot-long barracuda, which I threw back, but no signs of bonefish. I tied a fresh fly onto the tippet of her leader.

I checked the water temperature with a thermometer gauge, and it was eighty-three degrees, just right for the incoming tide. If the water was any colder, the fish wouldn't come up on the flats.

That afternoon, we returned to the flat where we had started that morning. I was reminded why they call bonefish "ghosts." I was staring at the water so long, my eyeballs burned. I looked in one direction, looked away, and a second later looked back, and there were dark fleeting shadows moving back and forth in the water like a herd of hunting dogs on the plains of Africa searching for wounded prey, but I could barely see them.

Mary turned around with a surprised look on her face, and I just nodded my head knowingly. The school was a good fifty yards away, and for the life of me, I couldn't tell which way they were headed. They darted about, following one fish in one direction and another fish in another direction. For all I knew, they could have just swum past us or around us without my positioning the boat for Mary to cast.

I poled harder and headed toward the mangroves, figuring the fish would take advantage of the high tide to search the shallows for shrimp. Instead, the fish headed for deeper water. Thirty yards from the mangroves, I turned around and waited. Sure enough, dead ahead, that dark cloud of adventure swept in our direction, darted away, and then swept toward us.

Mary was ready. She looked at the fish and then looked at me and then back at the fish again. Finally, when she looked at me, I nodded my head for her to cast.

She took a deep breath, turned, and focused on the school of fish at about ten o'clock. She relaxed her shoulders and released the fly in her hand, and it swung freely. She lifted the pole with her right hand and started to sweep the tip back and forth over her head like a pro, shooting out line all the time until there was just about no line left at her feet; that's when she released the cast. The line arched forward, the fly whipped about, and just when the line was fully extended, the fly gently touched the surface of the water about ten feet from the school of fish. The cast could have been closer, but at least the fish weren't spooked. The fly settled to the bottom, and Mary looked at me. I motioned a tug, and she gave it a tug. The dark shadow of fish came together like a funnel, and within a split second, they surrounded the fly. Mary was looking at me again, and when I saw the line twitch, I feigned another tug. Mary followed my direction, and one of the bonefish darted from the school and shot toward deeper water. Mary's line followed the fish in a sweeping arc, and the tip of her pole bent forward as the reel started to sing.

"Set the hook," I shouted.

She arched her back and gave that pole a good tug. The pole flexed, and the reel sang as the line ripped from the bail.

"Keep the tip of the pole high," I said. "Keep it high. Let the pole play the fish, or the line will snap."

She set the cork butt of the pole against her stomach and laid into the fish. The line ripped and ripped until I thought it was going to run off the reel. Mary looked down and saw what looked like the bitter end of her fishing line. She said, "John, I can't see any more line on the reel."

I scrambled back on the platform and started poling in the direction of the fleeing fish that now took an abrupt ninety-degree turn and swept across our starboard, the line making a wake in the water.

I did my best to relax and not holler orders, but I did mention for her not to dip the tip of the pole and keep reeling. Mary did as told, but I still didn't see that fish. It was that far away.

"Don't lose him," I kept whispering. "Don't lose him."

Finally, I made eye contact with the fish but only for half a second before it took off again.

That fish kept Mary in the bow for nearly half an hour as I poled all over that flat trying to catch up. She'd reel in some slack only to have the fish rip the line from the reel again. She'd reel, and the fish would heel. I could tell Mary's arms were tiring, because the tip of the pole would level off. Mary acted more tired than like she was having fun. Three times the fish made it to the boat, but when it swam in our shadows, it flicked its tail as fast, if not faster, than the first time it took the fly.

The fourth time the fish approached the boat, its tail barely moved. I reached for the net and came alongside the console, placing my left hand on the plastic windshield, watching the water. That fish got one more spurt of strength, and it took off around the stern. I watched as the leader dragged along the gunwale, hit the motor, and crept down the lower unit. Before I could say a word, like the split second before an accident when you see what is going to happen but can't talk or react fast enough, the line hit the prop and cut along the sharp blade.

Ping.

Mary's pole straightened, the line became airborne, and the leader was swinging effortlessly in the wind in front of her face. Mary stared at the end of the curled line. No fish. No hook. Mary looked confused.

I was shocked. My mouth sank open, and I dropped the net and just gawked at the free-swinging line. It was probably a twelve pounder, nearly two feet long, floating on the surface. Its tail weakly beat a retreat toward the deeper green water. Its gills hungrily pumped water for oxygen. The fish cruised toward the anchor line about five feet off the port side, now waving good-bye with its tail.

Son of a gun, I swore. I took two huge steps, the first one on the top of the cooler and the second on the gunwale, and then I straightened my body in a dive. Stretching out, I flew through the air with outstretched arms. My fingers were as pointed as the claws of a diving bald eagle. I came down on top of that slippery fish and grabbed it with both hand just as I did a big belly flop in the water. The fish squirmed from my left hand, but my right hand held the tail and kept it from sliding away. I crawled up on my knees and wrestled about, taking a firmer hold of the fish in both hands, my left hand now under its gills. I turned around and raised the fish above my head triumphantly. Mary was hopping up and down in the boat, clapping her hands and smiling. I splashed over in her direction and handed her the squirming fish. Laughing, she squeamishly took it.

I crawled back in the boat and said, "I'll take your picture."

Mary held that fish way out in front of her at arm's length, and I took the picture. What a photo. Mary was all white teeth and sunblock lips and pretty white nose. I set the camera on time delay, set the camera down on the paneled console, pointed it toward her, and ran over. I gave her a big hug with one arm, and we both looked at the camera as the shutter clicked. That was the greatest picture of my life. I was soaking wet, my hat was drooping, my sunglasses were askew, my arm was around Mary, and Mary was holding that fish. I made five copies of it. Bryan has one; there's one in my bedroom, another in the living room, and one in my wallet. And Mary has one.

Then, just as quickly, I jumped back into the water and said, "Now hand me that beauty."

Mary handed the fish back to me. I held it with both hands, kissed it on its lips, and quickly set the exhausted fish in the water. Its tail waved tentatively back and forth. I talked to it real quietly, congratulating it, thanking it, and telling it how pretty it was. Finally, the fish became energized and started wiggling. That's when I lowered my hands, and the fish slowly swam away, just a tad faster than the time it broke the leader.

Mary was in the water beside me. She threw her arms around my neck, and we embraced—first to congratulate each other on our accomplishment, and then we embraced as friends. We held each other and watched the fish swim away until there was nothing else to see but the setting sun against a bank of puffy clouds on the edge of paradise.

She moved her head slightly and said, "I can see the sunset better with my good eye."

18

JOHN GOES FOR THE HUEVOS

This whole king of Fantasy Fest idea was more than I could handle, and it made me fight a lot of ghosts from the past. Since 'Nam, I hadn't liked attention drawn toward me. I didn't like social engagements. I didn't like being the center of attention. I liked isolation. Peace and quiet.

I felt stressed. And of all things I could think of, the thought that predominated my mind the most was that I really needed to go to Sanctuary Key and talk to the squad. For the first time in my life, I acknowledged the squad's existence, sought their advice, and wanted to tell them the whole truth, as Hank had now freed me from the soldier's pledge I had made to him in 'Nam. I had expected the squad to show up at my house in Key West, but for some reason, they didn't. So I decided to go to them.

When Bryan and I arrived by canoe at Hangover Key, it was dark. Bryan started a small fire, and we sat down. I placed my black pouch on a rock opposite me and stared at the pouch, seeking direction. I felt hypnotized. I wanted to ask permission to change my life. I stood up, crept around the fire, picked up the pouch, and returned to my stump. That pouch was the only possession I had never given away. I sat and weighed it in my hands.

"What's in there?" Bryan asked as he hung my wet shirt on a makeshift clothesline.

"Memories." I unbuckled the flap and looked inside. Then I pulled out a war medal from Vietnam, a combat infantryman's badge (CIB). The medal was three inches long and half an inch wide. In the center was a shiny silver rifle surrounded by a silver laurel on a blue background. The badge was awarded to infantrymen and Special Forces soldiers who fought in active ground combat while assigned to an infantry, ranger, or Special Forces unit. It recognized the inherent danger and sacrifices of all infantrymen, in comparison to all other service people. Infantrymen (a.k.a. Grunts) fought the wars with guns and faced the greatest risk of being wounded or killed in action.

In 'Nam, it had taken twenty-four other service people to support one infantryman in the field. The other service people included the clerks, cooks, suppliers, drivers, intelligence, etc. Every soldier had his place in a war, but the infantryman fought the battles. It was the one medal I was the proudest of, because it united all fighting soldiers together.

I could see those stories dancing in my mind as I turned the pages in my memories. I was there again, in 'Nam.

Physical pain was very important to a soldier. Without pain, a soldier had no forewarning of death or imminent danger. Without pain, he could be shot and not even know it except for the impact and the blood. Without pain, he might not twist and convulse to avoid the next shot. Without the precursor pain, a soldier could die without even knowing it. So physical pain wasn't necessarily bad.

Emotional pain was something different. Two soldiers under the stress of war and constant threat of death could bond like brothers in their fight for life. Their love for each other could become so intense that if one of them died, the survivor could die emotionally and refuse to love again for the dread of more loss. In 'Nam, a soldier was better off without emotions, because it helped him avoid making physical mistakes.

I think that's what had happened to me when the squad had died. I'd loved them so much and had been so devastated by their loss that I'd shut down my emotional system and quit loving. After the squad had died, I'd still had another ten months in Vietnam, and my emotions had run for cover in what was technically known as denial. I had run into my cave and rolled the rock shut, sealing the entrance.

I'd felt like I was on an emotional train to nowhere across a highway as flat as the Keys. Whenever I had let out my emotions, they'd acted goofy and crazy and frightened me so that I'd locked them in my mind and had forbidden them to come out again.

I hadn't felt anything except an overwhelming wave of depression and sorrow and grief, but even that hadn't made me sad or made me cry. The isolation had been so overpowering, I had denied its existence. So I had quit feeling, and, in a way, I'd lost what I'd been trying to save by denying what I hadn't been able to have.

I'd wanted to die, and for the rest of my tour in 'Nam, that had been exactly what I'd tried to do—die. I had no longer been afraid of death, no longer afraid of fear, no longer afraid of anything. But unfortunately for me, or fortunately—whichever way you look at it—death hadn't wanted me that way. After all, how could death have enjoyed itself if its victim had been willing? Death enjoyed watching terror. Death wasn't interested in itself. Death was the end of pain, the end of sorrow, the end of emotions, feelings, thoughts, and ideas. Death was nothing, so death had avoided me like the plague, and I'd sought after it like the only answer to my misery.

Of course after I had lost the squad in that whorehouse, I'd volunteered for everything. That's what had gotten me into a mechanized unit. No matter how dangerous, no matter how death defying or how great the odds of surviving, I'd been there.

The problem had been, without fear, I'd become invulnerable.

Or so I had thought. But now the squad was telling me that they had been there watching my back.

One time I had volunteered to fly in a helicopter across the Cambodian border and reconnoiter the movement of North Vietnamese troops as they trekked south along the Ho Chi Minh Trail, a no-fire-zone trail that routed through a friendly country, Cambodia. I had spent three months on a mountaintop, sleeping in a cave during the day. At night I'd pulled out my three-foot-long starlight telescope and watched the enemy pass. One night I'd counted 3,217 regular troops, 24 jeeps, 2 flatbed trucks, herds of water buffalo burdened with sacks of rice, 7 nurses in white uniforms, a battery of canons, 4 mortar teams, 4 trucks full of AK-47 ammunition, a portable bridge, and a crate of RPGs. I had reported their position over the radio, and within an hour, the B-52 bombers had unloaded their cargo as the troops and supplies crossed the border into Vietnam.

The evening I'd left that position, I'd stood on a rock overlooking the trail, in plain sight. When the NVAs had looked up at me, I'd waved, flipped them the bird with both hands, dropped my pants, and mooned them. The NVA hadn't shot at me or even moved closer to investigate. They'd just kept marching south. They'd known an American would never have acted so insanely.

At the pickup point that same evening, the helicopter had been on time, but before it had landed, rifle fire had broken out from the tree line. Two lurking American gunship helicopters that had followed the Huey retrieval helicopter had strafed the tree line with machine guns and rockets while I'd run toward the Huey.

At the same time, another team of American forward observers had come charging for the helicopter from another direction. Two of them had been gunned down and had fallen in the rice paddy. I'd stopped and run back for them. When I'd gotten there, one of the soldiers had been lying facedown in the water. I'd picked him up and run him to the chopper.

As I'd rolled the body off my shoulder into the helicopter, the copilot had screamed, "Get in the fuckin' chopper—we're leaving."

Instead, I'd turned around, run back for the other body, and placed it in the helicopter alongside the first. The pilot had scrambled into the air before I'd gotten aboard, and I'd had to grab the rail of the fleeing chopper, lift myself up, and crawl inside. I'd sat in the open cabin and watched the NVA in the tree line fire at us, but I'd known they couldn't have hit us, because I hadn't cared.

But another of my soldiers had succumbed to fear, and he hadn't been able to shake it. He had been on an ambush one night, and when the ambush had been triggered, half a dozen NVA had been in the kill zone.

The problem had been that the column of NVA had been one hundred men long, and the NVA had finally overrun the Americans.

Tom Hersch had had NVA soldiers jumping over his head and had finally just given up. He'd set down his rifle by his side and just lain dead against the rice paddy berm.

The NVA had kept firing and lighting the sky with their rockets until, finally, a pair of NVA soldiers had stopped at his position. One of the NVA had shot a burst of machine-gun fire that hit Tom in the rib cage and stomach. Tom had not moved.

Then the two NVA had started to go through his pockets. They had removed his wallet, cigarettes, and lighter and then taken his hand.

Tom had been married and had had a gold ring on his wedding finger. One of the gooks had tried to pull it off.

The ring had not budged.

The other soldier had given it a tug, but still the ring hadn't moved.

Tom had known that the gooks would often cut off a finger to remove the rings, and Tom had decided right then and there if they tried to cut off his finger, he was going to wake up and go after them with the Ka-Bar knife on his waist.

Something had distracted the two gooks, and they'd picked up their AK-47 rifles and run into the shadow of the night.

Tom had survived, but ever since that night, Tom had been afraid of his own shadow.

I remembered going to a PX (post exchange) in Vung Tau to buy some snacks. The PX had been within a huge fortified concertina-wired, booby-trapped American camp, but still, instead of relaxing for a moment and going inside to buy a candy bar, Tom had sat at the turret of his APC, behind the .50-caliber machine gun, finger on the trigger, looking around for the enemy.

No amount of coaxing had gotten him to relax, lay down his weapon, and go inside. He hadn't been able to shake that fear.

Now, twenty years after the war, I fumbled with my medal, weighed it in my hands, and polished it with my fingers. I didn't know which way I was going. I could stand up and say to Bryan, "Let's go to Greece," and he'd go.

The little people in my head appeared. Glutton had a roly-poly belly with triple chins, and he was lying on a couch, gorging himself on a bag of potato chips, drinking beer, and watching TV. Hedonist was dressed in tinsels, which sparkled red and blue. He wore a ring on every finger and rings in his nose, belly button, eyelid, both ears, and forehead. He smelled like a bottle of cheap wine and preened his hair with a soft brush. Outrageous hung from the top of a mountain cliff by two fingers with a bag of chalk strapped to his waist. Excitement smoked cigarettes at a horse race with a $5,000 winning ticket in hand. Jester was frantically laughing, holding his side in hilarious hacking and coughing. Killer stood in the dark corner of a doorway, indistinguishable from the night, gripping a Ka-Bar knife. The one emotion that I wanted to hand the reigns of this dilemma to was Killer, the competent one. Killer never missed, and all the others were afraid of him. That's another reason my emotions refused to come out. Womanizer held a girl in each arm and looked for a third. Priest listened to the confession of a poor woman in rags. Love was tied up in a dark closet with his mouth gagged with tape.

I thought I was going crazy, but in reality I was becoming sane. I was listening to the voices in my head. I took a deep breath and looked around. I had the right to life and was capable of living like everyone else. I hadn't been afraid to die in Vietnam, but maybe now I was afraid to live. The sparkle was in my eyes, but the sparkles were the same ones I'd seen before when I'd gotten the yearning to run. I'd been going for it, like Ichabod Crane riding his horse after the headless horseman.

Bryan came over and put his hand on my shoulder.

"I think you are afraid to let go and to love."

I was startled. "Why do you say that?"

"Because death will be waiting for you. That's how death enjoys taking people, when they are exuberant and full of love. You told me that before."

"I'm afraid to love, because death will hurt all the more?"

"Exactly."

"Love held hostage."

19

I'LL DO IT

Just as suddenly, like uninvited houseguests for dinner, the squad walked up to the campfire and took their places in the circle. They all stared at the glowing embers—Billy Boy, Cameron, and Stuart. I said, "Good to see you, guys."

Billy Boy was the first to speak. "Only the truth can set us all free, Lieutenant. Remember?" He reeked of sarcasm.

I replied, "I think I am starting to understand you guys. Crazy… but acceptable."

Billy Boy said, "Don't mention that word 'crazy' around me. You know how sexy that makes me feel, and I don't want to be distracted." Billy Boy started crying. He stood up, tiptoed forward, wrapped his arms around my shoulders, and hugged me, slobbering a kiss on my shoulder.

I was stunned and pushed Billy Boy back. "OK, Soldier…remember protocol."

Stuart replied, "You're not through with life yet, Lieutenant. Don't forget the theme song of the Fantasy Fest parade this year: 'If you can't be with the one you love, love the one you're with.'"

I said, "I have to be straight with you. All these years I have kept a secret from you."

Bryan said, "Just like I kept a secret from you about the coins I took from *La Cruz*."

Cameron said, "Keeping secrets can turn into lies quickly…and you can't keep secrets that hide crimes. It is criminal."

I said, "I pledged to Hank that I wouldn't tell another soul—and souls are you—about what happened that night in Vietnam. I'm the guy who is keeping you in your purgatory."

"For Hank?" Stuart said. "That no-good scumbag. You promised him silence, and you are keeping that silence for him."

"It was my word," I replied. "My word. A pledge…my honor."

Cameron sat on the edge of a stump, placed one arm on a knee, and said, "Well?"

I inhaled deeply through my nose, stiffened my back, and said, "Hank has released me from that responsibility if I tell him where the *La Cruz* is located. That means you guys are going to be homeless."

Billy Boy sniffled. "We won't need that home if you set us free." Billy Boy stood up and came at me, waving his forefinger and shaking his booty. But before he got close enough, Stuart intercepted him and set his knife against Billy Boy's throat. Stuart said, "Let the lieutenant finish."

Billy Boy's anger turned to terror and then sorrow. He started to cry and play with his nose and his eyes with the backs of his hands.

I said, "First of all, it was my fault. OK? I killed you. Every one of you." I made eye contact with everyone, waiting for a surprised or shocked look, but they all remained focused on my words. I said, "I killed you through my negligence…my mistake."

"Go on," Stuart said.

That's what I did. I told it like I was still there, because in my mind, I was.

"Three weeks after Hank returned from the Saigon hospital with a bandage over his hand where that Cobra snake had bitten him, we went on that stupid night ambush in the whorehouse. Hank didn't want to get his bandage dirty, nor did he want to get it soaking wet in the rice paddies, so he convinced me to set up in that nearby whorehouse. I guess I understood. I didn't want his hand to get infected, so I went along with the plan.

"When we got to that whorehouse, the old mamasan greeted us at the door and was reluctant to let us in. But we barged in and took over the place."

Cameron said, "We remember all that. We all got blow jobs for five bucks a piece, and then Stuart and I watched out the window from one corner of the house and Bryan from another."

"Hank and I were together," I said.

Stuart lit another cigarette.

I continued. "About midnight, Hank came over to me by the window and asked, 'See anything?'

"'Not yet.'

"'I feel as safe as a baby here. Nobody is going to come blasting their way into a whorehouse, especially across that open field. They'd be nuts.' Hank looked up at the staircase and said, 'Why don't we go upstairs and sleep it off with a couple of whores? I could use some more nookie after seeing all those hot Red Cross nurses, Donut Dollies, in Saigon. I'm still as horny as a three-peckered toad.'

"So Hank and I went upstairs without telling you guys, and we took a couple of girls with us. I remember the one I was with smelled of Mennen's aftershave lotion. Hank took his girl into the other room, and I heard him laughing and glasses clinking as my girl and I lay on a real bed. I fell asleep and awoke to banging in the bathroom, a squeal, and thrashing about. Then I heard a stutter and gurgling.

"'Keep it down, Hank,' I shouted in a whisper. He wouldn't. There was thrashing about, and it sounded like Hank was throwing her around the room. I got up and knocked. No answer. The door was unlocked. 'Hank, you there?' I asked. I looked inside the bathroom and what I saw floored me.

"On the floor in the bathroom knelt Hank, bare-ass naked, his back to me, unaware of my presence. The girl was under him. She was motionless. I said, 'Hank,' giving Hank time to compose himself and clean up his act. Hank didn't respond. The girl certainly didn't respond. Her feet were about a shoe's width apart, the toes pointed outward. When Hank moved, the girl's feet moved, wobbly and lifeless.

"I crept closer. Hank had a knife in his hand and had carved a hole in her chest between her breasts. Blood was everywhere. Her blood was running off her chest and into the open floor drain. In shock, I asked, 'Hank, what the fuck are you doing?' Hank licked his bloodied fingers. 'Hank, what's going on here?' I asked, dumbfounded. 'Hank. What the fuck?' Hank rolled off her, exposing her opened chest and mangled body.

"I was totally freaked. I tried to swallow, but my throat was constricted. She lay still, her left leg twitching and her arms quivering. Then my girl appeared alongside me. When she saw her friend on the floor, she screamed. Hank jumped at her in a heartbeat, took her neck, and gave it a snap. There lay two dead bodies on the floor next to each other.

"Hank looked at me mercifully and said, 'You can't tell anyone what I did. You can't.'

"'Like hell I can't.'

"'No...I...we are on the same side. Those whores are the enemy. They all are.'

"'Hank, you need help. You just killed two innocent civilians.'

"'They weren't civilians, and they weren't innocent. That bitch robbed me blind. She was supposed to deliver a pound of weed to me, but when I left for the hospital in Saigon, she expected never to see me again and spent it all. Lieutenant, you can't tell anyone about this. I'll be court-martialed...go to prison...be dishonorably discharged.'

"'Hank, they have help for guys like you. You cracked, that's all. With all the shit you've gone through, they can't hold it against you that you cracked.'

"'I'll do anything you want. Anything. Just ask me, but don't say anything to anyone about this.'

"'No, Hank. I gotta tell.'

"'You betray me now, and you're turning on your own. I'm one of you. They are on the other side. Those whores were screwing the VC yesterday anyway. They are the real VC. They take money from us and give it to the VC. We all know that. Now there are two less enemies out there. I know it for a fact. Look. We drag the girls out back and make it look like the VC did it. OK? When we find the girls in the morning, we are the big heroes.'

"'No, Hank.'

"'You stay here then. I'll do it.'

"I sat there petrified and watched Hank do just that—drag the bodies out of the back door—listening to the bodies thumping down the stairs. I watched him do it a million times in my head that night. Hank went downstairs again, coaxed the Vietnamese cleaning boy out of the back door for a smoke, and cut his throat. I watched Hank from the window.

"Then there was noise from downstairs where you guys were located. I went out the door, looked down, and could just barely see NVA soldiers popping up out of a hatch in the middle of the downstairs floor. Firing broke out, but before I could open fire, something hit me in the back of the head, and I was out cold.

"I wanted to tell you this story the first time you appeared to me at Hangover Key, but I couldn't. I had made a pledge to Hank. I would have been breaking my word."

Bryan said, "Just like I would have been breaking my word to Black Jack about the gold coins."

Cameron said, "But you can't use the soldier's code of honor to hide a crime."

Stuart said, "But those bitches were VC. We all know that. We knew it then, but we didn't care."

"We still love you, Lieutenant," Billy said.

"Thanks, but I don't deserve it."

"You deserve it, and you deserve more than that," Cameron said.

Stuart sighed and said, "We are free to go."

"But how about the lieutenant?" Billy Boy asked. "We dragged him into this mess. How about him? The fight ain't finished yet."

Bryan said, "We are still a squad, and we have to help the lieutenant. It ain't over yet."

20

YOU'RE NEVER TOO OLD FOR A SURPRISE

The historic Hemingway home at 907 Whitehead Street was surrounded by a weaving, tilting redbrick wall. The bricks had been removed from Duval Street before it had been paved, and the bricks had been turned into a wall at Ernest Hemingway's bidding. Behind that wall was a lush tropical garden where the "Meet the Candidate Rally" would kick off my campaign. The theme of the Fantasy Fest was "feelings." For the occasion, I wore an Australian bush hat, a white shirt with the sleeves snipped at the shoulder to expose my oiled-down shoulders, Birkenstock sandals, and a pair of charcoal shorts. Bryan wore the same outfit, but he looked more like the Hulk.

Bryan and I walked to Mary's new residence, a small cottage next to the Wildlife Center. On the way, we reached the corner of Reynolds and South Streets, across from a circular house made from coral rocks. A world-famous photographer, Richard Harrison, had built the house in 1915.

Mary wasn't there, so we walked over to the Wildlife Center, where screeching birds greeted us. I thought I recognized some of the birds from Sanctuary Key, and I realized there was no better place for them to take up temporary refuge.

Mary was in the last cage hosing down the floor. She quickly turned off the faucet and came outside, clapping her hands and massaging them together. I gave her a quick hug. She looked exquisite in a knee-length white dress with fluffy shoulders.

"Don't worry," she said. "I didn't get sweaty."

"We have a party to attend, Queen Mary," I said. "We have some fund-raising to do."

Mary and I walked hand in hand to the Hemingway House, and Black Jack and Bryan followed. At the front-gate entrance was a life-size doll dressed in black silk, like the VC wore. A sign was propped against the doll that read "WELCOME HOME, GI." Black Jack lay down beside the doll and licked the leather sandals.

The inside garden was as thick with plants as Hangover Key, but there were American flags and banners everywhere. A Cajun band played on a small stage only big enough for themselves in the garden area. There was a drummer, a trombone player, and a female vocalist at the microphone under a white awning. They played a combination of jazz and Creole music. Three hundred folding chairs faced the band, and half the chairs were filled with couples fanning themselves with menus. There were posters of me on my flats boat and the word "feelings" all over the inside walls and on the trees. It was a picture of me in military uniform when I had graduated from Officer Candidate School in my youth.

Billy Boy, Stuart, and Cameron were waiting for us at the bar under the wooden porch. I smiled at them and said hello as if they were just regular customers. The squad had mischief in their eyes, like they were going to have fun at whatever cost, because it was party time.

I asked Billy Boy, "I thought you would be gone by now."

"Yes, we are free to go, but we don't have to go right away. We decided to stick around for the parade."

Billy Boy saluted me, but when I didn't return his salute, he dropped his hand and asked, "Are you too la-di-da to acknowledge your roots as an army officer?"

I waved diplomatically and replied, "Leave me alone, you guys." I downed a glass of coke and set the glass on the bar. "Just enjoy yourselves, and stay out of trouble." I turned around and shook hands with the city mayor, Scott Fitzgerald, and then hugged my aunt Wilhelmina. Everyone in Key West loved Aunt Wilhelmina. She made it her career to help others, no matter what their political or social status in life was. A nod from Wilhelmina brought results.

"You look absolutely wonderful," Aunt Wilhelmina said.

"Thanks for donating the outfit," I replied.

"It's the least I could do for our Vietnam veteran hero."

People were dancing, chatting, smiling, enjoying the music, flirting, and having a gay old time. This continued for close to an hour until the dinner chimes rang and the folks were herded to the southern lawn, where a line of tables held burning candles as centerpieces.

I sat at the head table with Bryan, Mary, and elected county and city officials, as well as representatives from the women's club Zonta, the president of the Veterans of Foreign Wars, and three actual veterans of foreign wars.

The oldest World War II veteran was eighty-six-year-old Tom Busbee. Tom sat in a wheelchair. He was as thin as a coat hanger and had sunken cheeks and snowy, frizzled white hair. You could tell that he took a lot of pride in that wheelchair, because it was plastered with army-unit stickers: the screaming eagle from the 101st Division, the flaming fire from the 9th Infantry, the Big Red One sticker from the 1st Division—on and on.

The day that Tom had been injured, his platoon had been unloading a resupply truck in the village of Valbonne, France. Tom had been on the upstairs porch embracing a beautiful young French woman and watching his men unload a truck. The girl had worn only a nylon slip and nylon bra, courtesy of Uncle Sam. She'd played with the hair on Tom's fuzzy chest. Tom had held a bottle of French wine in his right hand. As he'd lifted the bottle to take a swig, machine-gun fire had ripped through the air, and before the first mortars had struck, the woman had slumped in his arms with a bullet hole in her neck, another in the chest. She'd died in his arms, with her back blown into his rib cage, wet with blood. Tom remembered the face of the woman falling away from him. Her eyes had been closed. Her face had been bloodless. The heavy smell of smoke had engulfed him.

As Mr. Tom's wheelchair was pushed in place at the table, he raised his right hand into the air and shouted, "Shoot the rotten bastards."

His nurse handed him bottled water and said, "Tom, drink this. You must be thirsty."

In delirious moments of nonsensical intoxication, Tom said, "How about us stepping into the room and sharing some nylon stockings."

"Sure, Tom," she replied. "After you drink your water."

He sniffled, rested his head on his chest, and closed his eyes. Tom's American flag lay in his lap.

The Korean War veteran was disabled as well. Howard Hensley was the quietest of all. His division had been overrun by thirty thousand stampeding Chinese troops wielding machetes and chopsticks, which they skewered into the eye sockets of dying Americans and ate them like starving samurai warriors.

There was a Gulf War pilot who had lost his plane on the twenty-fifth day of fighting. Lieutenant Commander Lance Frith had had thirty-nine missions in all and had unloaded in three weeks four hundred thousand tons of ballistics, 10 percent of all the explosives detonated in World War I. An F-15E fighter-bomber pilot with the Tenth Squadron Fiftieth Tactical Unit, Lance had flown his plane more miles in two weeks than most people drive their cars in a lifetime. His sorties had destroyed scud missile sites, AGP70 radar installations, airfields, and three enemy MiG 29s—two of the MiG 29s in the air and one on the ground.

Lance was a tall and gallant man, the only honored veteran without a visible wound. He appeared to have no emotional wounds either. Lance appeared to be basically interested in being soberly polite. He never told the story of his downing, but everyone else knew it, because his weapons specialist ordnance man had been Hank's son, Marvin.

Their F-15E had been returning to the airfield in Oman on the Red Sea the evening of November 12, 1990, when the nose of the plane had lifted into the air, the wings had slid sideways, and the plane had crashed into the water, exploding in a ball of fire. Only seconds before the crash, Lance had ejected himself from the plane. He hadn't been high enough off the water for the parachute to open fully, and he'd slammed into the water at supersonic speed. Lance had worn a Saint Christopher medal that he'd held in his two hands as he'd skipped and bounced across the shiny blue sea. He'd prayed to God for his life, he'd prayed for God, and he'd prayed for himself until he'd made his final tumble and stopped in the water. When the rescue helicopter had lifted Lance from the water, Lance had been cursing and screaming at the sharks that had grown closer and closer. No one in the rescue helicopter had seen the sharks, but they did admit it was the last time they had ever seen Lance smile.

When Lance had returned home, his infatuation with speed had proven to be his downfall. He'd run over his wife in his brand-new Corvette. It was rumored he was quiet because if he relaxed and drank and got crazy, he'd admit that he'd run over his wife because she'd reminded him of his last moment of sanity as saltwater swimming with sharks had stung his nostrils.

A couple of Shriners were there, the commanding officer of the Naval Air Station at Boca Chica, some pretty girls, and a few long-haired hippies in shorts and T-shirts. Apparently the hippies were the children of military officers.

After appetizers of conch fritters, the Caesar salad was served. The entree was barbecued tuna, garlic-mashed potatoes, and asparagus soufflé. For dessert, tropical fruit ices donated by the Flamingo Crossing. Then the dreaded moment came for speeches. Aunt Wilhelmina was first, extolling the bravery of Key West's war veterans. Marty Grandau, owner of the latest shopping mall on North Roosevelt, was next. Marty told a story about me as a boy that had everyone laughing. Marty said that as youngsters, he and I used to feed raccoons sugar cubes, knowing full well the raccoons' habit of washing their food before eating. The raccoons would eagerly accept the gift and give it a dunk. When the sugar had dissolved in their hands, the raccoons had become frantic, digging into the water, swirling it, inspecting their empty hands, circling, frantically clawing the water, and turning their hands over. However, Marty said we had always finished our teasing with fresh carrots. The audience loved the story.

Then it was my turn. All eyes looked at me as I stood up.

"Good luck," Mary said. I bowed toward her and moved toward the podium.

Just as I got there and the crowd quieted, a stir of activity sounded from the entryway, and, as if on cue, in stumbled Hank Laser. Hank was plastered. He wore a party hat askew, his eyes floated in his head, and his body faltered. On his arm was a fresh young woman wearing a sleazy gold dress that exposed all her breasts except the nipples.

Hank focused on me and came at me like a brakeless truck on a downhill slide. He stood eye to eye with me, and, with his hand covering the microphone, Hank asked, "Are we partners?"

I shook my head. "Not yet, Hank."

He pushed me away from the microphone, steadied himself on the podium, and took a deep breath through his nose into the microphone, which made the speakers squeal. The audience looked stunned. Hank teetered a moment and fumbled for a piece of paper in his front pocket, removed it, and waved it wildly. He dropped it, fell over to pick it up, and, from his knees, returned to the podium. Leaning close to the microphone, he began. "It is with much shame and disappointment that I bring this news to you. You see, our candidate for Fantasy Fest king is a liar, and I was in his platoon in Vietnam, and there are some things I could tell you about John that would make your hair stand on end. I'm going to have to withdraw my support."

You could have driven a Mack truck into everyone's mouths. Hank continued. "John Marley took credit for deeds of bravery in Vietnam that he didn't deserve—deeds that made him out as a hero, but in reality, he was a fucking coward." The crowd gasped. "I've hidden this secret for years because of my own shame, but now I have to unburden my soul. The day John Marley lost a squad of three men in 'Nam, he was fucking a damn whore in the back room while his men were gunned down by a platoon of gooks. I'm sorry...a coward...a shame." Hank slammed his fist down on the podium and stepped back.

I was so embarrassed, I couldn't have pronounced my name if my life had depended on it.

The crowd was equally dumbfounded. You could have heard a mouse fart. Ceiling fans stilled, and the stars stopped shining. The leaves in the trees poised for an answer. The walls of the Hemingway House straightened in disbelief. I didn't know which way the crowd was going to go. They sat motionless, necks stretched forward and eyes staring.

With all the moralizing and fund-raising and hype about the election, I thought they might kill me for all the work they had completed so far, all in vain.

I approached the podium and said, "Ladies and gentlemen, my radio operator in 'Nam, Hank Laser, is probably right about me being a coward. There were times in 'Nam when my little pucker shook so fast, and I couldn't do a thing to calm it down except relieve myself, and then that didn't even stop it. There were times when I wanted to crawl back into my mother's womb and pass on my chance at life to someone else. That was when I cared. But there were no times when I did not love each and every one of my men under my command. I still do. Whatever mistakes I made over there, God forgive me, because I haven't forgiven myself. I'm sorry this happened. Hank didn't tell it exactly the way it happened, but yes, I did lose my squad, and I did make my share of mistakes. Forgive me. I hope it's not too late for you to find someone else for your Fantasy Fest king."

There was silence, except for the sound of my chair dragging the floor. I sat down. My hat felt like it was holding a sauna.

There was a commotion at the end of the table. Hank and the girl were fighting. Hank grabbed her by the arm, and she broke free, kicking Hank in the knee as she ran from the garden.

Aunt Wilhelmina was at the podium before I even saw her move. She tapped the microphone for everyone's attention.

"My nephew was a hero," she said. "And that's the truth. I know it in my heart, and now that he is home, I won't have some known scoundrel coming forth at this time and ruining this party and trying to drive my nephew from our midst again. When our soldiers came home from Vietnam, they were spit at and humiliated by antiwar protesters, and the veterans felt it in their hearts. War is hell, and those who survived need to be recognized for their ability to survive. John, as well as all veterans, should be thanked by each and every one of us. They risked their lives for our freedom, and their sacrifice cost them more than their time in that dread-awful country of Vietnam. That nasty war is over, and it's time we thank our vets. And, in the words of the great Buddha, 'He who has not sinned…probably drank too much beer and forgot.'"

Aunt Wilhelmina chuckled.

The crowd was still dumbfounded. They could have gone either way. Would they rip me from the stage and sling me over the brick wall? Eyes made contact and communicated without saying a word. Glares and stares penetrated me and then one another. Tension silenced the fan waving.

Then a very strange thing happened. Cameron appeared behind Wilhelmina and Harvey next to me. Cameron tickled her under the arms, and she began giggling. Cameron skipped to the next woman and tickled her, with the same results.

Snickering erupted from the crowd. Billy Boy jumped down from the stage and ran to a circle of young men, handed them each a beer, and saluted. The men clinked glasses, guzzled the beer, and hoisted the bottles high. As the crowd began to explode with ease, Billy Boy continued to distribute beers. The crowd became alive with commotion and comradery.

Stuart accosted a disgruntled gent with a painted frown on his face. Stuart held a knife to the man's throat and said, "Say something nice." The frightened man hollered, "I believe in you, John." Stuart moved his knife blade to the next man, and more accolades followed. The waves of excitement and laughter and tomfoolery crescendoed back and forth through the assembly. They screamed and cheered as loud as the organ at the Saint Paul's Episcopalian Church on Easter Sunday morning.

One woman screamed out, "I love you, John. I really do."

A man wearing a shirt decorated with rainbow-colored fish hollered, "I love you, man. I love you."

Tom Busbee rose from his wheelchair and screamed, "Let's have some nookie."

Lance began to fly around the table with his arms extended like the wings of an F-15A, his mouth sputtering like a revving engine.

The plump lady with the fingers of diamonds waddled up to the microphone, put her fat little cheeks up close to the mike, and said, "If anyone wants to talk about John, they'll have to talk to me first. We love our macho man."

Hank even started to smile like he had made a mistake, but he was probably afraid that the crowd might turn on him. He was sweating, his eyes darting, and the young floozy had disappeared from his side. Hank backstepped and fell over the VC doll, and Black Jack bit at Hank's cuff.

I stepped down from the podium, and there was Mary, standing right in front of me. Mary kissed me on the cheek.

The kiss lasted no longer than half a second, but it was one of the most marvelous experiences of my life. I felt so proud and cleansed. I was still in love. I was in love with Mary and with life. I felt overwhelmed.

The night sparkled with love and trust and harmony, and the next day, the *Citizen* newspaper wrote about the veterans and their contributions to the Keys as servants of the people. The pride in veterans rumbled through the city like an earthquake. And that's how things went for me, like I was in a rocket ship headed for the moon. My engines were burning pure jet fuel, and I felt clean.

21

THE ELECTION OF THE CENTURY

The next morning, I stood like a regular army soldier at attention, ready to be inspected. I said to John, "I'll do anything to help you win, sir, both me and Black Jack, and I mean anything. I'm just so happy."

I'd never seen his cheeks spread so wide in a smile. He patted his little belly and replied, "Bryan, Key West is strange, an odd place to live. People here like extremes. That's what it's going to take to win this election, so tuck in that chin, stick out that chest, and prepare yourself for the unfathomable."

When he told me to stick out my chest, I thought he meant like a man, but then he entered me in the "Walk on the Wild Side Tea Dance and Southernmost Costume Contest" at the Atlantic Shores Resort. Believe it or not, I wiggled my way into a yellow plastic dress adorned with a red-cherry neckline and matching hemline. John's election committee, three men and two women, placed two coconut halves on the front of my dress and two coconut halves on my butt, just so everyone would get the idea. They plucked my eyebrows and turned me into a curly redheaded floozy with blue gloves that reached my elbows—that is, after they shaved my upper chest and my legs to above the knees. Of course if anyone had looked carefully at my legs, they'd have noticed calves the size of a football lineman and knobby, scarred kneecaps. No eyes got that far.

John handed me a red plastic purse that had nothing in it but tissues.

I told him with a shaky voice, "I'd only do this for you, John."

He patted me on the coconuts and said, "Go for it."

I stood behind a plywood partition to hide from the crowd, and when I stepped out, spotlights hit me from four directions, and the whooping and hollering vibrated the water in the lighted pool. The cacophony was so loud, I wanted to hold my ears. Embarrassed, I raised the purse in front of my face with both hands and peeked over the leather strap. I swear there were five hundred people. There was no place to run. The place was packed. Even the backstage had filled. So I jumped in the pool. For a second there was a gurgling silence until I stood up and spun around. All eyes were smiling. My coconuts were too tight, and I adjusted them to more screams of delight. I was about to panic until I saw Billy Boy at the edge of the pool. He placed his hands behind his neck and swung his hips. As I gawked, his nose curled, and he did it again. Billy wanted to help. A bouquet of yellow daffodils landed in the water next to me. I picked up the flowers and did just as Billy Boy showed me. Billy Boy gave me the big OK sign.

I would have never thought I could arouse so many people just by walking up three short steps out of a swimming pool, but I did. Billy Boy pointed to the stage, and that's where I headed. When I got there, I hid my face behind that purse again, looked through the flowers, and focused on Billy Boy gyrating his hips and making pelvic thrusts. I mimicked him, twirling and slinking around the stage. I felt proud and relaxed, swaying and cuffing my wrists. Then I felt a surge of power and flexed my biceps, triceps, and deltoids. I couldn't do anything wrong. They loved me. And you know what? I won first place—a check for $500! I no sooner took the check than I said, "Mr. John, this check is for you and your campaign to become the Macho Man Fantasy Fest king. Good luck."

John gave me a big hug, and that was that. We could have gone home right away, but I danced the night away with all the guys who seemed to be as happy as if I were Marilyn Monroe herself.

Afterward I asked John why there had been so many guys hugging and dancing with each other, and he explained that it was men's night out, and the drinks were half-price.

"But when do the girls come out?" I asked.

"Bryan, for now at least we seem to have acquired a lot of male support, possibly because of Billy Boy."

John was supposed to crown the winner of the Hawaiian Tropic Contest and give her a body massage with hot oil. The contest took place at the Southampton Inn swimming pool the following Saturday. I don't remember how crowded that place was, because all the girls were ogling over John, asking him questions and trying to cuddle up to him so they could be one of his princesses. I don't even remember how many of those pretty girls were there, because I'd see one in a pretty swimsuit and think she was the prettiest until another came along looking even prettier. There were hundreds of them.

I wanted to dress up like I had at the Atlantic Shores, but John thought it best that the cheering be left for the girls. And he was right.

Hank turned up again—the devil's advocate.

At the sunset ceremony at Mallory Square, John and I were on a pedestal between the cat trainer and the sword swallower. A skinny little man with a xylophone volunteered to play background music while John answered questions about his life and times, from Alaska to Panama, Rome to Bangkok.

I could listen to John forever.

Hank weaseled his way into the crowd of listeners and asked, "Is it true that you killed women and children in Vietnam?" It was the last question Hank would ever ask John in public.

Even the cat trainer stopped his act and turned his head to listen. The man on the tightrope quit juggling and just stood there on the rope with his ears cocked, all his weight on one foot, frozen in interest.

John's expression froze in surprise.

Hank asked, "Did that experience qualify you for this election?"

The passengers on the crew ship docked alongside stopped eating and talking, leaned over the rail, and held their breath. John turned up the loudspeaker so that his voice could reach down to Duval Street. He cleared his throat. (He should have done that before he turned up the volume.)

John answered, "Hank, this is getting old, but let me try to explain one more time. When I was a freshman at Key West High, I got a D in algebra from a teacher named Mr. Bawdin. From the day I walked into his class, sat down, and made eye contact, we never got along. Bad chemistry. I didn't flunk his class, but I came damn close. In 'Nam, I had a couple of D days. When I was nose deep in mud with leeches sucking at my nostrils and my asshole spitting out diarrhea just from touching the water, and some VC I couldn't see shot and hit one of my men, who fell in shit-smelling water and drowned, I did start shooting at anything that moved. My sanity suffered dearly under the circumstances, and my sense of right and wrong faltered, but I was trying, because I love you, man. I really do. I love all of you."

It seemed like Hank couldn't ask a question without bringing down the house with applause for John. The more Hank followed John around and harassed him, the more John's popularity blossomed.

Black Jack even got in the act at the Pet Masquerade Parade at Marriott's Casa Marina Resort. I dressed her up so she looked like an elephant with a big, long snout. On her side, I tied a poster that said "Sanctuary Key Macho Power." That sign alone must have brought in a thousand more votes.

Everybody in the city took pictures of Black Jack and petted her and wanted her autograph. So that's what we did. We set her paw on a blue inkpad and let her walk all over whatever people gave her to walk on—restaurant menus, photographs, or T-shirts.

At the same time, an amazing thing happened to John's guiding business as well. He became the most popular guide in the Keys for Washington politicians. They not only wanted to fish in the Keys, but they wanted to hear his philosophies on politics, leadership, and the precious environment of the Keys. John's ideas were fresh, unadulterated, and not born of bribes or friendship, but of a philosophy for the people.

When the senators and congressmen flew down from the north, John gave them time to reflect on their goals and philosophies while they reeled in boners or tarpons.

To the senator from Alaska, John stated, "You have to sit back and just look at the situation and decide, in a calm and purposeful manner, whether your gut says these matters are for yourself and for the good of the nation and the people, or whether you are a victim of special interests that hold the carrots. The best interest in nature and world peace should be the carrot for you. Act from your heart."

I tied flies for John, day and night. Robert Dole caught a fourteen-pound bonefish, and he said the experience made him feel better than winning any election. Senator Kennedy caught a fifty-seven-pound permit. He wanted to have it mounted, but John explained that he couldn't mount the fish without killing it. Senator Kennedy returned to Washington and instilled the same philology into the welfare reform bill.

Fletch Bowen, our next-door neighbor, was after the Guinness World Record for the heaviest man alive. The record had been set in 1993 by Abigale Lucas from Tennessee. She had weighed 947 pounds. Fletch Bowen was up to 904. He had to eat a minimum of twenty-eight pounds of food daily to maintain his weight. If he dropped below that level, he started losing pounds. The problem was that, at his weight, he was very susceptible to diseases, since his immune system was so overwhelmed by protein mass that it lost its purpose in life. Bacteria and diseases were running rampant in his body, and his skin was beginning to crack. Lucky for him that the diseases were consuming each other in a feeding frenzy.

Every morning the Publix Super Market in Key West delivered two bags of groceries at nine o'clock sharp. The same boy, Al Catione, wearing a T-shirt, baseball cap, and white tennies, came whistling up the path. Although Al was a strong boy, he appeared to struggle with the load. One time one of the bags ripped, and there was ice cream and milk and chocolate and cake mixes and syrup all over the pavement. Al frantically loaded everything back into the truck and returned in an hour with two full cloth bags, recyclable.

Fletch had a handler for all the food—his brother, a gourmet cook.

Volunteer carpenters had removed doors from the house and hammered and nailed larger ones, as well as larger sinks and skylights.

Mr. Bowen set the world record a week before Fantasy Fest and said he did it all for John.

While all this was going on, I was celebrating and doing all sorts of things that I'd never thought I'd do in Key West. I entered the celebrity look-alike competition at Celebrities, the street-side bar in the Holiday Inn La Concha Hotel on Duval Street. First of all, I stripped down to my nylon briefs, which I had been getting used to wearing by this time, and then one of John's voters pulled out his paints. I refused to let him shave my chest, but what he did was outline the shapely figure of a curvy woman's body on mine. He painted her right down my front. In the crotch, he painted an Eve-type leaf.

By the time the artist had finished, he even had me confused as to who I was, because when I looked only at the drawing, I saw a woman, and a good looking one at that.

Hank was there, alone now and jeering in vain. He had lost a lot of weight, and his eyes had sunk deep inside his skull. He asked a lot of questions, but all to himself.

John stated, "Only in Key West can a queen be a king and a king be a queen."

Of course you probably don't know what a Sunday tea party is, but I'll tell you. It has a lot to do with all those coconuts and lipsticks. I was there too, a hit—more votes for John.

There were more masked parties, toga parties, marches, and celebrations. People stepped outside of themselves, in social and relationship roles, and took a stroll on the wild side in a celebration of diversity. I rented a motorcycle for a weekend and went to the Poker

Run, where ten thousand bikers from all over the country invaded Key West to raise money for charities.

After President Clinton fished with John for the weekend, he boarded Air Force One smoking a cigar and returned to Washington. The first thing the president did when he landed was dispatch a secret-service team to investigate the possibility of opening President Harry Truman's southernmost White House for himself. President Clinton wanted his own winter getaway to smoke hand-rolled cigars and fish with the best. At John's request, the president petitioned the Olympic Committee to reconsider fly-fishing as a sport for the next Olympics. John was certain to win a gold medal, because he could place a shrimp fly in a shot glass from fifty feet away on a windy day.

There was no stopping John—not Hank and not the NVA, who hadn't been seen in so long that I suspected they had given up the war. The Lower Keys of Florida had found themselves a native winner, and the election committee decided it the weekend before the Fantasy Fest parade. It was unanimous: John Marley was the king, and his queen was Mary Laser.

22

SHAME MELTS MY TUMMY

As soon as John left the house to take Vice President Al Gore bonefishing, I walked my favorite route to Sippin's Coffee House—up Southard Street and through old town, past the pretty white porches and flowering bougainvilleas. Once I crossed Duval Street and turned up Eaton, I headed for two white pillars marking the entrance to the coffee house.

I was happy for John, but I felt lonely at the same time. With the election over, the squad had left. After twenty years, I was completely alone with my thoughts. Don't get me wrong—I was happy for the squad. But at the same time, I felt the loss of their friendship.

Hank stepped out from behind one of the pillars. "I give up," he said, extending his arms in an embrace. He repeated, "I give up."

Black Jack's leash grew taunt, and I looked to see her choking herself on the collar and her legs digging into the cement like a stubborn mule refusing to move. Ignoring Hank, I knelt down and calmed Black Jack with a pat on the head and soothing words, but her eyes never left Hank.

Hank stood there with his arms extended. Just to avoid embarrassment, I stood up, meekly gave him a hug, and let go. Hank led me over to an outside table where two cups of coffee were steaming. He said, "Sit down and have a cup of coffee and talk to me." He shoved one of the cups toward me. It was black, just the way I liked it. Then he sat down behind the other cup.

Hank said, "The Kona Sunrise coffee blend, decaffeinated—I believe, your favorite brew."

I folded the *Citizen* newspaper under my arm, tied Black Jack's leash off to the back of my chair, and sat there, looking at the coffee.

Hank twirled his white plastic chair around and swung his arm over the back. He said, "Nice day, isn't it, Bryan?"

I nodded.

He said, "This is what I love about the Keys. The mornings are the greatest. Perfectly still, sweet air, nice and comfortable. I'll never leave. I love it here. How about you?"

I nodded my head again.

He smiled sheepishly. "We used to talk a lot in 'Nam. We were the best of friends. Do you remember?"

I squinted and replied, "Not really. I remember talking to the lieutenant a lot, and Cameron and Billy Boy, but I don't remember talking to you that much."

"Oh yes, you talked a lot. We were the best of friends."

I sipped the coffee, and it was just the way I liked it—strong and piping hot.

Hank said, "I just want to talk to you like old times. You see, after that party at the Hemingway House and I mentioned that whorehouse incident, it was a cleansing experience for me. John and I made a pledge in 'Nam that we wouldn't discuss that story with anyone. When he returned here last spring, he wanted me to break our pledge, but I wasn't ready. Now the tables have turned…so goes life. I've learned my lesson, and I'm willing to move forward and forget the past."

"I'm sorry," I said.

"You don't have to be sorry about anything. You have been the victim all along. I'm the one who should be sorry, and I am. You told me a story in 'Nam one time. I'll never forget it. And that story gained my respect."

"I did?" I asked. "I told you a story? I love stories." My defenses relaxed, but my body stiffened with anticipation. I looked at the cup of coffee in a new light and took another sip.

He said, "The one about you growing up in a mansion in Asheville, South Carolina, and your pet turtle."

"I did? I told you that? What did I tell you?"

"You are some guy," Hank said. "You always loved animals. Just like now." Hank reached out to pet Black Jack, but Black Jack retreated to the end of her leash and growled deep in her throat.

"She'll let you pet her when she gets to know you better," I said.

"And I'm the patient type." He sat up and continued. "You told me the story about catching a big old turtle in the pond in front of your home. The turtle was a big fat green one. I think you called it a soft shell. You put it in a plastic swimming pool and filled it with water and made an island of sand. Every day after school, you fed it chicken feed from the henhouse. Then one day you came home, and there was a crater in the sand with broken eggshells and baby turtles crawling all over the place. I think you said there were twenty-four, and you took care of those babies like a proud papa."

"I did?" I smiled, feeling all warm and fuzzy inside. "I did? I did!"

"Yeah, you told me a lot of stories about those turtles. You were going to raise them and sell them to your friends so everyone in your school could have a pet turtle. They had tiny little legs, green shells with yellow stripes, and pencil-size heads."

"Oh," I beamed. "They're so cute. I love turtles."

"After a while you quit feeding them chicken food and switched to dog food, and they got twice as big. And mama turtle got to liking you after a while. She quit biting. She was about six inches in diameter and as heavy as a shot put. That's what you told me anyway."

I laughed. "I like that story. I'm so glad I did that. I'm so glad I told you, because I don't remember a thing."

"You did, and you were happy then too, real happy, until your friend Lance Silvers—I think that was his name—do you remember him?"

I shook my head. "Kind of."

"Anyway, this Lance got a hold of them."

I leaned closer.

Hank got a whiff of my breath, waved at the air between us, and sat back. "Your very best friend. The best friend you've ever had. You were inseparable, especially when it came to doing things outdoors, having fun."

"How old was I?" I asked.

"You must have been around ten or eleven."

I smiled and cuddled closer. "It sounds like me."

"Yes, and then, then Lance betrayed you."

"He betrayed me?" I asked.

"Yes, he did. You don't remember?"

When I shook my head, Hank continued. "Maybe I shouldn't tell you anymore."

"Oh no, please. Tell me what happened. I won't be able to sleep another wink until you tell me."

"Well, that Lance fellow was a businessman, and he took the whole brood of turtles and used them for bait to catch some large-mouth bass in the pond up the road a ways. He wanted that hundred-dollar prize money from the fall fishing contest. He won that contest too, with your turtles."

"He did? He killed my turtles?"

Hank looked down and said, "Every last one of them."

I ground my teeth and stared around the room, wanting to hurt someone. My voice cracked when I asked, "Why did he do that?"

"Greed, I guess. He said the whole lot of turtles wasn't worth more than ten dollars, and he made a hundred off them. He said he might have gotten carried away a little, but he did help you raise those turtles, and he was the one who pointed out the mama to you in the first place. He offered you half the prize money."

"Oh no," I said as I shook my head. "Oh no. He killed my turtles. Now I remember. Lance killed my turtles. I remember. I think I remember."

"Do you remember what you did to Lance?"

I peered into Hank's sunglasses and replied, "No, I don't...remember a thing."

"You took one of those bass that he caught, and you beat Lance with it. You didn't stop hitting him until there was no fish left. You tore Lance up real good with those scales, and if it weren't for your mother hearing the commotion and her pulling you off Lance, you might have killed him."

"Well, he deserved it," I exclaimed, sticking out my neck. "He deserved every last one of those hits."

"And you gave him justice. Justice was served."

"That's right." I shook my head. "I don't remember real good, but he deserved it. Yes, sir."

"I guess I shouldn't tell you any more stories, because I can tell that I'm upsetting you."

"Oh, please." I sat forward again, saw him recoil, and sat back myself. "Please, tell me some more."

"I don't know if I should be putting myself into your life like this, but we were such good friends."

"You can," I pleaded. "You can butt in all you want, Hank, and any time too. Just tell me some more."

"There're just some things I should tell you, and there are some things I shouldn't tell. I just want to be honest and fair with you."

"Go ahead—tell me some more."

"It is about John."

"Oh." I caught my breath. "John? John is my best friend."

"I know he is, and that's why I have to tell you about him."

"What about him?"

"I'm having a party for him."

I started to play with my ear again, real fast and hard—pushing and shoving, squeezing and twirling.

"It's a surprise party." He smiled. "What are friends for? And I want you to come with me now and help me set it up. We've got a lot of fixing to do."

"But I'm supposed to go home now. John is guiding today, and I'm not supposed to go anywhere."

"His client is coming to the party too. It's a surprise. Mary will be there, and so will John's committee and key players in the election. Well, come on." He stood up and pointed for me to follow.

I looked at Black Jack, and she was straining at the collar again, trying to stay at the table.

"Come on," Hank said. "Let's go. We don't want to disappoint John."

I dragged Black Jack alongside me and followed Hank across the street to a parked van with tinted windows. I saw his friend Eduardo in the driver's seat, just sitting there listening to a Cuban song on the radio.

Hank said something to him in Spanish, and Eduardo started the engine. Hank got up front, and Black Jack and I took the seat right behind them. They talked in Spanish now, and the tone of their voices was rife with tension.

"Where are we going?" I asked.

"Like I said, to Little Palm Island. I rented one of the cottages out there. It has a big deck, a beach for swimming, and plenty of room."

"Maybe I shouldn't be going anywhere without telling John. He might worry about me."

Hank turned around in his chair and faced me. He said, "This is a surprise party. You can't tell anyone."

"If nobody knows about it, who'll be there?"

Eduardo turned his head in surprise, and Hank said, "Just don't worry."

We drove up the Keys, and I counted birds. By the time we stopped at Little Torch Key, I had counted fourteen great white herons, a flock of white ibis so big I lost count—but probably between thirty and forty—two ospreys, and a blue heron.

We boarded the speedboat, and Eduardo untied the lines and pushed the bow away from the pier. Hank sat in his comfortable white seat behind a large control panel and gunned the twin engines.

Black Jack sat on my lap in the cushioned seat just in front of Hank. We cruised down a channel between stilted houses. At Newfound Harbor, Hank accelerated, and we sped into the Atlantic toward a small five-acre island easy to identify, because it was packed with towering Jamaican coconut palms.

When we reached the dock, Eduardo tied off the boat, and Hank turned off the engines and hopped ashore. I set down Black Jack and followed Hank. Hank said, "You know President Kennedy visited this island back in the 1960s when Warner Brothers used this island as the location for the film *PT 109*, the story of JFK's war exploits."

"He did?"

"And his old man, Joe, ran electricity and water to the island so that JFK wouldn't have to listen to a generator hum at night."

Hank saw my surprised look and said, "Nothing but the best for your friend."

A roseate spoonbill waded in the pond below the cascading waterfall.

We approached a thatched-roof guesthouse, and Hank opened the door and stepped back.

It looked beautiful with the shiny Mexican-tile floor, huge lofted ceiling, bar, and colorful rattan and wicker furniture.

Hank said, "We need a few more decorations. I thought I could do some fixing up here, and you and Eduardo could go out to that Sanctuary Key that you are always talking about and maybe pick up something nice that John would be proud of."

I gasped and squirmed, looking for an escape route. I answered, "I don't talk about that place, and you're not supposed to know."

"Everybody knows. Remember the pet parade at the Casa Marina? Black Jack had the sign on her back."

"I don't think John would be happy if I told you. John told me not to tell anyone, and that includes you."

"But look what I've got planned, big fella. How can you do this to me?"

I scratched my head and replied, "'Cause John said so."

"Do you do everything John tells you?"

"Yeah, I do," I grinned. "All the time. Except one time when Black Jack got sick. But you know about that."

"Come on, big fella. Let's go into the dining area and talk over some snacks."

We walked into the other room, and I saw more food than I'd ever seen packed on one table. There were chocolate pies, apple pies, apple fritters, gummy bears, foot-long hot dogs right next to a container of mustard, jugs of Kool-Aid, sticks of cotton candy, boxes of Russell's chocolate candy, silver mint paddies, and bite-size candy wrapped at both ends. My mouth watered. I hadn't eaten any breakfast, and my stomach was growling. I said, "Oh, I don't think I should be here, Hank...I don't think so." I tried to backstep out of the room, but Hank blocked my way. Hank physically turned me around, slapped me on the back, and said, "Look, big fella, sit yourself down on that nice, comfortable couch in front of the television, and give yourself some time to relax and unwind. When was the last time that you watched TV?"

"Oh, I think it was when that one president quit his job."

He thought a moment and replied, "Well, it has been a while then, hasn't it? You deserve this." He extended his hands toward the food.

"John doesn't think so. John thinks it will make me real sick."

"John doesn't know everything, now does he?"

Hank took me by the arm, led me to the couch, sat me down, and then turned on the TV and used the remote control to start the VCR. It was a tape of The Three Stooges entitled *Dizzy Doctors*. The captions read "The people places and things in this movie are fictitious. Any resemblance to real people is a miracle." I slowly lowered myself onto the couch and started laughing right off. Larry, Curly, and Moe were medicine men in the Wild West and accidentally replaced the medicine they were selling with soap.

Hank offered me a soda and a box of cookies, and I took them without taking my eyes off the screen. The food was as fun as the movie, and I stuffed my mouth with cookies and laughter. Crumbs and soda flew everywhere. I smiled, wiped my face clean with the back of my hand, stuffed another cookie inside my mouth, and softened it up with bubbly soda.

Hank stood back and watched the TV as the comedians chased each other around a stagecoach. Moe shot an arrow at Curly, missed, and hit the picture of Geronimo behind Curly. Geronimo fell over dead. I laughed and stuffed my mouth with M&Ms. Black Jack placed her head on my lap and closed her eyes.

When the three episodes on the tape ended, I thought I felt sad and sick because it had ended, but when I touched my stomach, I realized that wasn't the case at all. I was sick. I looked at that table of chocolates and saw the damage I'd done. Finger marks were in every one of those dishes.

I sat there slowly petting Black Jack with one hand, moaning and groaning.

Hank sat in the chair across from me and offered me another box of chocolates. "Care for some more?"

I groaned and moaned and tried to say something, but I couldn't say a thing.

He said, "After all these nice things I've done for you, are you going to tell me where Sanctuary Key is?"

All I could do was groan. I missed home. I missed Black Jack and all the birds and the turtles and the alligators and the panthers and the egrets. I didn't want any more food. I just wanted to go home. I said, "Home."

Hank drew closer and said, "Tell me, and I'll take you there, right now. Let's go."

"I miss home."

"Let's go then," he said. "Right now."

I could feel myself failing. I could feel the spiritual side of my body move away from my body and look down at it. But I didn't feel any pain. I didn't feel any pain even when Hank stood me up and I fell over on my face. I saw the blood on the tiles, and my head throbbed, but I felt no more pain than if a mosquito had bitten me. Hank rolled me over on my back, got on my chest, lifted my head by the collar, and got in my face, hollering, "Tell me. Tell me where."

I didn't feel anything. I just felt warm and fuzzy inside, and I had an out-of-the-body experience. I was looking down at myself with Hank on top of me, blood pooling around my head. Then I was looking up at Hank, and then I was looking down at Hank, and then up again. Hank grabbed me around the throat and started bouncing my head up and down on the tiles. I could hear him screaming, "Where? Where?" My body shuddered and convulsed and made all sorts of rattling noises, and then I looked down at myself and then up again, and then down, and down for a longer time, and longer still. Then I was totally looking down. What I saw didn't move.

I had left my body for good. I was dead.

23

THE SPERM BANK

Death is like the feeling you get when you need to urinate on a bus ride without a toilet, and you hold it for four hours. Death is when the bus stops, you get out, and you can finally let go. That toe-tingling relief is death.

I was back at the Sanctuary—not on land, but in the galley of the *La Cruz* with Stuart and Cameron and Billy Boy. Stuart and Cameron were playing poker at a round table in the captain's quarters. Billy Boy looked like a waitress. He wore a short skirt (with shaved legs), a sleeveless blouse, and a white crown. He served cocktails to the card players from a platter.

"What happened to Mary?" I asked. "Where is she?"

Nobody answered.

"She didn't like the working conditions and went on to another life."

Cameron looked up from his cards and said to me, "You finally made it."

"I guess I did," I replied. "But what is going on?"

"You're dead," Stuart said. "Stupid shit. You did just what John told you not to do, and it killed you. You deserve to be dead."

"But what is death?" I asked. "I'm still here."

Billy Boy shook his booty, set his serving cap straight with both hands, and replied, "Honey, death is whatever you think it is. If you think it is reincarnation, that's it. If you believe in heaven, that's where you go. If you think there is no life after death, there you be. Death is everything."

"But what is this?" I asked.

Stuart replied, "Dumb shit, limbo. You are still part of the squad, and we ain't finished yet."

"But I thought you guys were free to go."

Cameron said, "We are, but we are AWOL." He chuckled a moment, laid down his winning hand on the table, and said to me, "The lieutenant still needs our help. That asshole Hank plans to take down the lieutenant the night of the parade, and we're going to stop him." Cameron raked in the chips from the middle of the table as Stuart shuffled the cards.

"How is that?"

Stuart said, "He plans on kidnapping Mary. He plans to kill her unless John tells him where we are right now. And when John tells, and we all know he will, Hank will then dispose of his newly acquired partner and have the treasure to himself."

I asked, "Hank would kill John?"

"Don't act so surprised."

Stuart said, "We have to save his ass. That's the least we can do for him."

"I'm in the same boat as you guys?" I asked.

Billy Boy replied, "This isn't a boat. It's a ship." He offered me a beer, which I refused.

Billy Boy said, "You can drink now. You don't have the same disabilities as you did when you were alive. Have a beer."

I shook my head and said, "I know John's upset with me."

Cameron replied, "Upset about what? He doesn't even know you are dead. He thinks you are home with Black Jack. John is fishing."

"How long will I be here?" I asked.

"Fix him a stiff one," Stuart said to Billy Boy.

Stuart kicked out a chair for me, and I sat down. I held my head and just groaned.

"You are here as long as you want to be. Like the rest of us, you are free to go at any time."

Living aboard the *La Cruz* was luxurious. I didn't need to breathe, so it didn't matter that I was underwater, and the benefit of death was that the ship was as bright and cheerful and newly painted as the day it had been launched. Its beam was 33 feet and length 104 feet, so the ship was roomy enough. Cameron stayed in the camarote above the captain's cabin with all the gold. Stuart stayed in the master gunner quarters with the artillery supplies just aft of the mainmast. I stayed with Billy Boy in the captain's quarters, which was exquisitely designed. There were wood-carved chairs and leather couches, and masterful artwork was on the walls. Four polished silver kerosene lamps brightly lighted the entire room. I enjoyed sitting in the captain's chair with my feet on the teakwood table and watching the fish swim past the three plate-glass windows. The multicolored parrot fish with the white buckteeth were my favorite. They gnawed at the tube worms growing on the glass partitions and spat out puffs of inedible white sand. Billy Boy slept in the captain's bed, a four-post mosquito-covered feather bed. I slept on the floor on a throw-out mattress.

When I got bored, I thought of things to watch: Black Jack pacing the floor, wondering where I was, or Sandra Bullock showering naked under a tropical waterfall, all sudsy and enjoying the brisk, cleansing water. I stared at her breasts so long, they turned into the Milky Way Constellation, where stars collided with each other and exploded into fireworks, planets disappeared into black holes, and millions of colorful meteors raced through the galaxy. I could watch earthlings, which was fun, but I couldn't intervene—at least that is what Billy Boy told me.

"Why?" I asked. "How about when Stuart was going to kill Hank and hang him by the balls?"

"He was bluffing, trying to move the lieutenant to action."

"How about you guys at the Hemingway House fundraiser?"

Billy Boy waved his hand and said, "That was all your imagination. We, the dead, can only interact with other dead. There is only one way to interact with the living. I told you about it at Sanctuary Key, in the shower."

Cameron chuckled and covered his mouth.

Even the newly dead have a learning curve, and I knew a little bit of what he was talking about, because I could walk through walls and be wherever my mind wanted me to be, but I couldn't touch anything. My fingers went right through it. In some respects that was good, because it made me relax as an observer, but in other respects it was frustrating, like dying of thirst in the hot Sahara Desert while you watch a belly dancer drink a fresh glass of lemonade.

Emotionally, I was still alive and hooked into John.

"Aren't we all?" Cameron asked.

I hadn't even said a word to him, and he had read my mind. Surprised, I didn't want to gratify his haughty, condescending manner with a question. Instead, I asked Billy Boy, "But how did you hand me the towel in the shower at Sanctuary Key?"

"You were half-dead and so screwed up, anybody could mess with you. That explains a lot of things. You were half-dead, one foot in the grave."

"You know what I don't understand?" I asked. "I don't understand why I still feel stupid. I thought that would go away when I died."

"*Eeeekkk*," Cameron replied. "Wrong answer. You'll become smart when you leave this place."

Billy Boy answered, "That is the drawback."

I pondered that concept all night long until I saw John leave the Casa Marina hotel after entertaining his fishing client at the bar with stories of adventures. John went home, looked into my room, saw my bed empty, shook his head, and went to bed.

Early the next morning, he cancelled his guiding trip with Frank Hesseman, CEO from General Motors, and walked to the City Marina to the floating dock where we had last tied off the canoe. He was about to launch the canoe when Hank came out of nowhere and greeted him.

John acted annoyed, which made me feel good, because it showed how much he was thinking about me. Then I felt sad, because we could no longer be the best of friends.

Hank said, "I know you don't want to talk to me."

"You got that right." John continued his business. "But I do have a question for you…one that has been bothering me for a long time. The night the squad died, I got knocked on the back of the head by something."

"That was me. I'm not even sure why I did it. That was not the best of my days. Sometimes a person does something for no reason at all. Maybe just stupid."

John pushed from shore, and then Hank called out, "I know where Bryan is."

John dug his paddle in the water to stop the forward movement. He turned the canoe around to face Hank and said, "Speak."

"He's in a safe place."

"He couldn't be all that safe, because he didn't come home."

Hank cleared his throat and replied, "Believe you me, I want you to have him back too. The sooner the better."

It occurred to me that John didn't even know I was dead. I wanted to tell him, but I didn't know how to make myself visible, even though I talked and waved my arms to attract his attention. "He wants to kill you, John," I shouted. "He's planning on killing you. He already killed me."

John acted like a mosquito was buzzing in his face.

"Tell me," John said to Hank.

I could tell they were both sitting on a whole bunch of emotional baggage that made them stubborn. This confrontation had been provoked by my disappearance, but it certainly wasn't the only point of contention, nor was my absence the only point to be discussed.

Betrayal, slaughter, disappointments, adultery, more disappointments, hatred, and now, the climax of their hatred—me. Of course I wanted John to win, but when I thought about it, I couldn't figure out what there was to win.

Hank said, "If you would be so kind as to tell me the whereabouts of this coin's companions"—he held up one of the gold coins that I had given to that perverted veterinarian between his fingers. Hank flashed the coin proudly, smirked, and continued—"I will gladly tell you the whereabouts of your friend."

John replied, "You are the cesspool of the world, Hank. You never grew beyond the hate and disgust and anger and sickness of Vietnam. You wallow in the emotional filth like a baby in a puddle of mud, not knowing clean from dirty, not caring until the next hunger pang strikes."

Hank snickered. "How about you, fella? You weren't exactly Mother Teresa over there. You had a couple of romps with revenge yourself."

"But it will never happen again, and I've done everything in my power to grow beyond that experience."

"I learned a few lessons about life in that rice-eating cesspool myself," Hank bragged. "Number-one lesson: I am the most important person in the world, and if I let down number one, I'm a loser. Self-gratification is the key to happiness." He laughed like a child, silly and hasty-like. Finally, he held his side with one hand, pointed with the index finger of his right hand at John, and said, "You're as sick as the day you left 'Nam."

"No, I'm not. I let go of that hate when I picked up Bryan from the hospital. You, in spite of a marriage to a wonderful woman, never let go."

Hank ground his teeth in silence and then said, "I took Mary from you because I thought that whatever you wanted in life was good. But she wasn't good for me. In college, I told her that you had met someone else and were in love with Teresa Snatch. I tried to beat happiness into her..."

Hank nodded his head. "I did everything in my life to make Mary pay for her love for you. I loved to hate her. It made me feel that good. Hate...love to hate...hate to love...love hate...hate her for loving... love her for hating. You might say we never did balance our act, but right now, I don't give a shit. All I care about is the gold and the glory it will bring to me."

"But they are all fleeting experiences."

"That's my problem then, isn't it?"

"Yes, it is. I want Bryan."

"He is feeling no pain, but he does need your help. He gets homesick real fast. Tell me where the *La Cruz* is?" Hank asked. "So we don't stand here baking in the sun, sweating hate."

"If I tell you, you might not tell me where Bryan is."

"Once I know where the treasure is, I won't give a shit about Bryan."

John walked to the end of the dock, jumped down onto the sandy beach, picked up a twig, and used it as a story knife to explain the position of Sanctuary Key in relationship to the Marquillas, Drift Point, and the Egret Game Sanctuary.

"No wonder I never found it," Hank replied. "It's so shallow, even a flats boat would go aground. I thought it would be in deeper water. That's where I was looking. I followed you a couple of times in my boat, but we always grounded out and had to turn around."

John nodded his head. "And the mud is like quicksand. And Bryan?"

Hank laughed. "He is in cottage C-Twelve at Little Palm Island Resort, feeling no pain."

24

NAUGHTY BOYS HAVE THEIR FINGERS CUT OFF

Like the positive poles of two magnets, the forces of nature dueled in the skies over the Lower Keys. Thunder rumbled over trembling water, and fiery arrows of lightning crisscrossed the voluminous dark clouds and whipped the frothing waves.

At Little Torch Key, John boarded the ferryboat that transported passengers and guests to Little Palm Island Resort. He took refuge from the rain under the white canopy bimini. Only half a dozen people were aboard, and the captain, attentive behind the wheel, gazed at a wall of clouds swirling above the dancing mangroves. John hurried toward the captain and asked him, "When are we leaving?"

The white-haired captain had a puffy pockmarked nose, like someone had taken a bite out of the tip. The captain replied, "Yeah, the fish are jumping everywhere."

John spoke louder this time. "A friend of mine is staying in the cottages, and I've come to visit him."

"Yes, sirree, people come from all over the world to stay here, all year around. One of them girls from France took off her top the other day. The prettiest set of hooters I've seen in a while. I'll be darned."

Goofy old fart, John thought. John retreated under the bimini and regrouped, thinking to himself, I'll just pick up Bryan and take him home, and that's that. Of course Hank will probably be out at

Hangover Key by then, but so be it. The squad is free to leave, if they haven't already left this planet. I don't give a shit about those gold coins anyway...just my squad.

"You little shit," the captain shouted. John looked up to see a little boy leaning over the side of the boat with his hand in the water. The captain continued. "Stay in the boat, or I'll call security on the radio, and they'll drag your sorry ass off to jail the moment we land. You hear me? I don't want any barracuda chomping off your arm like it were a needle-nose fish."

The kid retreated to the stern of the boat with his eyes as big as his mouth, screaming. He climbed onto his mother's lap, clawing wildly.

The old man grumbled, shot lip-smacking side-glances at John, spun the wheel, revved the engine, and motored into high seas.

After ten minutes, the ferry approached a flotilla of large yachts anchored to a floating dock. In the background was a prototype Tahitian village with steep grass-roofed cottages and swaying coconut palms.

When the boat reached the docks, John was the first off. He ran through the bar, into the hotel lobby, where he glanced back at the captain, still on the boat. The captain eyed John suspiciously, so John ran around to the back of the restaurant, where he could no longer be seen, looked back once more, and then headed around the bar and disappeared along the scruffy coastline.

All the cottages faced the water, and it was easy for John to find C-12, since there were only a dozen or so cottages. A wooden mermaid held room number C-12 on her lap. John knocked on the door. When no one opened it, he stuck his head inside the room and called out, "Bryan."

Since I was sitting in the rafters with my legs crossed, looking down, I wanted to answer him and tell him that in spite of my being dead, I was OK. I really was, but no matter how much I shouted, he couldn't hear me. I wanted to calm John's anxiety, but there was no human way I could reach him. I always hated to hurt John, and I had done enough of that living with him. I never meant to; it just seemed a consequence of my forgetfulness or stupidity or infirmity—whatever you want to call it. He had rescued me from that mental hospital, and for that I was still grateful. He was like an older brother I had never had, and even though I acted somewhat retarded—maybe a whole lot—I don't know what I would have done without him. I'd probably still be sitting in that VA hospital, waiting for my next dose of medicine, fearful of the fourth-floor Thorazine drip. In spite of John's gruffness, he was a little kid inside.

John crept into the room and stopped in the foyer alongside the picture of Gauguin on a straw bed cuddling a topless native girl. John's nose twitched. The cottage smelled like someone had shit all over the light fixtures and turned on the power. He waved his hand in front of his face to clear the air, but it didn't help. Squelching up his nose, he called out, "Bryan...Bryan."

He walked into the room to the left, where my body still lay. The television was still on and the volume blaring. An episode of Ren and Stimpy played, but for some reason, I wasn't interested in cartoons anymore. I looked at John and remembered how I should feel sorry for him, but I didn't feel anything. John walked closer, pushing aside an overturned bed mattress and then an armoire. He came upon the black leather couch from behind and peeked over the top. I turned away. I heard a gasp and looked again. John knelt and felt my pulse, but by now my arm was stiff. He put his ear up to my mouth and listened for a breath. It never came. John leaned closer and whispered like a prayer as he touched my hand, "Bryan, what the hell are you doing here?" He acted like he didn't know I was dead. He looked hurt. He touched my face, my hair, my eyes, and my cheeks again. Standing up, he moved to the television, turned it off, spun around, and looked at me again. I was smiling, but stiff and hard. John moved closer, knelt down, shook me by the shoulder, and said, "Bryan."

I wish I could have gotten back in that body and awakened, but there was no way. I was stiff as a board.

John shook me harder this time, because he knew how deep I could sleep—nearly on the brink of death, with nothing less than the good Lord to awaken me. One time in Missouri, we had taken a nap alongside the Mississippi River on a summer afternoon. I'd leaned against a great oak tree, hands on my lap, and fallen asleep. I'd had a dream that John had given me a pet monkey for Christmas, and I'd been so happy, I hadn't been able to contain myself. The next thing I'd known, I'd been in the Mississippi River, cold and silty and sputtering for air. John had said he'd tried to wake me, and no matter what he'd done, I'd kept sleeping there, smiling. Finally, he'd rolled me out into the water.

That's what I thought about when John shook me, saying, "Hey, Bryan. Get the hell up."

John leaned closer and stared at my mouth, and then he put his index finger in front of my nose and waited. Eternity ran through his finger, waiting for me to dribble some snot or saliva, which would have made him the happiest man in the Keys.

John pressed his ear to my mouth and listened. Nothing. Then his brow showed the fight that was starting inside his heart. He got all twitchy. "Come on," John whispered. "Come on." He grabbed me by the shoulder and lifted me up, and I could tell right then he knew I was dead, because I was already starting to harden up like an old leather coat. John knew the touch of death. He set me back down, and his mouth puckered, and he started to cry. That's the first time I'd ever seen John cry (aside from him faking it for Dr. Howe), and I knew he was hurting. He sobbed and sobbed and kept it up longer than I thought he could. I don't know if he was crying just for me or for his own life and the mistakes he had made and the dead-end roads he had traveled down, but it was all coming out now.

"Bryan, I love you. I always did. God hold you in his hands." He said a prayer. He touched my hand and said, "You were the best friend I ever had. I'm going to miss you, but I'm happy for you now, because now you can become the person you always wanted to become. Thanks for sharing your life with me. I love you. And you know what I'm going to put on your tombstone, don't you?"

I really didn't know, so I shook my head, but he didn't see it.

He said, "I bet you know."

I didn't. John continued. "You know...BRYAN MARLEY, LOVED BY HIS SQUAD. I love you, man."

John felt himself in the seat of his conscious awareness. It was full of light and peace. In the distance, he saw himself, the person he was: full of emotions, feelings, and thoughts. He took a deep breath and exhaled revenge that trickled into his soul. It came like the strike of a match that glowed to embers, trickled down the rivers of his lifeline, alerted each and every cell to action, and then turned on the fire, the speed, the adrenaline, and the rush. The emotion changed into a fire-eating, horn-rimmed dragon, fearless, with only one source of fuel—hatred. All other feelings and emotions ran for cover and hid in fear. Love wrapped itself in a warm blanket and ran for the closet, sucking its thumb and mumbling gibberish. Glutton slumped on its restaurant counter stool, round shouldered, hiding in fear of being cannibalized. Other emotions—understanding, caring, desire, lechery, compassion, and even the schemer and seducer—feared moving. They all stood stone still. Hatred spit its fire, roared its pain, and sought out its victim. Any victim would do, but reason shouted out, "*Hank...Hank Laser...Hank...just Hank...Hank.*"

John faced the uncontrollable urge to kill and with a deep breath tried to turn it into a cunning calmness. He centered himself, void of feelings, a time machine with all senses turned off. John could be shot at that moment, have his arm cut off or an eye poked out, and he wouldn't feel it, maybe because he didn't fear it any longer. There was only one thing he was battling: the urge to kill.

John had learned in Vietnam that at the depths of depression, his senses turned off, and he became monotone in feelings, protecting himself from the unbearable agony of maniacal manslaughter: the ripping of limbs from bodies, the defacing of lives, and the emasculating experiences of bowels cut out and fingers nails ripped from the bone. By denying such emotional experiences, he'd survived, but only as an emotional shell. It was the price of survival.

Now, challenged to experience living without killing to fulfill his satisfaction, John looked at "hatred" and said, "No. Not this time. I'm not returning down that road." He felt the tears welling up inside, and he let them go. Grief stepped forward. John cried. John took a deep breath and felt the fuel of revenge make his body perspire with an odorous sweat, the sweat that could hide the scents of other beings and not be detected—the scent of lurking fear.

Like a full-throttled engine, his hands shook with the emotion overtaking him. It wasn't the first time he had experienced revenge. No, revenge had been his buddy in 'Nam—his foxhole mate, his night-time companion, and his pitiless purity. Revenge had shared many a drink of Wild Turkey, many a case of beer and chugs of scotch. As powerful and as disgusting as revenge was, it was also consoling, because revenge comforted fear. John feared nothing for his own life.

He took another deep breath and kicked back the feeling of revenge, assuring the emotion that it was acknowledged, but its moment of glory was not today. Revenge was out of control, going way too fast. Calm…calm…let go of the emotion. Let it go by. If he didn't, John might not see something coming and make a mistake.

John fought the urge and fought himself. He remembered he had had promised Bryan and Dr. Howe, his killing days were over. If John let revenge go on a rampage, John would be no better off than the day he had returned from 'Nam. He would be no better than Hank.

John acknowledged the emotion and took control of the situation by first tending to reality. He dialed 911, alerted the female voice to the deadly situation, hung up the phone, and went looking for Hank Laser.

Hank's scent was in the air. His spiritual karma lingered in a trail of dust. John sniffed and smelled it, not with his human senses, but certainly with senses he didn't even know he possessed.

As I looked down on John and saw him fighting his demons, I knew that revenge was John's most powerful feeling. He wasn't proud of that, but it was there. Yet when he had picked me up from the hospital in Miami, he had sworn that he would never let revenge control his soul again. But I could see it in his eyes, and it was the last place in the world I wanted him to return. It would destroy a life that he had worked so hard to rebuild. I couldn't let John walk down that path again. I had to do something. I had to help him.

25

DREAMS CAN TURN ON A MAN FASTER THAN A FRIEND

Billy Boy looked out the ship's porthole, up through the depths of the pond, and saw Hank's canoe sliding through the water over the spidery mangrove roots. "Oh my God," he said. "Here he comes. Here comes Hank. That son of a bitch." He turned to the rest of us and asked, "What are we going to do?"

I didn't know what to say since I was so new to death and didn't know all the tricks and rules. I looked to Billy Boy for the answer. He touched his forefinger to his chin and then exclaimed, "An orgy? Maybe we can have another orgy, a sex party? A down-and-dirty, no-hold-back orgy." He brightened up. "Finally, I can stick Hank where he belongs."

Stuart pulled Billy Boy back from the window and looked.

I spied over Stuart's shoulder. Sure enough, Hank pulled the canoe over the diked area, got back in, and continued paddling. His neck twisted left and right with each stroke of the paddle, looking both fearful and gleeful at the same time, a lethal combination of greed and trespassing making him sweat and lick his lips as his eyes flashed.

I wanted to get on with life as fast as the rest of them, but the squad had spent so many years in life without my participation that they had turned into a calculating, time-warped commando team. I didn't want to interfere, so I crossed my arms, leaned against the wall, and watched.

Stuart picked up his M16 rifle, placed the barrel on Cameron's shoulder, looked down the sights, and placed the crosshairs on Hank's heart. Stuart closed his left eye and squinted through the peep sight with his shooting eye, his forefinger applying pressure on the hair trigger.

Billy Boy grabbed Stuart's arm and shook it, saying, "Don't hurt him, please—whatever you do, don't hurt him. We'll all lose, because we are no better than he is."

Stuart pushed Billy's arm free and slurred, "Quit balling. You know we have no other choice." He quickly aimed again and fired. The tracer round went right through Hank and hit a tree on the other side.

Hank acted like he didn't even hear the gunshot. He certainly didn't feel it.

Billy Boy said, "Now you've done it. You've unleashed your anger, and it doesn't work. We are powerless against him."

I had all this faith in Stuart, believed in all his guns and knives and grenades, and now I found out it was all talk. "You guys can't do anything," I said. "You're all full of hot air."

Cameron grimaced and replied, "That's not quite one hundred percent accurate. There is the heavenly court. But the odds aren't good."

"And we're all scared shitless to do that," said Billy Boy.

They all bowed their heads, even Stuart.

I asked, "What is that, like...like the last judgment...before God or Saint Peter?"

"*No*," Billy Boy said. "It is more personal and tailored to everybody's personality. Totally frightening."

"I'll do it," I said. "I'm not afraid."

Billy Boy said, "You don't know any better. That's why you're not afraid. If you knew the consequences of the court, you would take it more seriously. These guys do not fool around, and most of the time, the defendant loses. If you lose, and that means Hank wins, you go to hell. No way you could go anywhere else."

"John has done enough for me. I'd do anything in the world to help him. I'm willing to take that chance. I'll do it. Where do I sign up?"

"But you're talking eternity, not twenty years or a hundred. This is eternity."

"I'll still do it. Because Hank's next target is John."

"Dante's inferno...no reincarnation...no other lives in this galaxy, no outer space exploration—just burning hell."

"Anything for John."

Cameron joined in. "The problem is that you will face a legalistic accuser: Satan himself, the prosecuting attorney. But he's your own personal Satan—Satan who wants to prevent your prayers from reaching God by accusing you of things that you might not even be responsible for. You might not even have done half the shit. They are in your spiritual DNA."

They all stood back from me as if I were going to beam up into another universe. I closed my eyes, and I wished. My mind wandered between thoughts of guilt and betrayal and humor. Sometimes I didn't feel dead at all.

Billy Boy breathed hard and whimpered, and I opened my eyes again. He said, "I hate it when death becomes so real. I truly hate it. This is the death of death...death death. I feel like I am going to fall off the end of the earth. All I want is love—the love and companionship and tender understanding that my father deprived me of. Maybe even a little compassion." He spat and then refocused on me and cried out, "Don't do it. We'll try something else. Maybe we can sink Hank's canoe...please."

I asked, "What else is there?"

Stuart said, "Hank doesn't give a shit about anyone except himself. There is no other way."

"Maybe we should talk to him first," Billy Boy asked.

"No way," Stuart replied. "He won't listen."

Billy Boy waved a handkerchief and cried into it. "You people are so cruel."

"Look at him," Stuart said, referring to Hank.

Billy Boy held the handkerchief over his mouth and looked out the window again. Hank was dragging the canoe through the shallow water, kicking up water, and cackling. The whites of his eyes as well as the aura of greed that pulsed from his being shone like a spotlight.

Stuart said, "I knew he'd come alone. No way in hell would he share this with anyone else, and I am sure that when he finds the mother lode, the first thing he will do is execute his partner, John. With John alive, Hank will get only half the booty."

Billy Boy asked, "You people are totally rude, crude, and malicious, especially you, Stuart. Let's talk to him first. He might just leave and agree not to kill John. He just might. Please." Billy Boy dropped the handkerchief on the floor, pushed his way past Cameron and Stuart to the window, cupped his hands over his mouth, and hollered as loud as he could, "Run for it, Hank. Run for your life."

Stuart grabbed Billy Boy by the shoulder and pushed him backward. Billy Boy caught himself on the back of a chair, swirled around, and raced up the winding ladder. The three of us ran after him at break-neck speed. Billy Boy was bawling and talking to himself. "The poor thing. Poor Hank."

Hank saw us coming and, for a moment, acted surprised. He stopped in his tracks and just stared at us.

When we stopped ten feet away, Billy Boy was the only one making noise, and that was sniffling and mumbling. "You're going to hell, Hank," Billy Boy said. "If I were you, I'd run for it right now. It's the only way."

Hank's greed took a rest, and he said, "Is this déjà vu, or did I have a brain fart?"

"It's a brain fart," Stuart replied.

"And you can talk too," Hank smiled. "I'll be damned. They didn't do much for your wounds though. They look as fresh as the day you died...still hurt?" He chuckled.

Stuart replied, "When I look at you, it hurts."

"Son of a bitch," Hank shook his head. "Son of a bitch. Bryan, you're here too. You look better dead than alive."

I didn't know how to reply.

Hank perked up. He asked, "Where is it?"

"If I tell you," Billy Boy said, "Stuart will never let you out alive."

"I'll take that chance," Hank replied, smirking at the lot of us.

Stuart raised his rifle to shoot Hank, but Hank didn't care. Hank looked at our footsteps and the tracks leading from the water, and he cackled, saying, "Thank you very much. I won't have to share it with a bunch of dead assholes." Hank cackled in his demented way.

Billy Boy hollered out, "It's going to be your death."

"Bite my ass," came the reply. Hank pulled out a .45 Magnum, the kind he had used to shoot at gravestones and grazing pigs along the roads in 'Nam from a speeding jeep. Hank aimed at Billy Boy and shot him in the forehead. Nothing changed. Billy Boy brushed it aside with the words, "Oh now he's done it again. When is he going to learn?"

Stuart laughed when Hank shot him in the heart. Stuart flipped him off with the back of his hand under his chin.

When Hank shot Cameron, Cameron fell on the ground and jerked and squirmed like he was dying and then began to laugh, holding his side. Hank looked at me but didn't bother to fire. He said, "I already killed you once. And when I find this treasure, the next person I'll kill is my partner, John." He threw the pistol inside the canoe and ran for the deeper water.

Stuart and Cameron stood there watching with their arms over each other's shoulders. Billy Boy had his head buried in his hands, balling.

Hank swam out twenty feet, reached the center of light, and dove under.

I clenched my fists and said to Billy Boy just before I closed my eyes, "I gotta do it. This time, there is no stopping me. I'm gonna do the heavenly court. Now."

I closed my eyes and wished for the trial to begin. I was willing to risk eternity for John. Let it be.

The squad stood back in wonder.

It didn't take long to get where I was going. It was an act of will. As a matter of fact, as soon as I closed my eyes this time, I was there. I stood in a courtroom before a judge who didn't appear very judicial. I looked at his long brown hair, tweaky eyes, and small mouth sucking on a marijuana joint and realized it was Mario Saveo, the 1960s free-speech radical from the University of California, Berkeley. He wore a T-shirt with the picture of a Rastafarian on the front. He was as skinny as a skeleton. Oh shit, I was in trouble, because I'd never liked Mario. He was much too radical and outspoken for the times. He was the guy who'd turned over a police car in front of the Rat Skeller's bar in Berkeley and torched it. The San Francisco Chronicle described him as Satan reincarnated. Mario had said he'd just been getting everyone's attention.

I turned to the jury and groaned. There sat a platoon-size jury of NVA soldiers—impeccably clean shaven, well groomed, and dressed right, with starched uniforms, rifle barrels sticking up between their legs, and helmets level. Not a pair of eyes were visible.

I turned to the judge and asked, "Do you allow guns in your courtroom?"

He exhaled a cloud of smoke and replied, "I need to keep law and order. How else can I do it without arming everyone?"

Oh my god, I thought. I turned to the gallery of spectators: Kent State students in their school sweatshirts looking as independent as the day in 1968 when their friends had been gunned down by the insane Ohio State National Guard Militia.

I cringed and looked to the prosecutor's table. What could be worse? There sat Charles Manson in a suit, looking like the day they had thrown him in jail for the murders of Sharon Tate and her friends. Manson had carved up the pregnant lady and her unborn child and smeared the blood on the walls of the house. *Helter-skelter.* Charles held a dragonfly in his left hand and pulled off a wing. He set the dragonfly on the table and watched it whirl in circles. Amused, and then bemused, he squashed it.

Next to Manson sat Hank, naked but for a ton of gold shackles and chains.

Cheers arose from the gallery.

Mario said, "Let the trial begin."

Manson jumped to his feet and said, "Mario, this son of a bitch"— pointing at me—"wants to put away one of our most infamous and tormented brothers. Hank Laser hated life with his very soul. He tortured his wife to divorce, abused his stepkid, robbed Cuban immigrants and murdered them, sold drugs to survive, and, in Vietnam, even sent marijuana back to the states in body bags."

"My kind of guy," the judge said.

Manson continued. "This is a man of character. Whereas"—he pointed to me—"this dude is a do-gooder. I say we need more Hanks in the world. I say we let Hank go for another ten years and let this kowtowing asshole take his place in hell." He turned to the gallery, who waved peace flags and tie-dyed T-shirts. Manson said, "Screw it," took a tote on his marijuana doobie, and said, "Sit down." As an afterthought, Manson flipped the judge the bird and then snatched a housefly that buzzed in his face and popped it in his mouth.

"Good point," Mario said and looked to me. "What do you have to say?"

I stood up, walked toward the spectators, and leaned on the rail. They all stopped playing with their flags and scowled. I withdrew and said, "No matter what John and I did in 'Nam, we didn't mean to hurt any of you Americans, and we didn't even want to hurt the NVA that much; we just wanted to go home, like I do now. At some point you have to go on with life and forget the past. Even you guys. I want to go home."

Mario said, "You don't seem to understand that you have to prove to us that you will cause more havoc on earth than Hank will, and then we'll take him instead of you."

"But this sounds like the opposite of whatever a jury should do."

"I didn't say that either of you are going to heaven. This is a court of evil. It's who goes to hell first."

"OK," I said. "This is my first time here. I'm learning. If I live, I promise to...to...to...destroy downstairs enclosures in the Keys, catch and keep only illegal-size fish and lobsters, pray for hurricanes, build a thirty-foot wall all along the border between California and Mexico...and what have you. John will be so jealous of my meeting you all. I can't believe this...oh, forget it. I don't know what I am saying."

Mario waved his hand in a circle. "You just don't get it, do you? You just don't get it!"

"I think I got it," I replied. "I think I just got it. Are there any of you interested in some gold?"

The jury lifted off their seats and stretched a good inch or two taller. The Vietnamese loved gold. Their eyes shone like silver dollars.

Mario said, "That's enough horseshit out of you. Go back where you came from."

I looked directly at the jury. "But the gold will destroy the Keys the way it is today. The gold will wreak havoc on the reefs, destroy the wildlife, change weather patterns, and actually discolor the ocean water. Gold is greed, and greed will destroy the world."

There was definitely some interest from the jury.

The key jury foreman stood up, looked me directly in the eyes, and said, "We loved those Red Cross boxes that we stole from you— the boxes with the candy bars and cigarettes and cookies inside. Those were the best."

Mario fired a handgun in the air and waved the smoking barrel at me, replying, "Get this jerk out of here before I shoot all of you."

I stuttered, "B-but did I win or lose?"

"*Loser.*"

The jury foreman, still standing, said, "The jury has come to a conclusion, and we find the plaintiff guilty as charged."

The courtroom held their breath.

The foreman continued. "But since he is a pet-friendly guy and can't remember half of what he did in 'Nam—and, unfortunately, the jury members share the same lapses in memory, because they can't remember what they were fighting for either—the jury actually likes capitalism now. We have come to a rather unusual conclusion. You see, Vietnam did not know what fried rice was until America came to its shores. The American soldiers did not like to eat white rice, so they showed us how to scramble eggs and ham and shallots and soy sauce into the white rice to make fried rice. Vietnam loves fried rice."

The courtroom exploded with the words "Fried rice."

The foreman said, "So we find the plaintiff guilty as charged, and we sentence him to another reincarnated life in this universe."

"But Hank?" I asked. "What about Hank?"

"Hank is an asshole. "

Two uniformed guards with ribbons galore and holstered guns moved toward Hank. Hank ran to Manson, grabbed the pistol on the desk, and emptied the revolver into the two guards. Manson yawned. When the unharmed guards closed in on Hank, Hank threw the pistol at them. The two guards grabbed Hank by the arms. Hank screamed, "I hate the world." The guards handcuffed Hank, draped him in gold chains, and dragged him through a side door. Hank was so overburdened by the weight, he couldn't walk.

When I closed and opened my eyes, I was back at Sanctuary Key, and only two feet behind Hank, underwater. He cleared his ears and swam even deeper. The answer to his dreams was only inches away. The gold slipped from his grasp deeper and deeper into a circle of light—deeper and deeper into a pond that knew no bottom. The gold was there, right before his eyes and within his grasp, but always out of his clutches. His greed sucked him deeper into the pursuit of happiness.

Then, like a snake moving into a rat's den, I slid into Hank's mind and short circuited his rationality with euphoria. I removed the battery from his time machine and ransacked his inner control box. His soul became a cluttering TV screen with nonsensical static.

I could see into his soul. Mary was there, the virgin she was, the harlot, battered and bruised after another lesson he'd taught her.

Her head was lowered, voice low, eyes to the ground, and face turned to one side. Hank loathed her existence.

John appeared as well. John, the man who had earned all the medals, whom everyone followed like little ducks in a row, said, "Spread out," as if he were still on a search and destroy mission in 'Nam.

The squad was there, in that 'Nam whorehouse, with their backs to Hank and doing their jobs.

Hatred dove deeper still into the pond. Hate was Hank's fuel and companion, the force that was always there to comfort him in his decision making, the friend few others wanted or admired, and the merciless sucker that would eat its own hand, as it was doing now. Hatred gnawed at Hank's heart, sucked his juices dry, dribbled on his dreams, and preened his self-disgust.

Dreams of success turned to schools of fish that twinkled in the rays of sunlight. Hank turned to the left and followed the light into the darkness of his soul. It was too much for Hank. He could go no deeper into himself without more air. He turned toward the surface, but I was there.

Face-to-face, he remembered me but showed no compunction. Even under the water, he laughed.

I said, "Here are all four tons of your dream, Hank." I handed him the gold. He held his arms out and accepted it gladly, with a gasp of water that filled his lungs with the heat of hell and the vindictiveness of war.

Hank wallowed in his squalor of hate and greed, tormented by guilt. He sucked in the devils of darkness and exhaled, for the last time, small bubbles of air percolating from his lips as he sunk deeper into the world of himself.

26

TAKE THAT, MIKE WALLACE

I buried Bryan alongside my parents' graves in the Key West Cemetery. The funeral was a bittersweet ceremony. On the one hand, I had lost my dearest friend, my teacher, who had helped transform me from an insecure veteran into the fun-loving and outgoing Fantasy Fest king that I was today. Yes, we'd won. We had been a shoo-in from the beginning, because of the city's support for its prodigal veterans. On the other hand, Bryan was with the squad, free from so many burdens that this life had set on his shoulders. Truly a dichotomy of emotions flooded my soul.

We dedicated the festival to Bryan and to the squad, since the festival was right on the heels of the funeral. It was either that or withdraw completely, and with all the work that Bryan had put into our campaign, we knew he would've wanted us to move forward.

Bryan's funeral was attended by over two thousand conchs. Billy Boy, Cameron, and Stuart were there, and of course the guest of honor, Bryan. The squad dressed in their camouflaged fatigues to watch the twenty-one-gun-salute ceremony provided by the Naval Air Station Key West. They watched from Frances Street, behind the black wrought-iron fence. Billy Boy was balling his eyes out, and Bryan was consoling him with his arms around Billy's shoulders, patting him on the back. Cameron stood with his head bowed, and Stuart had a gun and was looking around suspiciously.

It was difficult for me to be sad when I saw them there. Some of the conchs were emptying boxes of tissues with their tears, stealing glances at me and probably wondering why I didn't show more sorrow.

Mary was there at my side.

Love peeked its head out of the closet door and looked around nervously. Then love stepped forward and stood proudly in front of the crowd. Love was accompanied by courage and pride and a host of other good feelings.

I could feel a newness to my life.

All of a sudden, Black Jack showed up. Somehow she had gotten a wooden leg for her missing limb, and she sported sunglasses. I had no idea how she could put on sunglasses, but the shades were perched on her nose. Black Jack still limped, but not as ostensibly. At her side was a miniature collie shepherd, a male, who did not take his eyes off her. Black Jack gave me her famous nod and disappeared into the crowd with her new friend trailing close behind, wagging his tail and dangling his tongue.

Then the Fantasy Festival parade began.

My campaign committee had created a festival float that characterized the precious resources of the Keys. Dozens of injured animals from the Wildlife Center were perched inside cages, including cormorants, anhingas, ospreys, one immature bald eagle, scarlet ibis, green heron, tricolor heron, and a four-foot-long alligator.

Surrounding the cages were broad-leafed potted palms, billowing ferns, luscious bougainvilleas, and scented jasmine. In the middle of the float was a thirty-foot-tall golden hand, where Mary and I were to sit. Alongside it was a pot of gold coins, the real thing from the *La Cruz*.

Billy Boy designed my costume. The fabric was glitzy celluloid gold. The ribbons on my chest were daisies, petunias, and daffodils. My helmet was decorated with feathery down. I wore a belt buckle shaped like a swordfish. My boots were polished silver. I carried a pump-action rifle, but instead of shooting bullets, it shot gold coins. Then there was the CIB medal on my chest, which I now proudly wore.

Mary's costume was that of a green turtle, but her legs and arms stuck out where the turtle's legs should have been. She looked kind of funny, but happy.

I beamed with pride and said to Mary, "You look absolutely gorgeous, love." The word caught on my tongue and stayed there for the longest time before flowing down to my heart. "Love," I said. It was a word missing from my vocabulary. I had always loved the squad, but I wasn't talking about the squad now. I was talking about Mary. I wondered if it were true. Living a life without love was like swimming in the ocean with water wings—surreal!

I stood there eyeing my kingdom. The crowd was absolutely ecstatic.

This time I would do it. I would explode in ways that I was meant to live. I was going to let my emotions take charge of my life and live the way I was meant to live. I was going to come out of my emotional cave of hatred and fear, take chances, and let every one of my emotions play.

Mary kissed me on the cheek and said, "You look as handsome as the day you left for Vietnam."

"And you are as gorgeous as the first day I set eyes on you, nearly forty years ago, my friend."

"Does that mean I have to move?"

"It means anything you want it to mean as long as you love me."

She hugged my arm and kissed me on the shoulder. That's all we needed. Our marriage was sealed in our hearts and witnessed by the parade festivals.

I looked up Duval Street all the way to the Atlantic Ocean. The street was packed with partygoers waving and shouting wildly. Crowds, I thought. Fear. I felt a bolt of fear that turned into sweat and shaky knees.

The entire scene changed. The street became quiet and empty. The music stopped, and all the lamps dimmed. I heard the bolt of a rifle slam a round into a chamber, and I tightened. Sneakily, people moved forward from the doorways, balconies, and alleyways. But they weren't normal people. There were NVA soldiers, emotionless care-takers of death. I looked to the rooftops, and they were there as well, all alike, not one making eye contact with me, but staring straight ahead. They were Hollywood clean, tight, and as straight as the teeth on a comb. They had pith helmets perched an inch above each ear, packs evenly balanced, and rifles at parade rest. No matter which way I looked, there was geometric balance.

Guilty conscience, I thought. I took a deep breath and looked heavenward.

"Help me out of this one, Bryan. Just this last time."

I opened my eyes, and the NVA had disappeared. They were re-placed by the people of Key West, minds afloat in sunburst freedom and tie-dyed colors, faces and bodies carved from individual experi-ences and incongruous genes. There was long hair and shaved heads, earrings galore, black leather outfits, and Gatorade baseball caps.

The float started with a jerk, and I stared up the length of the street. I felt pride.

Clearing my throat, I approached the microphone. Instead of speaking, I shot off a burst of gold coins into the crowd from my hip, first to the left, and then to the right, and then overhead. I was hot. The crowd's first reaction to the coins was to peel off the wrapper and eat the chocolate. When the revelers realized the coins were not fake, they danced in circles, holding the coins high.

I spoke into the microphone. "*Here's to love.*" I laughed. The crowd hollered and screamed, not totally for me, but for their spirit of zeal. I said, "I want to say that I am proud to be here, to have been chosen to represent this magnificent city and concept. All these open hearts yearning for charity, this greenery and clean water and breathing trees—they all mean so much to me. My friends, I am no longer bur-dened with the shame and guilt associated with Vietnam. I am free. *Free.* Thank you for being so kind and listening to me. I love you all. I love you."

The crowd was ecstatic, but Mary said, "John, the microphone is off."

I shrugged my shoulders, and when I turned around, the squad was sitting around the treasure chest—Billy Boy, Cameron, Stuart, Bryan, and the man who surprised me most, Hank Laser. Hank had his radio on his back and looked at me meekly.

"I guess I got a little out of hand there, sir," Hank said. "I thought you were headed for no man's land. The squad forgave me and helped me back."

"If they can forgive you, I certainly can, Soldier," I said.

"Thank you, sir."

Bryan said, "But I thought you were headed for hell."

"I don't think hell was quite ready for me yet. They said they would take a rain check. Something about I gave ass holes a good reputation."

I inspected each of the soldiers from head to foot. They were all impeccably clean and spotless.

"You are something to be proud of," I said. "And I am going to do something that I never allowed you to do in Vietnam. But first, Stuart, you really shouldn't carry a loaded weapon in public."

Stuart inspected the rifle at parade rest, shrugged his shoulders, and flung the rifle into the air. It disappeared into the stratosphere.

Proudly, I asked Stuart, "Soldier, what are your plans?"

With a wry smile, he replied, "First of all, I am going to get a new heart, and then I am thinking of maybe heading for Saudi Arabia, Afghanistan, or Iraq—someplace where I can do what I like to do best."

"A mercenary to the core. You were trained well."

"Yes, I am, sir. And thank you. You were a good leader."

I turned to Billy Boy. "Well, Soldier?"

Billy Boy was painted silver from head to toe. He wore a tiny G-string, and on his head was a bouquet of artificial flowers. Around his waist were a silver holster and a toy gun with a long barrel. He shot confetti into the air with the gun and kissed the smoking barrel. Billy Boy wagged his tail and swooped his head back, his hair cascading in a wild wave of color. "You know what I'm going to do, you little devil."

"No. Honestly, I don't."

"Lieutenant. Shame on you. I am going to stay right here in Key West. While you were running all over after Hank, I found my eternal soul mate. He is absolutely gorgeous."

"Who is he?"

"He is a hunky fisherman. He owns the forty-two-foot shrimper the *Engorged*, and I am going to be his first mate, his second, and his third."

"Well, good for you, Billy Boy. I'm happy for you." I turned to the eternal oddsmaker Cameron. "And you, my friend?"

"Guess."

"Win the Florida lottery?"

"Now that I have some inside contacts, that isn't a bad idea. But I plan to cast my fate to the gods of fortune and take the next hand dealt to me. I'm excited to see what happens."

"Good, and Hank? I see you're back in and composed."

"Yeah. With Stuart around, how could I be anything but…"

"You going after more treasures?"

"Yeah, but this time, treasures of the heart with a Zen Buddhist philosophy."

"Good luck then…and Bryan?"

"As my tombstone says, 'Bryan Marley.' Thank you."

"It was the least I could do. And I want to thank you for helping me fight my demons: revenge and hatred in particular. I can see them now for who they are, and I am in control of them, and not vice versa. Billy Boy told me about what you did for me. I know I would have handled it myself, properly, but thank you."

"No doubt about it, John." Bryan smiled. "You are the man."

John smiled, "You look so relaxed. So comfortable. So terrific."

"I've never felt better, sir, and I think I could read a thousand words a minute with the mind I have. It's purer than gold, and insatiable."

"I'm glad it is all over for you."

"Amen."

"What are your plans?"

"Not to get shit at and hit again, that's for sure." Bryan chuckled. "With your permission, I'd like to become your guardian angel. I'll be there to remind you to be compassionate, sensitive, and caring in your safe new world—a new world in which you belong and which you fought to express yourself in."

I smiled and replied, "I accept."

Stuart asked, "Any regrets, sir?"

I sighed. "Only that we couldn't have spent more time together."

"Hold on," Stuart replied. "In this crazy world, you just can't tell."

I knew he was thinking of the future. I said, "I love you, guys, and I'm sorry for everything. Sorry for all the misery I caused each one of you. Please forgive me."

Billy Boy replied, "It wasn't all your fault, sir. And besides, although we complain a lot, just like in 'Nam, we've done OK for ourselves."

"Yes. I guess you have. I love you."

They popped to attention in their own unique ways. Stuart was as sharp and crisp as a nail. Cameron squinted through the smoke of his cigarette. Billy Boy turned his salute into a wave. Hank stood proud, and Bryan wiped a tear from his eye. I moved forward to shake their hands. I stopped, because I realized that they were still soldiers and awaiting their due respect. I stepped back, saluted, and said, "Men, the war is over."

They returned the salute, and then Stuart, Billy Boy, Cameron, and Hank turned around and walked away, at first slowly, with their feet shuffling. As they reached the treetops, picking up speed, they changed into the speed of sound and then into the speed of light. They raced toward the universe and flashed into oblivion in a clear spark of dusty flame as pure as a star.

Bryan perched on my shoulder. I looked at him, and he said, "You would not believe this dream I have for you. It is filled with meditation and yoga."

I cuffed him on the ear and laughed. "And fishing!" Then I turned to Mary. She was in awe of the crowd. I couldn't remember ever looking at anyone so precious. Those big brown eyes were spar-kling stars. She was good for me.

Mary took my hand, and out of the side of her mouth, with a smile, still looking at the crowd, she asked, "Do you talk to yourself a lot?"

I chuckled, winked at Bryan, glanced back at Mary, and said, "Get used to it, honey. Get used to it."